I KNOW YOUR NAME

A WOLF LAKE THRILLER

DAN PADAVONA

GET A FREE BOOK!

I'm a pretty nice guy once you look past the grisly images in my head. Most of all, I love connecting with awesome readers like you.

Join my VIP Reader Group and get a FREE serial killer thriller for your Kindle.

Get My Free Book

www.danpadavona.com/thriller-readers-vip-group/

1

B lack clouds gathered overhead and blotted out the night sky. The car smelled of gasoline and fast food. The fuel filter was clogged, and fries covered the floor mats. Slumped in the passenger seat of Polly Hart's car, Shawn Massey fiddled with his phone. Why wouldn't his mother answer?

Polly brushed the blonde hair off her cheek and peered through the windshield. The girl directed a concerned scowl at Shawn.

"Are you sure you want to go through with this?"

No, he wasn't. Three years ago, Shawn's mother had walked out on their family and moved across Wells Ferry to live beside the lake. Shawn had expected Megan Massey would remarry, yet she didn't have a boyfriend. Not as far as he could tell. She had neither the time nor the inclination. The woman cared about nothing but work.

A rising star among criminal defense attorneys, Megan would accept a position at a big city firm before long. A job in Buffalo or Albany. Maybe even New York City. Then Shawn would never see her again. She called him every day. Once or twice a week, he ate dinner at her place, an expensive lake house his father could never afford. Their strained conversations spoke volumes. Megan wasn't comfortable around her only child. She'd leave him at the first opportunity.

"I have to confront her," Shawn said, glaring out the window as the manicured properties grew.

"You aren't going to do anything stupid, right?"

Polly held his eyes. Shawn didn't reply.

A quarter-mile from the house, Shawn pointed along the shoulder.

"Drop me off here."

"It's nighttime, Shawn. What if a car comes along and doesn't notice you?"

"Stop worrying." He hopped out of the car and leaned his head inside. "I'll call you in the morning."

Worry creased her forehead.

"What if I stick around for ten minutes? Just in case it storms."

"It's been threatening to shower all day, and nothing has happened. I'll walk home afterward."

"I'm uncomfortable leaving you here."

He forced himself to grin.

"I'm not afraid of a little rain, Polly." He tapped the roof of the car. "Talk to you tomorrow."

She huffed as he slammed the door. Then she drove off and left him along the road, the darkness suffocating as peepers sang from the lake shore. He stuffed his hands inside his pockets and shuffled down the road. The houses along the water ran upwards of four-hundred grand, the properties spaced out and bordered by trees for privacy. You didn't need fences in the lake district. Sprawling estates gave you all the isolation you wanted. His sneakers squeaked along the blacktop. Headlights approached from the end of the road and vanished after the driver turned down a side street.

A humid wind shoved him from behind. Insistent. As if nudging him forward. All week, the news had predicted severe weather—thunderstorms with torrential downpours, flooding, high winds. The Wells River roared in the distance like a monstrous beast consuming the land.

The trees rustled off the road. Shawn pulled up and stared into the shadows, convinced he wasn't alone in the night. Walking faster, he lowered his head against the breeze. The sensation that someone watched him grew with each step.

Before he realized it, he stood in his mother's driveway, bouncing on his toes as he reconsidered. It was one thing to imagine the argument in his head, but quite another to go head-to-head with a lawyer who masqueraded as a parent. Not that his mother would belittle him. But how did you win a debate with a woman who argued for a living? Three years ago, at the impressionable age of fourteen, he'd heard his parents yelling from the bedroom. They'd fought before, but never like this. A chasm formed between Kemp and Megan Massey, and neither seemed willing to build a bridge. Then one evening, after Shawn finished putting the dinner dishes away, his parents sat him at the kitchen table and gave him *the talk*. Mom was moving out. It wasn't forever, just until his parents worked out their differences.

Even then, Shawn had known better. She wasn't coming back.

Shawn drew a breath and raised his gaze to the house. Something was wrong. From outside, it appeared his mother had gone to sleep early. But he knew Megan Massey. She never turned in before one in the morning on the weekend, preferring to sleep late. The lights were off, no flicker from the television screen. Yet he sensed movement inside the house.

He glanced over his shoulder. Nobody watched.

Shawn strode up the walkway, past the potted palms, sneakers scraping along paving stones, as he climbed the stoop. The mailbox rattled when the wind gusted. A wet shoe print glistened on the stoop. He raised his knuckles to bang on the door and stopped. The door stood open a crack.

Though Wells Ferry was rich with old money, the town had its problems. Crime grew on the east end of Wells Ferry and spread like a blight. There was no chance his mother would leave the door unlocked at night.

Shawn's heart thumped, his instincts on high alert as he paused outside the entryway.

Voices traveled from somewhere in the house. From the kitchen?

Shawn set his hand on the door and edged it open. The hinges didn't groan and give him away. Now he stood in the foyer, the room thick with air freshener and cleaning solution, impenetrable darkness daring him to step forward. Shadows lurched off the furniture and crept across the floorboards. He wanted to call out to his mother, but he kept quiet, sensing danger hid around the corner.

Dread deadened his legs. He moved along the wall, sticking to the dark. Pictures of boats, sunsets, and shimmering lake waters adorned the walls. No photographs from family vacations. No memories of the loved ones she'd left behind.

A thought popped into Shawn's head. What if his mother had brought a date home and entertained him in the kitchen? If so, why were the lights off?

A thump brought him to a stop. A squealing noise came from the kitchen as someone shoved a chair across the floor.

"You don't have to do this," his mother said from around the corner.

"Too late," a voice whispered.

"Please, no. I'm sorry. It doesn't have to end this way."

Shawn's legs locked. He didn't dare move a step closer. Someone was in the house and threatening his mother. Swallowing, Shawn forced himself to move. He wished for a weapon, something he could use to defend his mother. In his bedroom, he kept a multi-tool with two sharp knives, one serrated. Little good that did him now. Scanning the hallway for a makeshift weapon, he found nothing.

"You never should have crossed me, Megan."

Burgeoned by a need to defend his mother, Shawn pushed off the wall and turned the corner. He saw her. Eyes beseeching, Megan hunched over in a chair with the shadowed figure towering over her.

"We can work this out," she sobbed.

The LED clock on the microwave reflected off the knife before the man jabbed the blade into Megan Massey's stomach. Her mouth opened in a silent scream. Blood trickled off her lower lip.

"Mom!"

The man whirled around. He hadn't noticed Shawn until now.

Smooth and confident, the man focused on Shawn. Razor-sharp eyes peered out through holes in the ski mask. The stranger dressed in black to blend with the darkness, down to the leather gloves. As though he had all the time in the world, the murderer cleaned the knife with Megan's shirt. His mother's eyes fluttered as her life slipped away.

When the man stepped toward Shawn, the boy turned to run. There was nothing he could do to save his mother from the fatal wound. Now he needed to save himself.

A snicker escaped the killer's lips.

"I know your name," the madman whispered.

Shawn scrambled down the hallway as footsteps thundered out of the kitchen. Slipping on the floor, the teenager knocked a photograph off the wall. The frame smacked the hardwood, shattering the pane. Shawn righted himself and raced for the door. Glass crunched behind him under a booted foot.

The killer burst out of the house as Shawn ran into the night.

2

Raven Hopkins lay on the precipice of sleep, half-aware of the lightning flickering outside the cabin window. This was the third time this week she'd spent the night in Darren Holt's cabin in Wolf Lake State Park, and she wouldn't have wished for anything else.

A private investigator with Wolf Lake Consulting, Raven curled beside Darren and listened as he snored, massaging the knot out of his shoulder while he muttered something indecipherable inside a dream. He'd worked his fingers to the bones all day, maintaining the park trails and fighting against the weather. After a snowy winter, April had arrived with unseasonable warmth and ceaseless rains. Two mudslides closed the west end of the ridge trail, and water roared over the cliffs of Lucifer Falls, carving out the stream bed where they'd excavated the skeleton of a murder victim last summer.

Thunder rumbled and shook the walls. The clamor caused Darren to stir before he draped a pillow over his head and fell asleep.

Raven turned to her back and glanced at her phone. Maybe she should check on her mother.

No, that was a bad idea. Since last April, Raven had watched Serena Hopkins like a hawk, worried her mother would relapse. After her brother, LeVar, and Thomas Shepherd, now the sheriff of Nightshade County, rescued Serena during a heroin overdose, Serena entered rehab. She'd come so far over the last twelve months. Serena never missed a Narcotics Anonymous meeting, and she'd proved herself capable of handling a high-pressure sales position at Shepherd Systems, where she worked with her best friend, Naomi Mourning.

Still, Raven fretted. As Serena often acknowledged, one never conquered addiction. The temptation forever lingered. But it was time to cut the strings and let her mother survive on her own. Give her space and allow her to thrive. And Raven would earn more time with Darren.

Nobody comforted Raven as much as the ranger. The sprawling state park grounds and rustic cabin lent Raven peace. This was their sanctuary, their endless adventure. Since winter's end, Raven had considered selling her house to Serena. As much as she loved the little house on the west ridge above Wolf Lake, it didn't speak to her the way the cabin did.

Happiness fluttered through her chest as she imagined a new life inside these cabin walls.

Darren's phone rang, dragging him up from sleep. He flicked on the light, rubbed his eyes, and stared at the phone.

"It's Kemp," he said, giving Raven a confused glance.

Darren's cousin, Kemp Massey, lived with his son in Wells Ferry on the western edge of Nightshade County. Raven met Kemp and Shawn over Christmas. She recalled Kemp's wife had left him three years ago, and Shawn hadn't taken the separation well. Why would Kemp call Darren this late? Raven worried something had happened to Shawn. As she climbed off the bed, Darren sat upright and grabbed her arm. She questioned Darren with her eyes as he fumbled for a pen and paper.

"Dead? Are you sure it was murder?" Darren scribbled on a memo pad. "Where is Shawn now?" Another pause as Darren grabbed his clothes off the foot of the bed. "Call the sheriff's department. Raven and I are on our way."

Darren tucked his phone into his pocket and tossed a sweatshirt over his head while Raven pulled on her clothes.

"What was that about?"

"Someone murdered Megan Massey at her house, and Shawn saw it happen."

Raven placed a hand over her heart.

"Oh, my God. Who killed her?"

"Shawn didn't see the man's face. He called Kemp a few minutes ago and said the guy was still after him. Then Shawn's phone died."

"So Kemp doesn't know where Shawn is?"

"No," Darren said, slipping his gun into his shoulder holster. Before taking the ranger's position at Wolf Lake State Park, Darren had worked the force with the Syracuse Police Department.

Raven grabbed her gun and threw her beaded hair over her shoulder. Thunder rumbled when they stepped into the humid night. Water sloshed off the ridge and rushed toward the lake. The last thing Nightshade County needed was another round of storms. Concern etched into his forehead, Darren surveyed the horizon as lightning flashed. Shawn was out there somewhere, running for his life.

"I can't assess the trails in the dark," Darren said, running a hand through his hair. "The hikers won't be happy, but I'll close the ridge trail until I'm sure it's safe."

Raven helped Darren carry a roadblock from the storage shed behind the cabin. Their sneakers slipped in the mud as they traversed the slick grass. Darren had outfitted the roadblock to read *Trail Closed Until Further Notice*. The sign wouldn't stop a hiker intent on breaking the rules, but it was the best he could do for now.

Darren started the engine as Raven slid into the passenger seat of his midnight blue Dodge Silverado 4x4. Turning on the high beams, Darren backed the truck out of the welcome center's parking lot and took the winding road into the village. Rain splattered the windshield. He activated the wipers and leaned forward, hands death-gripping the steering wheel.

Why would anyone murder Megan Massey? Raven considered the possibilities as they drove down the lake road toward the interstate. Criminal defense attorneys represented unsavory characters. Had Megan crossed a client?

The truck slowed as Darren pumped the brakes. Around the bend, water rushed across the road and cascaded down the hillside. Raven's heart pushed into her throat until they made it through the washout.

"Tell me everything about Megan Massey," she said, distracting herself from the flooding.

"Megan and Kemp had issues even when Shawn was younger." Darren pulled his lips tight as he remembered. "She's driven. I never pegged her for a small-town attorney and figured she'd end up at a major law firm. Not sure if Kemp would have allowed her to take a big city position."

"So Kemp controlled the marriage."

"You could interpret it that way. I'd rather say he looks out for Shawn's best interest and wouldn't drag his son away from his friends just so his wife could earn a promotion."

Raven tapped her sapphire nails against the armrest.

"What about Shawn? You mentioned he had trouble fitting in at school."

Darren wiped a raindrop off his nose. He turned off the high beams when the truck encountered ground fog. As long as nature kept throwing hazards in front of them, Raven wouldn't relax until they reached the highway.

"Shawn got along with his classmates until the separation. Then his grades dropped, and the school suspended him after he started a fight."

"Rage issues aren't unusual for teens from broken homes."

"Kemp doesn't know what to do. Shawn refuses to see a counselor, and Megan is... was too focused on her job to notice her son spinning out of control." Darren took a sharp turn onto the interstate ramp and punched the accelerator. "I still can't believe someone murdered Megan in front of Shawn. We have to find that kid. Can you call Chelsey?"

Besides being Raven's best friend, Chelsey Byrd ran Wolf Lake Consulting, a private investigation firm in the village center. Though Kemp hadn't hired Wolf Lake Consulting to find his son, Raven and Darren needed all hands on deck.

"Chelsey might already know if Kemp called Thomas."

Chelsey dated Thomas Shepherd, the sheriff of Nightshade County. Thomas lived in a lakeside A-frame down the hill from the state park, and Chelsey often spent the night with the sheriff.

After confirming Chelsey had heard about the investigation, Raven turned her attention back to the road. She worried about hydroplaning as Darren stepped on the gas.

"I know you're concerned, Darren. But slow down. It's a twenty-minute drive to Wells Ferry in sunny conditions, and we haven't experienced a dry day this week."

He exhaled and eased back on the truck's speed.

"What if the killer caught Shawn?"

"Stay positive. We'll find your cousin."

Darren glared through the windshield as the mile markers whipped past in green blurs.

Raven hoped they'd find Shawn before the murderer did. Megan's killer couldn't allow a witness to escape.

3

Thomas pulled the cruiser into Megan Massey's driveway and killed the engine. A gust nudged the vehicle as he assessed the entryway. The door stood open, letting in wind and stray sprinkles. The phantoms of wet footprints dried on the walkway before angling toward the lawn. A few hundred feet separated the victim's house from her closest neighbor.

After radioing his position to dispatch, he stepped out of the cruiser and glanced up the road. Any minute now, Wells Ferry PD would arrive, igniting the usual territorial pissing contest. Wells Ferry perched on the western edge of Nightshade County, so close to the border that some residents argued over which county the town belonged to. Tensions between Wells Ferry and the Nightshade County Sheriff's Department ran deep and predated Thomas's arrival. Stewart Gray, the former sheriff, always complained about their long-running feud with Wells Ferry PD.

Thomas blinked twice before he got moving. If he blinked an odd number of times, he'd need to stop and blink again. It was an obsession he couldn't shake when pressure mounted, and after multiple homicides in his county, Thomas had faced a life-time of pressure over the last twelve months. His hand moved to his spine and lingered an inch from the old bullet wound. While he'd worked as a detective with the LAPD, his task force fell into the crossfire between two rival gangs. The gunfire struck his back. He still felt the phantom bullet digging beneath his skin, a horror he'd never vanquish.

Headlights swept around the corner. Thomas let out a breath when the vehicle passed. It wasn't a Wells Ferry PD cruiser. Born with Asperger's syndrome, Thomas avoided arguments. He preferred to work alone and struggled to express his feelings, though he'd opened up in the last year. It helped to have so many close friends.

Wanting to investigate the scene before the police arrived, Thomas captured photos of the shoe prints. Wearing gloves, he squeezed between the open door and the jamb and stepped inside the foyer. A wall switch stood to his left. He paused before he clicked on the lights. What if the killer was still inside the house?

Kemp Massey had phoned the sheriff's department a half-hour ago. His son went missing after witnessing a murder. How did Thomas know the boy hadn't killed his mother and fled the scene? Darren vouched for his cousins, but Kemp and Megan Massey were headed toward a messy divorce.

Thomas moved in silence down a long hallway. A broken picture frame lay on the floor. A nail protruded from the wall where the photograph once hung. As he stepped around the broken glass, a knocking sound pulled his attention upstairs.

He found Megan Massey sprawled on the floor. A blood streak marked her struggle as she crawled from the table to the back door. He touched his fingers to her neck. No pulse.

Blood soaked her sweatshirt and pooled on the floor. A chair lay broken beside the table, and a hole marred the plaster. These didn't strike Thomas as signs of a struggle. More likely the killer smashed a hole in the wall and broke the chair in fury. When he lifted the camera, the noise came again from upstairs.

Standing beside the stairwell, he looked up into pitch-black. Speaking into the radio on his shoulder, he requested backup. In his mind, he pictured the psychopath stepping through the upstairs, unaware of the sheriff's presence.

He followed the staircase to the second landing and cleared the bathroom. A perfume bottle rested on the sink. Otherwise, Megan Massey kept a tidy bathroom, free of clutter. The next door opened to a guest room, empty except for a bed tucked into the corner. Thomas doubted Shawn stayed overnight in this room. Nothing was out of place, and the carpet was recently vacuumed.

Thomas paused beside a closed door at the end of the hallway. He edged it open.

The master bedroom lay before him. A handcrafted armoire stood against the wall, a dresser to his left. Shoes lay on a rack on the closet floor, and Megan Massey's wardrobe draped off hangers. Moving his eyes across the room, Thomas spotted a briefcase beneath the bed. He stepped around the bed.

A shadow flashed across the window. Thomas raised his gun and released his breath. A loose shutter banged against the outer wall, causing the noise.

He phoned the department. Deputy Veronica Aguilar was working the swing shift this evening and would need to stay late.

"I need the county to send their forensics team," he said, studying the scene. "How soon can you make it here?"

"Half an hour. I'll call Virgil on my way to Wells Ferry."

At sixty-two, Virgil was Nightshade County's veteran medical examiner. His assistant, Claire Brookins, was a prime candidate to take the position after Virgil retired. No doubt Virgil would grumble when he learned of the Wells Ferry murder. Like

Sheriff Gray, Virgil wished Wells Ferry would defect to the next county. Or fall into the lake. Thomas wondered how far back the bad blood stretched between the rogue lake town and the county.

Thomas wished Aguilar was already here. Though his lead deputy stood five feet tall in shoes, Aguilar exuded confidence and intensity that gave hostiles pause. She wouldn't back down against Wells Ferry PD. Neither would Thomas, but he abhorred confrontation.

As if he'd summoned Wells Ferry PD with his thoughts, emergency lights swirled across the windows. Two male officers with football player physiques stepped out of the cruiser and approached the stoop. An officer with a goatee shot the sheriff's vehicle a derisive glance as he passed.

Thomas met them at the door. Better to initiate the conversation, he figured.

"This is Wells Ferry jurisdiction," Goatee said as he pushed past Thomas. "Why are you here?"

"The county sheriff's department received the call," Thomas said.

Goatee grunted. His partner stood beside him with his thumbs hooked in his belt loops.

"We'll clear the house," the partner said.

"Already taken care of."

"Then we'll double check."

Thomas didn't care. Let them waste time prowling around the upstairs while he assessed the crime scene. As their shoes thumped up the staircase, they whispered and watched Thomas from the corners of their eyes. He returned to the kitchen and took pictures, careful not to disturb anything.

The killer could have shot Megan for a clean kill. A stabbing was an act of rage, and knives were silent killers. A neighbor would have heard a gunshot. Anger fueled this man to murder his victim.

The hole in the wall and the stab wound in Megan Massey's belly pointed to a deranged killer who sought vengeance.

Which meant he couldn't rule out Kemp or Shawn Massey.

Baritone voices traveled from the upper landing before the officers clomped down the staircase. The jurisdiction war was just beginning.

4

"Can you think of anyone who'd want to hurt Megan or Shawn?"

Cupping his elbows with his hands, Kemp Massey paced the kitchen while Darren and Raven sat at the table. Like his son, Kemp wore sandy brown hair parted at the side. A shade over six feet, Kemp was almost as tall as Darren. Kemp's cinnamon skin tone and leathery, weather-beaten face proclaimed he was no stranger to the outdoors.

"Nobody would hurt my son," Kemp told Darren. "As for Megan, I can't say what she was involved in. We haven't spoken in months."

Raven raised an eyebrow when Kemp turned away. Darren set his hands on the table.

"So you aren't aware of any cases she's handled over the last year."

"How would I know? She had her life. We have ours."

"Please, Kemp. We're trying to help. Anything you can remember might help us locate Shawn."

"Don't you think I'd tell you if I knew anything? He's my son. I'll do everything I can to bring him home."

A shiver rolled through Kemp's shoulders as he stood at the window and peered into the stormy sky. Rain slithered down the pane.

"I'd like to look inside Shawn's bedroom."

Kemp turned around.

"There's nothing in Shawn's room that will tell you who murdered Megan."

"It might give us a clue where Shawn is hiding."

Kemp exhaled.

"Be my guest. Shawn's room is the first door at the top of the stairs. But this is a waste of time. We should search for my son, not overturn his bedroom."

"The police and county sheriff's departments are looking for Shawn. Right now, the best thing we can do is narrow down the locations."

Darren and Raven left Kemp in the kitchen and climbed the stairs, taking the steps two at a time. Sirens wailed inside the town as rain pattered the house. A gray morass of mist cloaked the land outside the windows.

"What are we searching for?" Raven asked when they reached the upper landing.

Darren lifted a shoulder.

"I'm not sure. Maybe we'll find something that will tell us who attacked Megan."

"It seems like you're rushing."

He glanced at the window.

"Wells Ferry PD will be here any second."

"Is that a problem?"

"The police have a longstanding feud with the county. I doubt they'll be happy to find private investigators rummaging through the house."

"You're a state park forest ranger, not a PI."

"That won't help our case."

Shawn's bedroom appeared like a typical teenage boy's—A Thirty Seconds to Mars poster on one wall, a Twenty-One Pilots poster over his bed. An autographed picture of a hip-hop artist Darren didn't recognize lay on the desk. Wearing gloves, Darren picked up the photo and tilted it toward the light.

"Scout would get a kick out of this," he said, laying it down. Scout was Naomi Mourning's teenage daughter. The wheelchair-bound girl leveraged internet sleuthing skills to aid their investigations.

The bedsheets were crumpled, the blankets and comforter bunched at the foot of the bed. A dirty shirt hung over the desk chair, and a stray sock poked out from beneath the desk. A paper plate with a pizza sauce stain lay next to a computer monitor.

Darren dropped to his stomach and aimed the flashlight beneath the bed. More unlaundered clothes and a dust bunny the size of a rat. On a whim, he peered between the mattress and box spring. Nothing hidden.

A bookcase stood against the near wall. Darren couldn't move the bookcase. A furniture anchor held it in place. He removed the books—Stephen King novels, a historical encyclopedia of rock music, the *Harry Potter* series—and sifted through the pages. Shawn hadn't tucked secret notes inside any of the books. Next, he stood on tiptoe and ran his hand over the top of the bookcase. His glove came away dusty.

Raven checked the bedside table, then moved to the dresser and pulled the drawers open. As she searched beneath the clothing, Darren rounded the desk. A mixing board stood beside a keyboard and turntable. Studio quality headphones hung from a stand. Darren whistled.

"I never realized Shawn was into making his own music."

Raven closed the drawers and joined Darren beside the desk.

"Creating art is a great way for teens to deal with home issues."

Darren nodded. Kemp and Megan's failed marriage ate at him. It was one thing to separate and move on after a relationship unraveled. But what about Shawn? The teenager deserved better. Any hopes Shawn had of rekindling a relationship with his mother had disappeared. He couldn't imagine what the boy was going through.

Sliding the computer desk's drawers open, Darren sifted through papers. Musical notation, penned lyrics.

"No wallet," he said.

"He probably took it with him."

Darren jiggled the mouse and awakened the monitor. A password prompt greeted him. He glanced at Raven and shook his head.

"I'm not much for cracking passwords."

"Ask Kemp."

Raven followed Darren down the stairs. Kemp hadn't moved from the kitchen. The LED lights exaggerated Kemp's blood-drawn face, making him appear like something that crawled out of a crypt in a horror movie.

"We found nothing of note in Shawn's bedroom. Any chance you have his password?"

Kemp fidgeted with a pepper shaker beside the sink. He glanced up when Darren's question registered.

"Password?"

"To his computer."

"No idea."

Darren set his hands on his hips. He wasn't getting anywhere.

"Let's start over. Tell me about Shawn's relationship with his mother."

"They didn't have one." Kemp turned back to the window

and rubbed his hand. He seemed to favor his forefinger. "She brought him over for dinner every week. Window dressing to make it appear like they were still family. But that ship sailed three years ago after she left us."

"Were you home all night?"

Kemp's shoulders stiffened.

"Of course I was. What kind of question is that?"

"The police will ask."

"If you're inferring I murdered Megan in front of my son—"

"I'm not. But it's important you give the interviewing officers a complete time line."

Kemp moved to the refrigerator and stared at a picture of Shawn water skiing. Darren's stomach fell as he imagined the smiling boy in Megan's house, witnessing her murder.

"The police always suspect the spouse. Isn't that right?"

"Statistically, most murder victims know their attackers."

"Well, I didn't kill my wife. She ruined our lives, but I wouldn't harm her."

"Did Shawn tell you he planned to visit his mother tonight?"

"No."

"So you don't know why he wanted to speak with her?"

"I told you. I wasn't aware Shawn visited Megan until he called." Kemp dropped his head. "Shawn has been furious with Megan since the separation. He blames her. But the truth is, the separation was mutual. Megan and I hadn't gotten along for several years. She didn't belong in Wells Ferry, and motherhood never meshed with her career aspirations. We never should have married. Unfortunately, Shawn paid the price for his parents' breakup."

Raven leaned in the doorway.

"Was Megan seeing anyone?"

"Not that I'm aware of."

"Any old boyfriends who gave you a bad vibe?"

"Megan's business was her own. I stayed out of her life after she left. If I were you, I'd focus on her clients. She was a criminal defense attorney, and she didn't defend boy scouts."

Darren pulled a chair away from the table and turned it around. He sat with his forearms resting on the chair back.

"Any clients capable of murder?"

"Too many," Kemp said, running a hand through his hair. He scrunched his brow. "There was one guy. Hanley Stokes."

"Hanley Stokes," Darren repeated, copying the name onto his memo pad. "What about him?"

"Known drug dealer, in and out of jail over the years. Megan represented him."

"Did Stokes contact Megan in recent weeks?"

"Last I heard, he just got out of prison. Perhaps one of his scumbag friends went after Megan. Your guess is as good as mine."

Darren opened his mouth to reply when headlights swept over the window. Wells Ferry PD had arrived.

5

The two Wells Ferry PD officers shuffled past Darren's Silverado with caution. A bearded officer with a milky complexion aimed a flashlight inside the cab. The second officer gazed from the truck to the house, counting the silhouettes mirrored against the curtains.

Years of working overtime had taught Darren to recognize the faces of officers just called into the field. Harried, tired. Irritated to be working a case instead of enjoying their time off.

"Wells Ferry PD," the bearded officer announced, pounding on the door.

Suffering from a head cold, the officer spoke through his nose.

Kemp let them inside.

"Mr. Massey?" the clean-shaven officer asked. His turquoise eyes darted from Darren to Raven.

"Yes."

"And you are?"

When the officer glanced at Darren, the state park ranger stepped forward.

"Darren Holt, and this is Raven Hopkins."

"Darren is our cousin, and Ms. Hopkins works for Wolf Lake Consulting," Kemp said. "Have you found my son?"

"Not yet," the sick, bearded officer said. Black, curly hair poked out from beneath his cap. His nameplate read *Barber*.

The other officer acted as though he led the investigation. He wore a nameplate that read *Neal*. Tension thrummed through Neal, raising veins in his muscular arms. As he spoke, his eyes never left Darren. Neal peered over their shoulders and studied the room.

"Our men are searching for Shawn now. We could use a better description to help us find him."

"He's about five feet, nine inches," Kemp said. "A hundred-sixty pounds."

"Do you have a recent photograph?"

"I believe so."

Kemp dug through his pockets and removed a wallet. Sifting through the pictures, he slid a photograph out of the sleeve and handed it to Neal. The officer raised the picture to the light, nodded, and handed it to Barber, who turned his head and sneezed. Darren's eyes fixed on another photo in Kemp's wallet. A younger Shawn wearing a little league baseball uniform with a Mets logo on the cap. The kid's smile appeared so genuine, so innocent. This was before the problems started at home.

"When was the last time you saw your son?"

"Around nine."

"You let your son wander the streets all night?"

"He's seventeen."

"Lots of problems in Wells Ferry, especially on the east end. And as tonight demonstrates, sometimes those problems spread to the lake district. What was your son doing tonight?"

"He went out with his girlfriend."

"Give me her name."

"Polly Hart. She lives on Fennel Street. I'll get you the house number. They usually grab food or go to a movie, and Shawn always returns before his midnight curfew. I trust my son."

Officer Neal inched a step closer.

"We'd like to look through the house."

"That's unnecessary."

"Your son is missing, and someone murdered your wife. Are you unwilling to cooperate?"

Kemp glanced at Darren for help.

"Unless they produce a warrant, they can't search your property without your consent," Darren said, drawing Neal and Barber's ire. "But time is short. The only thing that matters is bringing Shawn home. I suggest you cooperate."

"Listen to your cousin, Mr. Massey," Barber said. He glanced at Darren. "Don't I know you from somewhere?"

"I worked for Syracuse PD for over a decade."

"I know the boys in that department. Next time I run into them, I'll bring your name up and see if they remember you."

Kemp stood aside and let the officers through. Neal and Barber strolled through the living room, both officers' hands uncomfortably close to their guns. Their eyes twitched back to Kemp, Darren, and Raven as they investigated the room.

"What are they looking for?" Kemp asked.

"They're just doing their jobs," Darren said, though the way both officers glared at him as if he was a suspect made him uneasy. "Let's get out of their way. We can talk in the kitchen."

They sat around the kitchen table. Kemp winced when something crashed to the floor in the living room. Raven warned him with her eyes not to protest.

"Back to Hanley Stokes," Darren said. "If I understood you, Megan represented Stokes and lost the case."

Kemp studied his reflection on the table.

"I'm not privy to the specifics. The newspaper said it was a drug bust. Stokes swore someone set him up. The usual bullshit argument."

"If Stokes pushed drugs in Wells Ferry," Raven said, crossing one leg over the other, "he probably didn't work alone."

Footsteps trailed off toward the back of the house.

"So we need to determine if Stokes blamed Megan for the court loss and sought revenge," Darren said.

"Or if he paid a partner to murder Megan."

Kemp looked up when Officer Barber entered the kitchen. Neal stood behind him, interrogating Kemp with his stare.

Barber coughed and said, "We need you to come with us, Mr. Massey."

"What's going on? Am I under arrest?"

"You need to explain something we found in the bathroom."

Darren's back stiffened. He'd advised his cousin to allow the officers into his home. Had he made a mistake?

Raven set a hand on Kemp's back. As they crossed the living room and turned down a hallway, Neal fell in behind them. The officers boxed them in, and Neal's fingers rested on his nightstick.

A bathroom stood at the end of the hall. A bar light shone above the mirror. While Neal blocked the hallway, Barber gestured at the basin.

"Care to explain all this blood?"

Darren peered over Kemp's shoulder. Raven hissed. The bathroom sink looked straight out of a gory movie. Blood stained the white basin. Specks dotted the faucet, and three splotches of blood marred the floor tiles.

Kemp blew out a breath.

"I cut myself fixing a hinge."

Kemp pointed at the wood cabinet beneath the sink. Then he raised his hand. Until now, Darren hadn't noticed the deep gash along Kemp's forefinger.

"You didn't clean it up," Barber said. "It looks to me like you were in too much of a hurry to bother."

"You've got it all wrong." Kemp met Darren's eyes, as though he needed to convince his cousin. "I was working on the hinge when Shawn called. After he told me what happened, I didn't have time to clean the sink. I just pressed a washcloth to the wound until the bleeding stopped and called the police."

"You phoned the sheriff's department," Neal said from the hallway. "Or have you already forgotten? It's tough to keep your stories straight when you have so many."

"What's that supposed to mean?"

"Can anyone verify your whereabouts at the time of the murder?" asked Barber.

"Your records should show the time I dialed 9-1-1."

"You could have called from the victim's house. Did you argue with your wife tonight, Mr. Massey?"

"What? No. I haven't spoken to her in months."

"You expect us to believe you had no contact with your son's mother, even though she lived only two miles away?"

"It's the truth."

Kemp's eyes pleaded with Darren and Raven, but there was nothing Darren could do. Why hadn't Kemp told him about the injury? Kemp concealed the laceration as if he had something to hide. Darren didn't want to believe Kemp murdered his wife. But someone stabbed Megan tonight, and a deep cut ran along Kemp's finger. There wasn't enough evidence to justify Neal and Barber arresting Kemp. Not yet, anyway.

"Check the rest of the house," Barber said to Neal. He puffed out his chest. "I'll stay with Mr. Massey."

Neal's eye twitched before he turned away. The officer looked ready to whip his nightstick against Kemp's temple.

Barber folded his arms.

"All right, Mr. Massey. We're starting over. I want a minute-by-minute breakdown of where you were this evening. If you lie to us, we'll find out."

Inside Kemp's living room, Darren leaned against the wall as Raven worked the phone. She'd called Thomas, urging the sheriff to hurry over before Wells PD arrested Darren's cousin. Then she'd contacted Chelsey to run background checks from the office on Kemp, Megan, and Hanley Stokes. The case spun out of control the moment Officer Barber discovered blood in the bathroom sink. Darren chided himself for advising Kemp to allow the search.

Kemp sat on the couch with his face buried in his hands as Officer Barber loomed over him with a page full of notes. Kemp accounted for his whereabouts between ten o'clock and midnight, but nobody could corroborate his story. As Kemp scrubbed a hand down his face, Officer Neal descended the stairs with an evidence bag in his hand. Kemp saw the bag's contents and shot off the couch.

"You can't take my son's comb. Not without a search warrant."

"You allowed us to search the premises," Barber reminded him.

"They'll compare the hair on the comb with fibers gathered at the scene," Raven said.

Kemp blanched.

"But Shawn didn't hurt his mother. He's innocent."

"Standard procedure," said Barber.

"You already knew Shawn was inside his mother's house tonight. This proves nothing."

"Does your son own a knife?" Neal asked.

Kemp shot Barber an incredulous look.

"One of those Leatherman multi-tools. So what? Lots of kids own them."

Neal glanced at Barber.

"We raided an underage party last summer. Lots of kids drinking. Your son was there."

"I found out and grounded him."

"While we're at it, I'd like you to provide us with a DNA test."

"No way. I want to speak to a lawyer before I grant you any more favors."

"It's for your own benefit. If what you say is true, we'll match your DNA to the blood in the sink and confirm your blood isn't at the murder scene."

Kemp glanced at Darren for advice. Darren pressed his lips together. He kept steering his cousin in the wrong direction. With consternation, he nodded.

"Make it quick. I'm not spending another minute here. We need to find Shawn."

Thunder boomed, shaking the walls. As Neal prepared the swab, Darren swiped his phone. The weather radar showed a line of storms heading at Wells Ferry. A flash flood watch covered the county, and nobody knew where to find Shawn.

Darren spotted the sheriff's cruiser pulling into the driveway. Finally. He exited the house and closed the door behind him, not wanting Neal and Barber to eavesdrop.

"We need you in there, Thomas."

"What's the problem?"

"Wells Ferry PD is forming cases against Kemp and Shawn. I know my cousins. Kemp didn't murder his wife, and Shawn wouldn't harm his mother."

"What do they have so far?"

Darren told Thomas about the evidence.

"Everything is circumstantial. Shawn's phone call places him at the murder scene. The hair fibers shouldn't implicate him."

"And your cousin's injury? Admit it, Darren. That doesn't look good for Kemp."

Darren rubbed his eyes.

"I understand. But I swear, Kemp isn't capable of murder."

After shaking the rain off his hat, Thomas led Darren inside. He wiped his shoes on the mat and touched the brim of his hat when he noticed Barber and Neal. Neither officer returned the courtesy.

"We have a rising river out there, and another round of storms moving in," Thomas said. "Where are we on finding our missing teenager?"

Neal straightened his back.

"Four officers are searching for Shawn Massey. We put in a call to your department. But your staff is already stretched to the point of snapping."

"My lead deputy arrived to aid the medical examiner and forensics team. Dispatch is attempting to reach Deputy Lambert. That gives us enough bodies to cover Wells Ferry and figure out where Shawn ran off to."

"We'll help," Raven said, moving beside Darren. "Just tell us what you need."

"We're not finished with Mr. Massey yet," Officer Barber said.

Thomas lifted his chin.

"We need everyone in the field. If another inch of rain falls, that river will spill out of its banks and flood the neighborhood. We need to find Shawn before that happens. Give me the location on his phone." Barber glanced at Neal, who worked his jaw back and forth. "Don't tell me you haven't contacted the cell provider. That should have been our first move."

Darren spied the fire in the sheriff's eyes. Thomas rarely got upset, but he had a right to be angry. Why hadn't Wells Ferry PD asked the cell company to locate Shawn's phone?

"Our department assumed you'd already traced the phone," Barber said, putting his notes away. "You were the first to reach the scene, correct?"

Thomas grumbled. While Barber and Neal completed their interview with Kemp, Darren and Raven followed Thomas outside.

"It's almost like they don't want to find Shawn," Raven said.

Thomas surveyed the boiling clouds.

"I just got off the phone with Chelsey," said Thomas. "She's still running background checks and will get back to us." He pulled an iPad out of his cruiser and called up a digital map of Wells Ferry. A yellow dot marked Megan Massey's house. A second dot rested over their current location. "I checked with Shawn's girlfriend, Polly Hart. She claims she dropped off Shawn down the road from his mother's house around eleven o'clock."

"Why didn't she wait for him?"

"According to Polly, Shawn told her to leave. The storm hadn't started yet, and Shawn wanted to walk home."

"So how do we find him?"

Thomas swiveled the iPad so Darren and Raven could view the screen.

"I'll call his cell provider and begin a search. In the meantime, it's a two-mile stretch from Megan Massy's house to here, and the Wells River lies in between."

"The river is near flood stage," Darren said, looking over Thomas's shoulder.

"There's a bridge in the town park. That's the only direct route between the two houses. I suggest we start the search here, arrow toward the park, and fan out along the river."

Darren bit his lip. He understood what Thomas inferred— that Shawn might have fallen into the river while fleeing from the killer.

"We'll need more than the three of us and Kemp."

"Aguilar will join the team after Virgil transports Megan's body to the morgue. I expect Deputy Lambert will arrive within the hour. Between our group and the Wells Ferry PD, we'll have enough bodies."

Darren paced.

"I don't like this, Thomas. Wells Ferry PD is already trying to pin the murder on Shawn and Kemp. I'm worried the officers don't have open minds."

"Let me worry about Wells Ferry PD. Focus on finding your cousin and think of places he might go if he's in trouble."

Glaring back at the window, Darren wiped the rain off his shoulders. The door opened. Neal and Barber led Kemp into the driveway. Barber's face twisted with frustration. The officer was determined to arrest Kemp for his wife's murder.

"Gentlemen," Thomas said, glancing skyward. "We're about to get blasted by another line of thunderstorms, and we have a lost teenager to find. I suggest we get moving before the weather shuts us down."

Neal dipped his cap and spilled water off the brim.

"Wells Ferry PD will lead the search."

Thomas didn't argue. The officers held jurisdiction in their town, though Darren wished they'd deferred to the sheriff's department. He didn't trust Barber and Neal, or how they jumped to conclusions. Darren's eyes drifted to his cousin. Kemp had donned a yellow rain slicker with the hood drawn over his head. The man shifted from foot to foot.

Was he nervous because they needed to find his son before the river flooded? Or because he'd murdered his wife?

7

SATURDAY, APRIL 17TH 12:55 A.M.

Footsteps echoed behind him. His own, or the killer's? Rain fell in sheets as Shawn Massey moved from one tree to the next. Each breath scraped broken glass through his chest. He needed to slow down before he collapsed from exhaustion. If he did, the maniac who'd stabbed his mother would gain ground.

I know your name.

The killer concealed his face beneath a ski mask, and he whispered so nobody recognized his voice. The possibility that Shawn knew his mother's killer sent shivers down his back.

Wind whipped rain against his face. Shawn shielded his eyes and pushed forward, his sneakers sinking into the mud. Between the storm and the dark, he wasn't sure where he was. Somewhere north of the park, though he wasn't certain if he was closer to the lake or his house. To make matters worse, he'd lost his phone and wallet running from the madman. That left him no way to call his father or the police...not that he trusted Wells Ferry PD. All they did was harass teenagers and bully people who stood their ground.

As he moved through a clearing with the clouds rushing

overhead, his feet flew out from under him. He splashed against the waterlogged terrain. Sucking wind, he fought to regain his breath as his strength waned. Branches crackled through the forest. It might have been the wind, animals running from the storm, or the killer.

After he pushed himself up to his hands and knees, he glanced around the clearing. The forest thickened ahead. A creek shimmered beyond the trees.

He was somewhere between the park and the lake inlet. Running blindly, he'd drifted off course. Home was at least a mile away, and the going would be slow if the rain didn't let up soon. Experience taught him the Wells River was out of its banks by now, making it impossible for him to cross unless he retraced his steps to the park. With the killer somewhere in the forest, he couldn't risk turning back.

Thick woods loomed behind him. It was too dark to see into the trees.

Shawn struggled out of the clearing and reached the forest, his ears attuned to the surrounding sounds. As he descended the land and staggered toward the creek, a cold hand wrapped around his heart. When he was in elementary school, a rapist snatched his classmate, Chad May, while the boy hiked through the forest. The police found Chad's body a week later, naked and bloated, face-down in the creek and covered with leeches. Until then, Shawn had considered Wells Ferry a safe place. After the rape and murder, parents banned their children from playing near the woods. Perverts were everywhere, they said. You couldn't trust your neighbors.

The police never caught the rapist. As lightning flashed, blasting harsh, momentary light through the forest, Shawn imagined Chad's rapist still hiding in the woods, waiting for the next kid to wander past.

A tree rustled in the dark. Shawn turned his head toward the sound and froze in place. Inky shadows poured off the trees.

An animal growled back near the clearing as Shawn leaped the creek and landed on the far bank. The mud tried to swallow his sneakers as he grasped at saplings and pulled himself out of the creek bed.

He ran without looking back, dodging trees. Branches whipped at his face, and roots tripped him. All around, the forest swelled with breaking branches and the ceaseless wind.

The woods thinned. He was close to the inlet now, civilization somewhere in the distance.

Shawn stopped to catch his breath. Leaning over with his hands on his knees, he flinched when lightning exploded. The flash left him blind, his hearing dulled by the thunder crash. If he stayed here, the storm would kill him before his pursuer caught up.

When he broke out of the forest, he didn't believe his good fortune. The lake battered the shore. Pinpricks of light shone from residences across the water. No chance of reaching those homes, but the blue-gray marina stood before him. Last summer, he'd rented kayaks with his father at the marina. The windows were dark. The marina didn't open until eight.

A gust of wind nudged him out of hiding. He crossed the vacant parking lot and ran to the first window. Cupping his hand over his eyes, he peered through the glass. Too dark to determine if anyone was inside. The ghostly memory of Chad May's rapist followed him from window to window as Shawn circled the marina. The doors were locked. No surprise. But the window on the far side of the marina was open a crack. Shawn struggled to fit his fingers into the opening. The wood shrilled when he tugged up on the pane.

He poked his head inside. No alarms ringing. Then he lifted himself onto the sill and hauled his body inside.

Shawn dropped to the floor and landed on his hip. Pain shot through his leg as he took in his surroundings. He shivered, his clothes sodden and muddied, his sneakers soaked by filthy rainwater. Canoes and kayaks lay stacked against the near wall. The silhouette of the front counter drew a black rectangle against the darkness.

Crouching low, he moved between the aisles and located the storage room at the back of the building. He pulled the door open and squinted into the dark, afraid to turn on the light and give himself away. After his eyes adjusted to the pitch-black, he noticed the space heater tucked in the corner. A flashlight lay on the shelf. He closed the door before he turned on the beam. There were no windows in the storage room, but Shawn worried about light spilling beneath the door. He flicked the light from wall to wall until he found an outlet. Leaving the flashlight on the floor, he hobbled back to the space heater and carried it to the outlet. Fiery warmth enveloped his body when he plugged in the heater.

A thud outside brought his head up. He shut off the light and sneaked back to the door. Grasping for the knob, unable to see anything, he located the lock and twisted it. Even if the killer tracked him to the marina, he'd need to break down the door to reach Shawn. It was quiet outside now, except for the rain.

An orange rectangle reflected off the concrete floor beside the heater. Favoring his hip, Shawn shuffled back to the space heater and peeled his shirt off. After he wrung the shirt out in the corner, he stripped off his pants, sneakers, and socks. Without a rack to hang his clothes on, he left them on the floor to dry.

He wiggled beside the warmth, wary of getting too close and burning his flesh on the grates. His body trembled uncontrollably, water dripping down his skin as he rubbed his arms and legs.

Shawn wouldn't stay here long. Though he felt safe for the first time since he'd rushed from his mother's house, he needed to leave before the marina opened and the owner found him inside. Which meant sleep was a huge risk. What if he didn't awaken before eight?

It suddenly occurred to Shawn he might be a fugitive. It wouldn't surprise him if the police pinned the murder on him. The killer had worn gloves, careful not to leave evidence inside the house. If the police found Shawn's fingerprints or hair inside the kitchen—and they would, for he'd eaten dinner with his mother once per week for the past month—they'd paint him as a killer. He couldn't ask the marina owner to call the police on his behalf. Nor could he pound on a random door and expect a good Samaritan to help him. Shawn might be a wanted man.

Needing someplace to hide after he left the marina, he sifted through his options. Sometimes he partied with Polly's cousin, Camilla. There was a finished room above the garage, the perfect place to hang out and knock down a beer without their parents noticing. Crossing Wells Ferry to reach the garage was a helluva risk. But one he had to consider.

When the heat seared his chest, he turned and placed his back to the grates. Gradually, the space heater melted the cold away. The orange glow revealed a life vest on the rack. In a pinch, the vest served as a pillow. He set the vest on the floor and lay beside the heat. Whenever he closed his eyes, images of the knife plunging into his mother's stomach jolted him awake.

Shawn needed to reach his father. Dad was the only person who would believe he hadn't killed his mother. He promised himself he'd leave after three hours of rest. Just enough to take the edge off.

As Shawn curled beside the heater, he drifted into dreams.

8

SATURDAY, APRIL 17TH 1:30 A.M.

The driving rain made it difficult to hear the search party.

Thomas shook the water off his hat and surveyed the park. A paved walking and biking path wound between evergreen trees and led to a bridge at the far end of the grounds. The river sloshed against the crossing, threatening to engulf the bridge if the rain didn't stop. Raven's teeth chattered as she hooked elbows with Darren. Aguilar, Kemp, and Deputy Lambert huddled together, their shoes sinking into the mud.

Officers Neal and Barber stood before them. Neal barked orders as lightning flickered through the clouds. Barber barely kept his eyes open. The officer appeared on the verge of collapsing as he shivered in the rain.

"Officer Barber and I will take the north end of the park and search for Shawn Massey. The rain gave us one advantage. If he came through the park, we'll find his tracks. Be careful. The grass is one big mud pit."

"Where do you want us to search?" Darren shouted over the storm.

"Down by the pavilion. Maybe the kid found a way inside to escape the rain."

Thomas scrunched his brow and asked, "Why not check between the soccer field and the bridge? That's the most direct route between his house and Megan Massey's."

"Nobody in their right mind would cross that bridge. The water is too damn high."

"If it's all the same to you, we'll check the bridge after we finish at the pavilion."

"Suit yourself. But if the water drags you in, don't say we didn't warn you."

Barber and Neal headed north past the trees. Thomas didn't understand why Shawn would head in that direction when a straight line would take the teenager across the bridge. Still, he wanted to get away from the two Wells Ferry PD officers, and he trusted his companions more.

Lambert and Aguilar swept flashlight beams through the night, the two deputies calling out to Shawn every several seconds. Kemp yelled his son's name with growing desperation. Thomas led the search party to a wooden pavilion between a basketball court and parking lot. He checked the door and found it locked. The deputies separated and walked from window to window, aiming light inside. Thomas squinted through the foggy glass. No wet footprints inside, no sign anyone broke into the pavilion. As he expected, the pavilion was a dead end.

"There's nobody in there," Lambert said as he rounded the building.

"Why wouldn't Shawn cross the bridge?" Kemp asked. "He would have run home."

Thomas set his hands on his hips and scanned the field. Between the rain and fog, it was impossible to see more than a hundred feet in front of them. Far in the distance, a flash of light marked the officers' progress.

"We'll spread out and walk in a single line," said Thomas. "Leave about ten feet between you and your neighbor. If we don't find any signs that Shawn came this way on the first pass, we'll shift eastward and make a second pass." He met their eyes. They were all tired, wary of the storm. Yet their determination to save the lost teenager pushed them forward. "Take it slow. We all want to find Shawn, but this isn't a race. You're more likely to miss an important piece of evidence if you rush."

The search team spread out as Thomas commanded, Aguilar flanking the sheriff on his right, Raven on his left. Kemp walked beside Darren at the end of the line, while Lambert anchored the opposite side. Each member had a flashlight. The crisscrossing beams distracted Thomas as they struggled toward the bridge. A quick glance at his GPS confirmed they were directly between Kemp and Megan's houses.

"See anything?" Kemp called out.

Thomas heard the frustration in the father's voice.

"Keep searching, Mr. Massey. If Shawn came this way, we'll find tracks."

Lambert shouted, drawing their eyes.

"I've got tracks at one o'clock," the deputy said, fixing his flashlight beam at the muddy indentations arrowing across the field.

"Shift your positions," Thomas said. "Spread out and walk on either side of the tracks. They have to be Shawn's. Nobody else would be out in this weather."

The sheriff's heart pounded. For the first time tonight, they had a bead on Shawn Massey. But a sick feeling bubbled in his stomach. The Wells River roared a hundred yards ahead, and Shawn's tracks led directly toward the water.

"Notice the spacing of the tracks and how they weave erratically," Thomas called to Aguilar.

His lead deputy nodded.

"He was running."

Running from the killer, or fleeing because he'd stabbed his mother?

Thomas flicked the light behind him. A second set of tracks cut through the park and followed Shawn's, leading out of the trees near the park entrance.

"Someone followed him."

"I've got something," Darren called out.

Light sparkled off an object impaled in the mud. Kemp rushed toward the evidence before Darren put an arm out to stop him. Thomas jogged over and removed an evidence bag from his pocket.

"Don't touch anything."

Darren leaned over his shoulder.

"Is that a phone?"

Wearing gloves, Thomas wiggled the crushed iPhone out of the muck. It appeared someone had stomped the phone and shattered the screen. With the ground this soft, a drop wouldn't cause this much damage. The same person must have pried the back open, for the phone had no battery. As Thomas slipped the phone into the bag, he held it up for Kemp.

"Is this Shawn's iPhone?"

Kemp dragged a hand over his face.

"That's Shawn's. That's my boy's phone. Where is he?"

Thomas stood and studied the tracks. They kept weaving toward the river bank. Had Shawn run blindly into the river while fleeing his pursuer?

"Keep searching," Thomas said.

They marched to the river bank. Water rushed over the

bridge. Ancient support beams groaned as the river barreled against the structure. A fine spray wet their faces.

"He didn't cross the bridge," Raven said, kneeling beside the bank. She pointed. "There."

The footprints moved along the bank, as if Shawn searched for an alternate route across the river. The water had risen several inches since the teenager came this way. Soon, the water would erase his tracks.

As the search crew followed the bank, Kemp slipped. Darren snagged his arm and dragged him up before the river could sweep him away.

"Everyone step away from the bank," Deputy Lambert said.

Kemp staggered on, shaken.

"Did my boy fall in? Please tell me he made it across."

Before anyone answered, Aguilar fixed her flashlight on an oak tree lying across the river. The storm must have knocked the tree down.

"The tracks end at the tree," Aguilar said, glancing up and down the bank. "My guess is he used the tree to cross the river."

Kemp's head dropped. Thomas blinked the water out of his eyes and searched for an alternate route. There wasn't one. Walking across the tree over a swollen river was a death wish, but this was the only option.

A light blinded Thomas. The officers had returned from searching the north end of the park.

"What did you find?" Barber asked between coughing fits.

"You don't sound well, Officer. Why don't you head home before you catch pneumonia?"

"I don't take orders from the county sheriff."

Thomas bristled. He was tempted not to tell Barber about the phone. He gritted his teeth.

"We found Shawn's phone about fifty yards back in the field."

"You sure it's his?"

Thomas glanced at Kemp, who nodded.

"Mr. Massey recognized the phone." He lifted his chin at the tree. "With the bridge flooded, we believe Shawn used the tree to cross the river. The tracks end here."

"Or the river dragged him in," Neal said over Barber's shoulder.

"We'll assume he made it across." Thomas studied the forest on the opposite side of the river. "It's a long walk through the forest to reach his house, and he'd have a hard time finding the trail in the dark."

"There's no way across. We'll have to circle back to the parking lot and use the lake road to reach the other side."

"We can make it," Aguilar said, hoisting herself onto the trunk.

"Don't even think about it," Thomas said. But Aguilar was already crawling across the tree, her boots slipping on the slick bark as she wrapped her legs around the makeshift bridge. "Get back here, Deputy. It's too dangerous."

Lightning stroked down from the clouds and exploded. Aguilar slipped.

Thomas and Darren dove across the trunk as Aguilar's legs flipped over the side. Thomas snatched her forearm. The river screamed three feet away, branches and clumps from the eroded banks toppling through the waves. The toes of Aguilar's boots touched the water. In an instant, the force dragging her downstream increased tenfold. Thomas held on, refusing to let go. He'd never seen fear in Aguilar's eyes before now.

"Don't you drop me, Sheriff," she said, grinding her teeth as she locked eyes with him.

Aguilar's weight threatened to pull them into the river. Hands gripped his shoulders and tugged backward. Aguilar lurched onto the trunk with Thomas still gripping her forearm. Darren and Lambert urged him to hang on a little longer.

With Lambert's powerful hands holding Thomas in place, Darren crawled over his back and grabbed Aguilar's other arm. Together, they hauled the deputy away from the bank. Aguilar collapsed and lay on her back while the officers stood on either side of her. Neal radioed for help and shot Thomas a glare.

Thomas struggled to catch his breath as lightning lit the sky.

9

Water chuckled along the curb and poured through the storm grates as Chelsey Byrd ran up the sidewalk. She wore her dark, curly hair in a shoulder-length ponytail. Dressed in shorts and a tank top, she breathed through her nose as sweat broke along her brow. Each time her sneakers pounded the pavement, little puddles splashed and soaked her shins.

She'd taken to running every morning before sunrise. Arriving at work by eight o'clock had been a struggle until midwinter, when she started jogging before work. Now she fell asleep earlier and woke before the first signs of gray rose out of the eastern horizon. Exercise also helped her control her anxiety.

Fifteen years ago, during her senior year of high school, major depression struck Chelsey and crippled her. It took years of therapy and medication to piece her life together, and she refused to let depression win again. Last summer, an anxiety attack sent Chelsey to the emergency room after she collapsed at the mall. And on Halloween, she came within a fraction of an inch of dying when gunfire from fugitive Mark Benson grazed her scalp. Since the shooting, she'd jumped at every loud noise, every car backfiring. She didn't want to imagine what fireworks would do to her come Independence Day.

As if racing against her fears, she pumped her arms and legs, picking up speed. The exertion filled her with endorphins and lent her a sense of calm she hadn't experienced since before teenage depression struck. She ran faster, heart thundering through her chest.

The lights were dark inside the houses. And that was okay. She enjoyed waking up before her neighbors, preferred getting a head start on the day. After running background checks until well after midnight, she'd awoken at five-thirty, fed Tigger, the stray tabby cat she'd rescued, and dressed in her workout clothes. Instead of driving, she ran from her house to Wolf Lake Consulting, where she'd shower and cook breakfast before Raven and LeVar arrived. Working inside a converted single-story, two-bedroom house had its advantages.

She turned into the village center and jogged past the closed businesses. Only Ruth Sims's Broken Yolk had its lights on. By the time she reached Wolf Lake Consulting, she was wide awake and primed to run another mile. But she had work to do, so she slipped the key into the lock and opened the door.

Gloom pooled inside the main office. Three desks with computers and a filing cabinet comprised the workspace, and a television hung against the wall. Turning on the lights, she booted up her computer and limped on achy legs to the bedroom. Chelsey had furnished both bedrooms, so she or Raven had somewhere to sleep if work ran late. From her bedroom, she removed clothes from the dresser and carried them down the hall to the bathroom. The old water heater and pipes took a long time to heat, so she ran the water while she peeled off her sweaty clothes. After the shower warmed, she stepped under the spray and felt each muscle unravel.

As she washed, she thought about the case. According to Raven's message, Kemp Massey had officially hired Wolf Lake Consulting to clear his son's name and locate him in the wilderness. And that was a problem. In Chelsey's opinion, Kemp and Shawn Massey were suspects. Both held grievances against Megan Massey for walking out on their family, and Shawn's records depicted a history of violence, dating back three years to his parents' separation. Two fights, one school suspension. There was also a minor infraction involving underage drinking. Not a big deal in Chelsey's eyes. But it painted a picture of a teenager spinning out of control.

Then there was Kemp Massey. Kemp had drifted from job to job over the last decade. Last year, Wells Ferry PD picked him up for DUI. Most disturbing was the information Chelsey received from a Wells Ferry attorney. Megan Massey filed charges against Kemp six months ago after her husband showed up at her house, furious that she wasn't paying attention to Shawn. According to the attorney, Kemp tried to kick through the front door after she locked him out. Megan later dropped the charges. Chelsey didn't blame Kemp for wanting his wife to be a parent, but it was another strike against Kemp, a sign the man had a short fuse. But was he a killer?

Chelsey dried her hair and dressed. In the kitchen, she fried two eggs and plated them beside avocado toast. She sipped an herbal tea Deputy Aguilar swore by. As the fan buzzed over the stove, she paged through her notes. While Wells Ferry PD focused on Kemp and Shawn Massey, the sheriff's department homed in on Hanley Stokes, a known drug pusher in Wells Ferry. Stokes had completed his sentence two weeks ago. Megan Massey had represented Stokes and lost the case.

After washing her dishes, Chelsey carried the notes into the office and set them beside her computer. As she called up Wells

Ferry using Google Earth, her phone buzzed. Thomas's name appeared on the screen. Contentment warmed her body.

"Good morning," she said.

"It's night to me. We're still searching for Shawn Massey."

"Where are you now?"

"In the forest about a half-mile north of the town park. We picked up Shawn's trail in the park, but haven't found it since. Chelsey, we think he crossed a flooded river to reach the woods."

"And you're worried he didn't make it."

Thomas groaned.

"That's exactly why I'm worried. The river washed out the bridge. The only way across is a tree which fell over the water. Aguilar tried to shimmy over the tree and almost drowned. I don't know how a teenager running blind through the dark could do better."

"If he made it to the forest, he'd head for his house, right?"

"He'd try. But it would be tough for Shawn to find his way through the woods. Heck, we've already turned ourselves around a few times, and we have GPS units."

"Don't push too hard, Thomas. You're no good to anyone if you never sleep."

"The next shift comes in at eight. After we check the lake shore, reinforcements will arrive."

Chelsey leaned back in her chair and set her sneakers on the desk.

"Kemp Massey hired Wolf Lake Consulting to find his son."

"So Raven told me."

"What if Kemp Massey killed his wife?"

Chelsey relayed the information she'd learned from the Wells Ferry attorney.

"That's disturbing," Thomas said. "I'll pass the information along."

"It's possible Darren isn't thinking clearly on this case. Kemp and Shawn are his family."

"I'll keep it in mind. What's your first move?"

"Is Mr. Massey with you?"

"Yes."

"Let me know when he heads home. I need to interview him before our investigation moves forward."

Voices called from the background.

"Gotta go, Chelsey. We just found something."

"Shawn's trail?"

"I'll get back to you ASAP."

Chelsey pinched the bridge of her nose. Shawn fought mental issues, and Chelsey couldn't bear losing the teenager. His problems hit too close to home.

10

Morning light revealed footprints cutting through the mud. Officer Neal led the team along the tracks, the path marked by snapped branches and splotches where Shawn had fallen. Barber walked alongside Neal and blew his nose on a hankie.

Thomas spotted a piece of cloth torn on a blackberry thorn and bagged the evidence. It appeared to come from a gray sweatshirt.

"Didn't you say your son wore a gray Penn State sweatshirt?" Thomas asked Kemp.

"Shawn has a closet full of gray sweatshirts."

Kemp called his son's name. For the first time since they'd encountered the swollen river, Thomas saw hope in Kemp Massey's eyes. The father pushed toward the front of the pack, intent on racing after Shawn. Officer Neal grabbed Kemp and pushed him back.

"Get Mr. Massey under control, Sheriff, or we'll have to remove him from the field."

"You're wasting time!" Kemp cupped his hands around his

mouth and yelled again. Nobody replied. "This search is a sham. I'm not waiting."

Kemp tried to move past the officers. Barber's forearm stopped him. With a grunt, Barber muscled in front of Kemp and waited until Neal took the lead. After several minutes of searching, the tracks vanished. The grass grew thick here, concealing Shawn's path. Birdsong rang through the canopy as gray light filtered past the leafless branches. The forest looked dead and skeletal. As Kemp's desperation grew, Barber touched Neal's shoulder. Another muddy patch lay in the distance with tracks moving straight ahead. Thomas followed the officers out of the woods and found himself in a parking lot. A marina stood beside the lake. Muddy footprints weaved toward the marina and vanished in the grass surrounding the building. Barber glanced at Neal, who nodded.

The officers strode across the lot with purpose. Neal removed his weapon, causing Kemp to swing his eyes toward Thomas. The sheriff pressed the air down with his hands, a signal for Kemp to stay calm. Neal and Barber wouldn't shoot the teenager on sight, right?

Thomas picked up the pace and caught up to Neal and Barber. As he walked alongside, the two officers glared at each other, as if wondering why the sheriff was taking the lead on their investigation.

"Slow down," Thomas said, keeping his voice low so Kemp wouldn't overhear. "And maybe put the gun away."

"Shawn Massey remains a suspect in his mother's murder," Neal said. "I don't know about you, but I'm not taking chances."

"If he's in there, guns will only alarm him."

"Then you'd better hope he remains calm."

The two officers rushed ahead. When they reached the building, Neal gestured at Barber to check the door. Neal crept along the marina, testing each window. On the far side of the building, Neal waved Barber over. Thomas and the others stood back, ceding the investigation to Wells Ferry PD. A window stood open a crack. Two hand prints dirtied the sill.

"We have a break-in," Neal said.

The pane shrieked when Neal shoved it open. Darren and Raven shot questioning glances at Thomas as the two officers hopped over the sill and climbed inside. Lambert and Aguilar moved beside Kemp.

"Stay here," said Thomas. "And don't let Mr. Massey out of your sight."

For a sick man, Officer Barber moved with cat-like silence as he flashed his light down each aisle. Neal checked behind the counter before joining his partner. Drying mud led toward the rear of the marina. Thomas tilted his head toward the tracks, and the officers followed.

A storage room door stood closed at the end of the aisle. The mud ended at the threshold. Shawn had come this way.

Neal twisted the knob. Locked.

"There's no window to the storage room," Barber said. "If he's in there, he's not getting out."

Thomas rubbed his chin.

"What time does the marina open?"

"Eight," Neal said, eyeing the lock.

"We could wait for the owner to arrive."

"I'm not waiting that long. If that kid is hiding in the storage room, I want him out of there. Now."

"He can't leave. What's the rush?"

"Shawn Massey is the last person to see his mother alive, and we've got him on breaking and entering."

"We can't even confirm he's inside."

Barber pounded on the door. His eyes were red, his voice nasally and failing.

"Shawn Massey, this is the Wells Ferry Police. Open the door. We want to talk about what happened last night."

Silence.

Neal swung his gaze across the marina and stopped on a pry bar beside the counter.

"I'll get us inside."

"No," Thomas said, drawing Neal's ire when he placed a hand against the officer's chest. "The last thing we want to do is scare a kid who's going through hell. Besides, you'll damage the door. Do you carry lock picks?"

"We call a locksmith when we need a door opened."

"So do it. Or phone the marina owner and tell him to come in early."

Neal looked to Barber. The larger officer shook his head.

"We're treating Shawn Massey as a fugitive," Barber said. "We need to know if he's inside the storage room. If he's not, we're running behind and need to catch up."

When Neal strode toward the pry bar, Thomas held up his hands.

"Give me a second. Raven Hopkins is a PI. She might have the tools you need."

Neither Barber nor Neal appeared willing to wait as Thomas hurried to the window. He poked his head through the opening.

"Is Shawn inside?" Kemp asked, pushing past the deputies.

Ignoring the father, Thomas motioned Raven forward.

"Do you have lock picks on you?"

"Yeah, why?"

"We need your expertise."

Kemp continued to argue as Raven crawled through the opening. Thomas saw the protest form on Barber's lips.

"I take full responsibility if anyone asks questions." Thomas moved beside the door. "Raven, if you will."

Raven removed the lock picks from her jacket and inserted

them into the knob. Her tongue poked between her lips as she jiggled the mechanism. After a moment, the mechanism unlocked.

"She can't be in the building when we go inside," Neal said, positioned beside the door.

Raven shrugged and left through the window.

Barber threw the door open, and Neal spun inside with his weapon raised. Thomas gritted his teeth, afraid the officer would shoot the first person he saw. But the room was vacant. Barber sniffled and flicked the wall switch. A bare incandescent bulb hung from the ceiling. Thomas locked his eyes on the puddle in the corner. He studied the ceiling for a leak and found none.

"The kid was in here," Barber said, groaning. "He can't be too far ahead of us."

The officer spoke into his radio as Thomas paced the room.

"He came inside to escape the storm," the sheriff said, kneeling beside a space heater. Water evaporated off the ground in front of the heater. "It appears he was close to hypothermia, so he used the heater to dry his clothes and fight off the chill."

"Doesn't mean he didn't murder his mother," Barber said from behind.

"Officer, we found a second set of tracks pursuing Shawn Massey through the park. Who do you think those tracks belonged to?"

Barber's jaw pulsed.

"He could have doubled back, searching for an alternate route before he crossed the river."

"Except the pursuer's tracks were larger than Shawn's. There's a second man out there, and I believe he's the person who killed Megan Massey."

Neal scoffed.

Barber crossed his arms over his chest and stood face to face with Thomas.

"We'll see what forensics has to say about your theory."

Kemp looked between Thomas and the two officers as they exited the front door.

"Well? Where's Shawn?"

"He was here," Neal said. "Once we dust for prints, we'll have him on breaking and entering."

"You can't be serious. There's a maniac chasing him, and you want to arrest my son for hiding?"

"Shawn has a violent record at school. Until we prove otherwise, he remains a suspect."

Infuriated, Kemp lunged at Neal. Reacting quickly, Aguilar and Lambert threw themselves between Kemp and the officer as Darren grabbed his cousin and pulled him back.

"Mr. Massey just attacked an officer of the law," Barber said.

Thomas stepped in.

"No, he didn't."

"I want Kemp out of my sight. Get him out of here, or he'll spend the day in jail."

"Kemp, please," Darren said, dragging his cousin away from the officers.

"They can't call my boy a killer. Ever since the investigation began, they've done nothing but place the blame on me and my son. Shawn's in trouble. When will Wells Ferry PD do its job?"

Barber and Neal never took their eyes off Kemp as Darren and Raven pulled him across the parking lot. Lambert and Aguilar glared at the two officers.

"I've got this under control," Thomas called over his shoulder as he followed Darren and Raven. He set a hand on Kemp's shoulder. "Go home and rest. Your son is innocent, Mr. Massey. I promise we'll bring him home."

11

"Okay, let me rest for a few seconds."

LeVar Hopkins set the dresser on the floor and waited in the hallway while his neighbor, Naomi Mourning, caught her breath. They'd carried Scout's new dresser from the porch to the hallway before Naomi's arms gave out. The dresser was a donation from the Robinson family, who lived on the west end of the lake. Mr. Robinson had delivered the dresser in his pickup truck and pushed it up the ramp, leaving the rest to Naomi and LeVar.

As Naomi wiped the sweat off her forehead, LeVar peeked at the clock. Though it was Saturday, the nineteen-year-old had a final exam at eight o'clock. Today's test counted for twenty-five percent of his grade. He didn't want to rush Naomi, but he needed to leave by seven-thirty, in case he ran into highway traffic.

"All right, I'm good to go again."

Naomi grabbed the base of the dresser.

"Bend your knees," LeVar warned.

She nodded once and firmed her jaw.

"On three. One, two, three."

With a grunt, Naomi hauled the dresser off the hardwood floor. LeVar walked backward, looking over his shoulder so he didn't bang against the wall. Naomi struggled, the dresser fishtailing from side to side as she weaved in an erratic path. She gritted her teeth, her face beet-red.

"Why don't you set it down and let me pull it into the room?"

"You'll give yourself a hernia, LeVar. I can do this."

He admired Naomi's determination. The woman raised a wheelchair-bound teenager on her own, the deadbeat father nowhere to be found when Scout and Naomi needed him. It frustrated LeVar that Glen Mourning was fighting Naomi for custody. He hadn't paid attention to his kid since a tractor trailer crushed the rear of their vehicle and left Scout paralyzed from the waist down. The anger burning through LeVar gave him all the fuel he needed to move the dresser on his own, but Naomi insisted.

Naomi's arms quivered when LeVar turned the corner and directed the dresser into Scout's bedroom. A computer desk stood to the right, a bed to the left. The old dresser dated back to Scout's elementary school years. After the paralysis, she couldn't reach the top drawer from her wheelchair. The new dresser was longer than it was tall, a mammoth rectangle that weighed as much as an elephant and was just as unwieldy. Still, he wouldn't complain. He'd do anything for Scout.

When they set the dresser against the wall, Naomi dropped to the floor and rested her back against Scout's bed. She gave him an exhausted smile.

"Thank you. You did it."

"Not without your help."

"Stop," she said, waving a hand through the air. "You shouldered ninety-nine percent of the burden."

A squeaky wheel announced Scout's arrival. The teenager

had waited in the living room, staying out of the way. She took one look at the dresser and blew the hair out of her eyes.

"There's an interesting concept. A dresser that's short enough for me to reach the top drawer."

"I'm doing my best." Naomi moaned and touched her back. "I'm not as young as I used to be."

Naomi had turned forty-two over the winter, yet didn't appear a day over thirty. She wore her straight, brunette hair in a ponytail like her daughter.

"You didn't hurt your back, did you?" LeVar asked.

"My back is fine. But I'll sleep like a baby tonight. At least I don't have to work today."

Naomi ran daily operations at Shepherd Systems, the project management company Sheriff Shepherd had inherited from his late father, Mason. Thomas knew nothing about collaboration software and building operation plans for small businesses, but Mason had insisted his son take over the company so Shepherd Systems remained in the family. Until Thomas offered Naomi a high-ranking position at Shepherd Systems, she'd fallen into financial straits, unable to afford her daughter's medical bills while putting food on the table.

LeVar walked to Naomi and lent a hand. She smiled and accepted his help. The powerful teenager hauled Naomi to her feet. LeVar shifted his attention to Scout, who dragged the drawers open and closed, as though she'd found a cool new toy under the Christmas tree.

"Don't you have a criminal to catch or something?"

Scout was an amateur sleuth, an investigator who researched crimes over the internet and collaborated with teens across the country. LeVar marveled at the girl's skills. Last year, she helped the sheriff's department identify serial killer Jeremy Hyde, and she used her computers to research cases for Chelsey Byrd's Wolf Lake Consulting firm where LeVar's sister worked. On the side, LeVar, Scout, Raven, and Darren Holt investigated unsolved crimes in their semi-secret club, a group LeVar's mother referred to as the *Scooby Doo Mystery Gang*. Since last fall, Naomi and Serena Hopkins had joined the team.

The girl wheeled over to the desk and jiggled the mouse, awakening the laptop from sleep mode.

"There's always a bad guy to catch," Scout muttered. "Catch one, and two more pop up. I thought you had a test this morning."

LeVar had never seen Scout so depressed. If he had one wish, it would be for Scout to walk again. His heart ached for the teenage girl. Though her classmates treated her kindly, nobody invited her to sleepovers or asked her to go out for food or see a movie. It seemed her schoolmates didn't know how to act around Scout, didn't think she could have fun. But Scout was more fun to be around than they dreamed. LeVar spent entire days discussing hip-hop and listening to new artists with Scout. The girl was a living, breathing encyclopedia on the history of rap. Just once, he wanted to bring her into the field during an investigation. She worked cases in front of a computer screen. Despite her significant contributions, she didn't feel a part of the process.

As he mulled over the logistics, Naomi cleared her throat.

"I don't want you to be late. Come on, I'll walk you out."

Standing on the ramp outside the front door, LeVar glanced at his phone. A message had arrived five minutes ago. Raven and Darren were searching for a lost boy in Wells Ferry on the western edge of the county, and Chelsey wanted LeVar's help after he finished his exam. Chelsey Byrd had brought LeVar aboard as a paid student intern. Until he turned twenty-one, New York State wouldn't license LeVar as a private investigator. But he helped Chelsey and Raven solve cases, while building experience that might land him a law enforcement job someday.

It had been an unbelievable journey—from running the streets with the Harmon Kings gang, to earning his GED, enrolling at the community college, and declaring a major in law enforcement. It boggled his mind that his life had changed so much over twelve months.

"Looks like I've got a busy day ahead of me."

"Let us know how you do on your exam," Naomi said, shielding her head as sprinkles fell from a glowering sky. "I'm proud of you, LeVar."

LeVar started down the ramp and stopped.

"Is Scout okay? I realize it's early, but she doesn't seem herself."

Naomi sighed.

"She's stressed over the divorce and the custody battle. I still can't believe Glen is putting his daughter through this drama. He isn't emotionally fit to care for Scout."

"I'm sure the courts will see through his argument."

"Glen has money. He can afford the best lawyers. Anytime a custody battle reaches the court, there's a chance the decision won't go as planned."

"I wish I could help."

"LeVar, just being Scout's friend is enough."

LeVar blew out a breath. There had to be more he could do to solve their family crisis.

"I'll talk to Scout after I finish work."

"That means a lot to me."

LeVar glanced at Scout's window as the girl's silhouette wheeled past the translucent drapes. His throat constricted.

"You never have to ask, Mrs. Mourning. I'll do anything for Scout."

12

Chelsey parked her green Honda Civic beside the curb and confirmed Kemp Massey's name was on the mailbox. The Massey family lived in a two-story corner-lot residence with faded siding. A long porch ran along the front of the house, but there were no rocking chairs, no flowers or welcome mat that made the place seem like home. To Chelsey, the house was dying before her eyes, cast away from its neighbors and relegated to the corner.

The curtain pulled back, and someone peeked at her through the window. She didn't like this. Not one bit. Kemp Massey was Darren Holt's cousin, but Chelsey had never met the man. The more information she dug up on Massey, the less she trusted him.

Chelsey checked her hair in the mirror, procrastinating. She wished LeVar was here to back her up. Raven called before Chelsey could muster the courage to leave the car.

"You should be asleep," Chelsey said, staring at Massey's window. The man had disappeared.

"The day shift arrived. Darren and I are crashing at his place for a few hours. He wants to hit the woods again before eleven."

"So soon? That's not enough sleep."

"I'm well aware. Darren cares about his cousin. He won't rest until we find Shawn. Did you interview the father yet?"

"I'm sitting outside his house now."

Raven hesitated.

"Be careful, Chelsey. Kemp is Darren's cousin, but I don't trust him. He lost control in the field. Thomas needed to separate him from Wells Ferry PD. God knows what Kemp would have done had we not stepped in."

Raven whispered. Chelsey assumed Darren was nearby.

"I'll keep that in mind. Any progress on finding Shawn?"

"The trail turned cold outside the marina. The lake shore is rocky along the inlet, so he wouldn't leave tracks. Shawn could be anywhere."

"You think he killed his mother?"

"The Wells Ferry officers believe he did. He's the last person who saw her alive." Chelsey heard Darren's voice in the background. "I can't keep my eyes open. Let us catch some sleep, and we'll meet you at the office this afternoon. Say around two o'clock?"

"I'll be there."

"Remember what I said, Chelsey. Be careful around Kemp. He's not in his right mind."

Chelsey slipped the phone into her bag and opened the door. She leaped over a puddle to reach the curb, her senses primed as she approached the front door. Kemp Massey opened the door before Chelsey knocked.

"You Ms. Byrd?"

"Wolf Lake Consulting," Chelsey said, handing him her card.

He held the storm door open and motioned her inside. She paused before entering. Beyond the entryway, shadows eclipsed the downstairs. Swallowing, Chelsey stepped around Massey. A cluttered living room greeted her. Magazines lay strewn on a coffee table, and the cushions jutted halfway off the couch. He scrubbed a hand through his hair and nervously collected a pile of mail in the foyer. She spotted an overdue notice and a letter from a collections agency.

"Please, come in. Did you find our house okay?"

"Easy peasy."

He cleared his throat and glanced around the downstairs.

"Perhaps it would be best if we spoke in the kitchen. Follow me."

Kemp's bloodshot eyes couldn't sit still. They darted from side to side as if he expected demons to crawl through the walls. A stairway to her left led to the bedrooms. She glanced at the upper landing as he led her into the kitchen.

"Sit," he said, pulling out two chairs. "Coffee?"

"No, thank you. Mr. Massey—"

"Kemp, please."

"We should get down to business if we wish to find Shawn before it storms again."

"Of course."

He swiped a trembling hand across his mouth. She spotted a bandage wrapped around his forefinger.

"Did you injure yourself?"

Kemp stared at his finger as though it were an alien appendage.

"Oh, it's nothing. I cut myself working in the bathroom."

Blood stained the bandage. He slid his hand below the table.

Megan Massey was a highly regarded criminal defense attorney, and she'd chosen her career over her family. Any husband would harbor resentment, and Shawn displayed his frustration by acting out in school. Chelsey wouldn't rule Kemp and Shawn out as suspects.

"Let's start with places Shawn might run to. Places where he'd feel safe. Do you have family in town?"

"No," he said, rubbing the sleep from his eyes. "It's just us in Wells Ferry."

"Who would he contact if he was in trouble?"

"He'd contact his father."

"Understood. What about friends?"

Kemp drummed his legs beneath the table.

"Well, there's his girlfriend, Polly Hart."

"The sheriff already spoke to Polly. She hasn't heard from Shawn since she dropped him off at his mother's house."

"Who leaves her boyfriend by the side of the road in the middle of a thunderstorm? And the goddamn police. They were so convinced Shawn attacked Megan. Why would my son murder his own mother?"

"Kemp, please. Who else would your son contact?"

He closed his eyes and muttered to himself.

"I'm sorry. I should know the answer, but I can't think straight."

Chelsey softened her eyes.

"You're upset. Any father would be. Take your time."

"Uh, there's Phil Coplin. Shawn and Phil played baseball together when they were in little league. Best friends back then."

"Wasn't that several years ago?"

"Oh, right." Kemp clamped his eyes shut again and massaged his temples. After several seconds, he shoved the chair backward and stood. The father paced back and forth in the kitchen with his hands buried inside his pockets, a kettle over-heating. "It's the pressure and exhaustion. I just don't remember."

Chelsey wondered if Kemp knew anything about his son's friends. The father seemed caught inside his own private hell, furious at his late-wife, angry at Polly for abandoning Shawn, distrustful of the police.

She ripped a blank sheet of paper from her notebook and placed it on the table.

"I'll leave this here. When you remember who Shawn hung out with, write their names and addresses."

"He wouldn't run to his friends. I'm his father. I'll protect him."

"You know how teenagers think, Kemp. Shawn understands you're the best choice to protect him. But teenagers cling to friends during stressful times."

Chelsey wished she'd relied on her friends during her depression, rather than pushing everyone out of her life.

Kemp leaned against the counter.

"You're probably right."

She waited for him to write a few names down. It was obvious Kemp didn't know Shawn's friends, or was too stressed to recall.

"Who wanted to hurt your wife?"

A shrug.

"I gave the police a name or two. Clients who might blame Megan for losing in court."

"Hanley Stokes."

"For certain."

"Who else?"

"Megan and I stopped talking. She wouldn't tell me if there was a problem." His eyes lit. "They hang out at the lake all summer," he said, peering through the window. "Shawn and his friends."

"That's a good start."

"The lake is too cold during the spring. They don't swim until Memorial Day."

"Who swims with Shawn during the summer?"

"There was one kid." Kemp bit his lip and stared at the ceiling. "What is his name? Mike something. Shawn spent the night at his place a lot last summer."

"Do you remember Mike's address?"

Kemp shook his head.

"It doesn't matter. Mike is a year older, so he's away at college."

"Anyone else?"

He flashed an angry glare.

"Look, Shawn isn't hiding with a friend. Someone chased him through the woods, and he ended up at the marina. Where he went from there is anyone's guess. You saw the river, right? It's still flooding. If Shawn hid inside the forest, he's close to the river."

"Which is why we need to find him before dark."

A strained croak came out of his throat.

"I just want my boy to come home."

13

Shawn jolted awake when something rustled through the soggy leaves.

Propping himself up on his elbows, he studied the forest. After he grasped the first weapon he saw—a fist-sized rock—and crawled into a crouch, the teenager slipped behind a tree and pressed his body against the trunk. A centipede the size of his finger scurried over his hand. He flicked the centipede away. Though their poison rarely affected humans, they packed a painful bite.

When the sound didn't come again, Shawn crept out of hiding and stretched his achy legs. He'd slept upon a bed of rocks, and his back felt as if someone had clubbed him with a baseball bat. Shafts of milky light bled through the canopy. Judging by the strength of the light, he assumed it was midday. How long had he dozed?

His chest tightened when he thought of his mother. He'd hated her for leaving him. Now he only wanted to hear her voice one more time, to tell her he was sorry for not listening, not understanding. His parents had problems even before the separation. The late-night arguments, his mother spending more time at the office to avoid his father, the battles over whether to move to the city or stay in Wells Ferry. Separation and divorce were inevitable. Like a fool, Shawn needed someone to blame.

He'd never speak to his mother again. She wouldn't ask him about school or his girlfriend, wouldn't call Shawn and invite him to dinner, or help him move into his college dorm room next fall. Amid the sounds of the forest, he sobbed and wiped his eyes. Whoever killed his mother needed to pay.

I know your name.

Shawn cast a glance over his shoulder. The psychopath might have been watching from the forest. The trees grew thick in this part of the woods, bramble and pricker bushes spreading along the trunks like razor wire.

Though he'd dried his clothes inside the marina, his pants and sweatshirt were damp again. Sleeping on a soggy forest floor did that to you. The low sky warned him of more storms, and he needed to get inside, stay out of the elements, and put walls between him and his stalker.

He wobbled between the trees and tried to recall where he'd fled after leaving the marina. Without a watch, he'd only known it was late and dark, no sign of the coming sun after he climbed through the window and rushed into the forest. His feet ached, legs screamed in protest as he struggled onward. He was somewhere east of the inlet, the lake a short walk to his west. Shawn assumed he was a wanted man by now, and he didn't trust the corrupt police. As he approached the shore, he'd risk running into people. If someone spotted Shawn, the police would track him down. He couldn't trust strangers.

Running home seemed too dangerous. The killer would expect him to return to his house. If he hadn't lost his phone, he would have called his father. Or Polly. Or Mike.

Wait. Mike Nash.

Shawn's best friend was away at college until the end of the month, and his parents left for Florida in January and wouldn't return until Mike's semester ended. Which meant nobody was staying at the cottage. What he wouldn't do for a shower, even if it was cold.

He picked up his pace, invigorated by the prospect of escaping the weather. Maybe the Nash family kept food in the pantry, something to quell the hunger eating a hole through his stomach. And if they had a phone, his problems were solved.

Shawn pushed the flora aside and hurried west. In the distance, the lake whispered as it raked the shoreline. Keeping the water in sight, he climbed over a fallen tree and splashed through patches of mud before he broke out of the forest. The lake spread out before him. On sunny days, the water was a depthless blue. Today, it was a gray, churning morass, a reflection of the sky. He oriented himself along the shoreline. To the south, the marina poked out along the inlet. If he followed the shore, he'd reach the vacant cottage within an hour.

Sprinkles fell from the fitful clouds. He refused to endure another storm. Two boats floated on the water, heedless of the weather. Shawn sensed people watching as he struggled over the rocks. Intent on staying hidden, he walked along the edge of the forest and cloaked himself inside the tree line. It seemed he'd walked forever when the cottage materialized through the trees. Mike Nash's parents were wealthy. His father made a lot of money during the stock market boom and sold out before the crash.

Though he was certain nobody lived in the cottage this time of year, Shawn hesitated outside the property line and studied the windows for movement. The six-bedroom, hazel-wood contemporary home looked like nirvana after the night Shawn spent in the woods. A large deck sat off the back of the property, and the many windows offered views of the forest and the distant lake. It also allowed people to see inside. Shawn needed to be careful.

If he found a way inside. There was no guarantee the Nash family hadn't armed the home with a security alarm.

Shawn stepped out of the forest and surveyed the house. He moved to each window and tested the panes. Finding the windows locked, he checked the front door, then hoisted himself onto the deck. He stared inside and pictured himself on the couch beside Mike, video game controllers in their hands, their hair damp from a long day in the lake, an open pizza box on the table. He wished he could turn back time to last summer and forget this nightmare. If Mike was here, he'd know what to do. The open floor design lent him unobstructed views of the sitting area, dining room, and kitchen. A dark hallway led to the bedrooms and the bathroom. The shower. God, how he craved a shower right now.

He yanked on the sliding glass door. His breath caught in his chest when the door jiggled on its track. He peered over his shoulder and ensured nobody watched. Then he shoved the door until something popped. The lock released. Shawn grinned. Putting his shoulder into the door, he muscled it aside and stepped into the cottage. He held his breath and listened for an alarm. Nothing.

His sneakers left muddy tracks on the polished hardwood. This was his friend's cottage, and Mr. and Mrs. Nash always treated him well, never judging him for coming from a broken home. He slipped his sneakers off and tossed them on the deck. Then he located a broom and dustbin in the closet and cleaned his mess.

The refrigerator was empty. No surprise. But when he opened the pantry door, he smiled at the canned and boxed food. Soups, cereals, pasta. He could eat like a king for weeks.

Shawn flipped the light switch. The cottage had power,

which meant the electric stove worked. No phone. Like most people in Wells Ferry, the Nash family switched to mobile phones years ago. Before he ate, he needed to shower the filth off his body and change his clothes.

The dirt poured off his flesh as the warm spray washed over his head. All that mud circled the drain and descended. After soaping his body and shampooing his hair, he felt human again. Like he hadn't spent the night running for his life from a madman.

He toweled dry and stared at his reflection in the mirror. Scrapes crisscrossed his face, and a purple bruise rose off his arm where he'd landed after a tumble in the woods. Every bone, every muscle in his body pleaded with him to get off his feet and rest.

In Mike's bedroom, he dug a Nazareth lacrosse sweatshirt out of the dresser and found sweatpants that fit. He stole a pair of socks, but couldn't bring himself to confiscate underwear until he located a package of briefs in shrink wrap.

His stomach rumbled. As much as he desired food, he'd only slept three hours. Drawing the curtains across the window, he locked the bedroom door. He collapsed on the foot of the bed and closed his eyes.

Shawn fell asleep a moment before the police siren shrilled out of Wells Ferry.

14

By the time Darren and Raven stumbled into Wolf Lake Consulting, they were covered in a fresh layer of mud, their clothes soaked through and bodies dragging from lack of sleep and another fruitless search of the woods. Darren's shoulders hung as he followed Raven into the office. Chelsey took one look at them and shot off her chair.

"What happened to the two of you?"

"I tripped over a root and tumbled down an incline," Darren said, massaging his back.

"And I grabbed his arm and followed him down," said Raven.

"Let's get you cleaned up. There's a full shower at the end of the hallway." Chelsey wiggled her nose. "I don't have any clothes that will fit Darren."

"I might have something he can wear," Raven said, plunking herself down in a chair.

Chelsey ran over to her, waving her hands in the air.

"Nuh-uh. You're getting mud all over the workstation."

Raven released a long breath.

"I'll wash my hands in the sink."

"You can shower first, Raven," Darren said.

He felt as if he'd run a marathon. Failing to find his cousin left a hollowness in his chest.

"You sure?"

"I'll go after you."

"If you insist."

The bathroom door closed down the hallway. Darren glanced around the office, afraid to touch anything. He was a walking mud puddle, the silt and dirt ground into his hair.

"You look like hell, Darren."

"Thanks a million."

"When was the last time you ate?"

He touched his stomach.

"I scarfed a protein bar before we left the cabin."

Chelsey rolled her eyes.

"No, I mean real food, not something that comes in a wrapper."

Darren rubbed his eyes with his thumb and forefinger.

"I barbecued chicken breasts for dinner yesterday."

"Come with me," she said, pivoting on her heels.

He followed Chelsey from the office to the kitchen. She stood on tiptoe and removed a plate from the cupboard. Next, she opened the refrigerator and poked her head inside.

"I bought two pounds of sliced London broil for sandwiches."

"Two pounds? Are you feeding an army?"

"I figured we'd end up working late. It beats running out for fast food." She removed a plastic box of spinach and set a tomato on the counter. "We have condiments in the fridge— brown mustard, honey mustard, mayo. Pick your poison."

A smile formed on his face.

"You thought ahead."

"I told you. I've been down this path too many times. Nature of the business. Now eat before you lose another pound and blow away."

When the kettle whistled, Chelsey poured steaming water into a mug and set it on the counter. Then she scooped a green, powdery substance into the water, sprinkled a touch of cinnamon, and whisked the concoction together. Darren wondered if she was actually going to drink the strange brew. Instead, she pushed it in front of Darren and looked at him expectantly.

"What the hell is that?"

"Matcha tea."

"Am I supposed to drink this tea of yours?"

"Don't knock it until you try it."

"It looks like the scum you peel off swamps in the summer."

"Darren, you need healthy energy. If you don't drink my tea, I'll plug your nose shut and pour it down your gullet."

"Easy," he said, holding up a hand. He muttered to himself. "When did the world give up on coffee?"

Chelsey returned to the office and left Darren alone to build his sandwich. As he sipped his tea, he had to admit it wasn't half-bad. The taste was a little funky, but he suddenly felt wide awake without the typical caffeine buzz. He chose two slices of oat bread, slathered on far too much honey mustard, loaded a quarter-pound of London broil, and sprinkled spinach over the top. After slicing the tomato, he longed for diced onion. Opening the crisper drawer in the refrigerator, he gaped when he found a halved onion. If he wished for a sizzling filet mignon, would he find that too?

The sandwich wasn't the best he'd ever built. But it was heaven in his famished state. He closed his eyes and chewed.

After he finished, he cleaned and dried his plate and set it in the cupboard. He marveled at Chelsey's setup. Working at Wolf Lake Consulting was like working from home, only better because he was surrounded by friends. He scoffed at the dirt he tracked across the floor.

"Don't worry about it," Chelsey said from the doorway. "I'll run the vacuum while you shower."

"I'm making a mess of your kitchen."

"It's just dirt. I don't mind."

"How did your interview with Kemp go?"

She gave him a diplomatic smile.

"The investigation is off to a good start."

Yeah, right. The last time Darren saw Kemp, he tried to attack the Wells Ferry PD officers. Kemp wasn't just scared, he was out of his mind with grief. Darren gave Chelsey credit for speaking to Kemp alone. The woman had guts.

Before Darren could make an excuse for his cousin, the front door opened.

"Where's everybody at?"

"In the kitchen, LeVar," Chelsey called out.

Raven's brother leaned his shoulder against the jamb and grinned when his eyes fell on Darren.

"Bruh, you remind me of Pig-Pen in the Peanuts cartoons. You planning to plant a garden in your hair?"

"You're a million laughs, LeVar," Darren said. "If you must know, I spent the last three hours slogging through the forest."

"Try searching on your feet next time. It's faster."

"How did you do on your exam, wise guy?"

"Aced it."

"So you're confident you'll pull an A this semester?"

"One hundred percent."

Chelsey hooked her arm with LeVar's.

"Since you're well on your way to being a topflight investigator, maybe you can help us find Shawn Massey. Darren's cousin is missing, LeVar."

LeVar's eyes fell.

"Oh, damn. I didn't realize. Sorry for busting on you, man. I didn't know he was family. You must be worried sick."

"No worries," Darren said, dropping a hand on LeVar's shoulder. "Besides, the next time I traipse through the woods in the middle of a thunderstorm, I'm taking you with me."

"*Aight*," LeVar said uncertainly.

The shower gurgled at the end of the hallway as Darren and LeVar trailed Chelsey into the office. If Raven stayed under the spray another minute, she'd shrivel into a prune.

Chelsey loaded a digital map of the wilderness outside Wells Ferry and zeroed in on the marina. She ran a finger along the terrain as Darren and LeVar squeezed beside her.

"Here's the town park where you found Shawn's phone, and here's the marina."

"He's moving north," LeVar said.

"Could be by design," Darren said, rubbing his chin. "Or he might be lost."

Chelsey tapped a fingernail against the screen.

"He's from Wells Ferry. Even if he stumbled upon the marina by chance, he's not lost anymore. He knows where he's going."

Darren swiped dirt from the corner of his eye.

"We canvassed the area between the marina and the park where the river overflowed. I assumed Shawn would work his way back to his house."

"Not if he's worried the killer is watching the place," said LeVar.

"Dammit. We should have searched north of the marina."

"You had no way of knowing, *dawg*." LeVar scrolled the map. "What's north of the marina?"

"Nothing but forest for a mile before the residences pop up along the lake shore. Mostly seasonal cottages."

"Seasonal cottages," Chelsey repeated. "Shawn might have a friend who lives north of the marina. Someone the killer doesn't know about."

15

Chelsey waited until the bathroom door closed. The shower ran as she turned her attention to Raven, who wore a pair of Chelsey's jogging pants and a Broken Yolk T-shirt. A towel held her hair in place while it dried. Raven gave Chelsey a curious glance.

"What's with the secretive stare?"

"I didn't want to say this in front of Darren. But I haven't ruled out Shawn and Kemp Massey. Either might have killed Megan."

LeVar shared a look with his sister.

"Half the town is searching for Shawn. Are you suggesting he's the murderer?"

Chelsey exhaled.

"I'm unsure what to believe. Shawn had motive and opportunity. He's the only person the police placed inside the house with Megan. And he was upset with his mother and intended to confront her."

"Maybe they argued, and things spun out of control."

"In other words, he's not running from the killer. He's running from the police."

LeVar rocked back in his chair.

"Not buying this theory."

"Why not?"

"The park. Darren found Shawn's phone, and someone crushed the screen and removed the battery."

"He's right," Raven said, shifting her chair to face Chelsey. "Grinding the phone under your shoe might be an act of rage. But removing the battery takes forethought. Whoever found Shawn's phone wanted to ensure we didn't trace its location."

Chelsey tapped her nails on the desk.

"Didn't Thomas find a second set of tracks in the park?"

"He did. The prints appeared larger than Shawn's."

"So an adult male chased him."

LeVar leaned forward.

"What about the father? What makes you suspect he killed Megan Massey?"

Chelsey pushed the hair out of her eyes.

"Kemp Massey hated his wife." Chelsey recounted the attorney's claim that Kemp tried to kick Megan's door down in a fit of rage. "When I interviewed him this morning, he couldn't recall any of Shawn's friends. Either the guy is out of touch and aloof, or he doesn't want us to find Shawn."

"Because he's the killer."

"Possibly. There was something off about the guy. He's evasive." Chelsey turned to Raven. "What's your take on Kemp Massey?"

Raven lowered her voice and shifted her chair closer to LeVar and Chelsey. Darren was still in the shower.

"Thomas held Kemp back after he lunged at the Wells Ferry PD officers. The guy has a short fuse." Raven chewed a nail. "And there's something else. The police found blood in the bathroom sink at Kemp's house. He claims he cut himself repairing a hinge."

"I noticed the bandage. Seems like a convenient coincidence. Kemp Massey slices his finger open around the time someone stabs his wife. Could be he injured himself during a struggle."

"But the report says Shawn called his father at home to warn him about the killer."

"Shawn called Kemp Massey's cell, not the land line. Kemp could have been anywhere when he took that call."

"So we'll keep Kemp near the top of our suspect list," said LeVar. "But don't forget Kemp Massey hired us to find Shawn and clear the kid's name, not solve a murder case."

"Solving the case might be the key to finding Shawn."

"Understood. Who else belongs on the suspect list?"

Chelsey minimized the browser and called up a photograph of Hanley Stokes. Black, greasy hair trailed down to the convict's shoulders. A scar cut above his left brow.

"Hanley Stokes. Megan Massey represented Stokes after Wells Ferry PD busted him."

"He's the drug pusher, right?"

"Correct. Stokes's sentence ended. He's on the street again."

"And now Megan Massey is dead. Another coincidence?"

"If Stokes blamed Megan for failing him, he might have sought revenge."

"Huge risk," LeVar said, shaking his head. "Most convicts get out of prison and stay under the radar before they murder defense attorneys."

"Speaking from experience?" Raven asked with a mischievous grin.

"You watch *The Sopranos* too often." LeVar pressed his lips together in consideration. "All hell breaking loose the minute Stokes hit the street can't be a coincidence. He's involved somehow. Keep him on the list."

"How about a boyfriend?" Chelsey asked. "Megan Massey

was a good-looking woman. Hard to accept she never dated after the separation."

Raven unraveled the towel and swung her hair over her shoulder.

"Kemp claims he stayed out of Megan's personal life. We asked him who Megan dated. He doesn't know."

"Then we need to find out. What's our next step?" Chelsey leaned back and tapped a pen against her lip. After mulling the question over, she tossed the pen on the desk. "I ran background checks on Hanley Stokes, and Kemp and Megan Massey. Nothing stuck out. Let's run one more check on Shawn Massey, just to rule him out as our killer. I'll get started on that."

LeVar swept a hand through his dreadlocks.

"I'll call Scout and ask her to research Shawn's friends. Hopefully, we'll figure out where he's heading."

"Good idea. Tell her to focus on friends who live north of the marina."

"Bet."

"What did I miss?" Darren asked. They all swung their heads around. LeVar snickered at the Adidas sweatpants. The cuffs ran halfway up Darren's shins. Darren glanced down and scowled. "This is what you get when you borrow clothes from your girlfriend."

"We're planning our moves for this afternoon," Chelsey said, biting her tongue to keep herself from laughing. "Darren, take Raven with you and speak with Polly Hart."

"Why? Thomas already interviewed the girlfriend. She doesn't know where Shawn is."

"I'm more interested in Shawn's state of mind last night. If Shawn killed his mother, he'd show signs of instability."

"I assure you, Shawn didn't kill Megan."

"The police say he did. Let's rule him out before we move forward."

Darren furrowed his brow.

"All right, but it's a waste of time. We should go back to the forest and search north of the marina."

"And you will. LeVar will call Scout, and she'll look into Shawn's friends. If he has a friend in that area, she'll find him. No sense wandering around without a plan."

Darren exhaled through his nose. Chelsey could tell the state park ranger wanted to resume the search.

"If Scout doesn't find anyone by dinner time, I'm going after Shawn again."

Chelsey clasped her hands behind her head.

"We have work to do if we intend to find Shawn before dark."

16

Thomas hunched over a map inside the Wells Ferry Police Department's conference room. He hadn't slept this morning like he'd promised Chelsey, and the exhaustion was catching up to him. He rubbed his eyes when the terrain features crisscrossed in his vision.

With a groan, he set the map aside and scrubbed a hand down his face. He sat alone at the table while his deputies broke for a late lunch in town. This was hostile territory. The officers on the other side of the glass shot him disdainful glances as they went about their duties. He pretended not to notice. What the hell was the issue between Wells Ferry and Nightshade County? Like two feuding families, the rivalry dated back so far that nobody remembered what they were fighting over.

The door opened, and Officer Barber strode inside without bothering to knock. He looked worse than he had this morning. Barber breathed through his mouth, his sinuses cemented shut. His eyes hung like a mournful dog's. Red splotches on the officer's neck suggested he'd spiked a fever.

"You should go home," Thomas said, setting his elbows on the desk.

"And let the county run the investigation? You'd like that, wouldn't you?"

He tossed a folder in front of Thomas.

"What's this?"

"Preliminary report from the forensics team. They collected sandy brown hair from the entryway, hallway, and kitchen." Shawn Massey has sandy brown hair, Thomas thought. "The only other hair they found matched the victim's."

"So what are you saying?"

"That there were only two people inside that kitchen when Megan Massey died. Megan and her son, Shawn Massey."

"The killer wore a ski mask. That would explain the killer not leaving hair at the scene."

Barber clucked his tongue.

"Let's be honest. If criminals were intelligent, we'd never catch them. Ninety-nine percent of the time, we apprehend crooks and killers because they did something stupid. They don't think ahead, and they certainly don't clean up after themselves to avoid detection. Stop overthinking the issue. Shawn Massey blamed his mother for wrecking the family, and he murdered her to gain revenge. Maybe the bitch deserved it. You ever see Megan Massey in court? Spiteful whore considered herself better than the police."

Thomas ignored the diatribe and paged through the report.

"How long before the test results return from the lab?"

Barber blew his nose into a hankie and cleared his throat.

"Days, weeks. But we won't be able to match the hair to Shawn until we catch him."

"Did forensics pull fingerprints from the scene?"

"They did."

Thomas glanced expectantly at Barber.

"And?"

"They're running matches now. Shawn Massey's prints aren't

on file, but the father's are. Turns out Kemp Massey applied for
federal employment ten years ago."

"So if Kemp Massey was inside the kitchen, we'll match his
prints."

"If anyone besides the son murdered Megan Massey, it was
the father. I don't buy that story about him slicing his finger
open."

Thomas didn't want to argue. But Barber seemed insistent.

"Is there some reason you refuse to accept anyone besides
Shawn or Kemp murdered Megan Massey?"

"The evidence is crystal clear. No sign of forced entry. That
tells me Megan Massey knew her attacker and allowed him into
her house, or the killer had a key. The father admits his wife
gave Shawn a key to the house. It would've been easy for Kemp
to copy his son's key, or steal it."

"Is your partner just as certain?"

Barber rolled a knot out of his neck.

"Look, Officer Neal and I are both on overtime. I'm sick as a
dog and haven't slept three hours since yesterday morning. This
investigation is as clear cut as they come. The problems start
when big city detectives like you saunter into town and confuse
matters with far-fetched theories." A sardonic smile formed on
the officer's face. "That's right. We heard about your career with
the LAPD, the FBI task force you headed up. Too bad you almost
got everyone killed."

Thomas flashed back to the shooting. Bullets firing over his
head, his partners face-down in the grass, screaming for backup.
The searing pain when a stray bullet ripped through his back
and dropped him to the ground. Why would Barber throw the
shooting in his face?

"Give me what you have on Hanley Stokes."

"Stokes again?"

"He's a suspect."

"Whatever." Barber picked up the conference room phone and punched three numbers. "Yeah, Neal. The sheriff wants the Stokes file." A pause. "Yeah, I agree it's a waste of time."

A minute after Barber set the receiver down, the door opened. Officer Neal glanced between his partner and Thomas.

"There a problem in here?"

Barber shook his head.

"Just waiting for the sheriff to board the reality train."

Neal snickered. He tossed another folder on the table. Hanley Stokes stared back at him. In his mugshot, Stokes had a scrape across his cheek and a half-moon black eye, as if he'd skirmished with the arresting officers. Light brown hair grew past his ears. Thomas paged through the case file and lifted an eyebrow at Neal.

"You're still convinced the killer is Shawn or Kemp Massey?"

"They're the most logical choices. But if you're determined to prove Stokes did it, feel free to peruse the case notes. I have a witness who claims she saw Stokes outside Megan Massey's house three nights ago."

Barber turned to look at his partner. Apparently, Barber wasn't aware.

Thomas rose from his chair.

"Did he threaten Massey?"

"He pounded on the door for five minutes. Nobody answered." Neal tilted his head in thought. "Could be Massey wasn't home, or she spotted Stokes through the window and refused to answer the door."

"What did Stokes do next?"

"He left," Neal said, snatching the folder off the table and tucking it under his arm. "Didn't break in, didn't cause a scene. But it's plausible Stokes drove to his attorney's house to confront her."

Neal turned his head to Barber, as if seeking the officer's

approval. Barber gave a half-hearted grunt.

"So now we're investigating three suspects." Barber wiped the hankie across his nose. "I don't understand why we're making this case more complicated than it needs to be."

Officer Neal slapped Barber on the shoulder.

"No worries as long as we catch the bad guy, Barber. Right, Sheriff?"

Thomas didn't answer. He wondered how long Neal had held the Stokes information before sharing.

"Tell me about Stokes," Thomas said, sitting on the edge of the table.

"His reputation precedes him. Stokes deals coke and a variety of narcotics on the east side of Wells Ferry. Three years ago, he held up a liquor store in town."

"I didn't notice the robbery in his case file."

"The assailant wore a ski mask." Neal waited until the information sank in. Shawn Massey claimed his mother's killer wore a ski mask. "So we never proved Stokes robbed the joint."

"Yet you're certain it was him."

"Keep your ear to the pavement, and you'll hear rumors."

Part of Thomas wanted to celebrate. Finally, the Wells Ferry PD considered a suspect other than Shawn or Kemp Massey. But this news about Hanley Stokes seemed too sudden. Too convenient.

"Why the long face, Sheriff? This is your opportunity to take a violent offender off the streets."

As the two officers filed out of the room, Barber glared at Thomas over his shoulder. The door closed. It was quiet inside the vacated conference room.

Hanley Stokes sat at the top of Thomas's suspect list. He was a dangerous criminal with motive to murder Megan Massey, and a witness placed him outside Massey's residence.

So why didn't Thomas buy Neal's story?

17

L eVar scanned his computer monitor and sifted through Shawn Massey's call and text history. So far, their preliminary investigative work led to dead ends. Chelsey's background check into Shawn had come up empty. Except for school fights, there was nothing to suggest the teenager had a murderous bone in his body.

While Chelsey spoke with Wells Ferry PD in the kitchen, LeVar called Scout and placed her on speakerphone.

"What's up?" Scout asked.

She sounded as if she'd just awakened.

"Sorry, were you sleeping?"

"No."

LeVar glared at the phone, wishing he could see her face. Scout sounded so sullen, so defeated. No playful barbs or banter.

"Anyway, I'm searching Shawn Massey's phone history and wondered how you're doing on your investigation."

Scout sighed.

"Nothing interesting on Shawn's Facebook profile. He only posts a few times per month."

"Maybe he prefers a different social media site."

"No Twitter handle. He has an Insta, but he last posted a picture a year ago. Want me to keep looking?"

LeVar tapped a pen against the desk.

"Check his connections. Their profiles might tell us more."

"Okay," Scout said, yawning. "But it will take all day."

This wasn't like Scout. You couldn't hold her back from an investigation. LeVar's shoulders tensed when he thought about Glen Mourning's custody claim. Did he realize he was killing his daughter?

Switching the topic, LeVar tilted the phone toward him.

"Hey, I got some beats for you to check out."

"Yeah? Who?"

"Griselda."

"What's a Griselda?"

"It's a record label out of Buffalo. For hip-hop, that's practically our backyard."

"Cool," she muttered.

"But they're also a rap collective. Benny the Butcher, Westside Gunn, Conway the Machine. They recorded an album together, and it's pure fire."

"Whatever."

"I'll put them on next time you stop by the guest house, *aight*?"

"Yeah, sure."

LeVar wanted to scream. Scout's indifference ripped his heart out.

"Anything else?"

LeVar dropped his face into his hands.

"Nah, just wanted your help to track down Shawn's friends."

"I'll start in a second."

"Concentrate your efforts on anyone who lives north of the marina. You know where the marina is in Wells Ferry?"

"I have Google Earth, LeVar."

"Have at it. Gotta go, Scout. Work your magic."

The line died.

LeVar rocked back in his chair and rubbed the frustration off his face. Chelsey strode into the room and took a seat at the neighboring desk.

"Problem?"

He glanced at her between his fingers and exhaled.

"When we finish this case, let's open an investigation on Glen Mourning."

"Naomi's husband? Why?"

"Why is he fighting Naomi over custody? Since the accident, he hasn't given two craps about his kid. Suddenly, he wants to drag Scout away from her mother. Why the change of heart?"

Chelsey stretched her legs and crossed her ankles.

"People change, LeVar. Perhaps he realized how much time he lost with Scout, and he's attempting to make up for it by taking over her life."

"Talk about overcompensating."

Chelsey rolled her chair over to LeVar's and met his eyes.

"Listen, I agree with you. Glen Mourning doesn't deserve to win custody, and it would be a disaster for Scout if he did. But don't judge him before you walk in his shoes."

LeVar ground his teeth.

"Nothing worse than a father who walks away."

Chelsey placed a compassionate hand on his arm. Everyone knew LeVar and Raven's history. Their father, Dorian Hopkins, abandoned the family when LeVar was born and Raven was only seven. LeVar never met his father. Did LeVar resemble Dorian? If they passed on the street, would LeVar sense their relationship the way two magnets draw each other?

"Glen Mourning was behind the wheel when the tractor

trailer slammed into their vehicle. He blames himself for what happened to Scout."

"That makes no sense. How was it his fault?"

Chelsey flashed an ironic smile.

"Guilt knows no bounds." She patted LeVar on the knee and rolled back to her desk. "I'll help you look into Glen Mourning after we locate Shawn Massey. In the meantime, I need you to focus on this case."

"I'm on it."

"Tell me about Shawn's call history."

LeVar turned the monitor to face Chelsey's desk.

"Typical teenager. Only two calls over the last week, including the call to his father after Megan's murder. About three hundred texts, almost all to Polly Hart."

"What about the other caller?"

"I cross-referenced the number online. Dead end. It appears to be a telemarketing scheme, one of those car warranty expiration deals." LeVar's phone rang. He glanced at Chelsey. "It's Raven."

Chelsey set her mouse aside.

"They must have arrived at Polly Hart's house. Put her on speaker."

RAVEN PRESSED the phone to her ear and waited for LeVar to answer. The windows were down on Darren's Silverado. The sultry warmth rolling into the car reminded Raven of July and August. Growing up in upstate New York, she knew this type of heat always ended badly in April. From the passenger seat, she watched a monstrous cumulonimbus cloud explode in the distance. It wouldn't be long before another line of storms scoured Nightshade County, and these thunderstorms would be killers.

Darren fiddled with his keys beside her. Raven put the call through the speakers so Darren could participate. LeVar answered.

"LeVar, Darren is on the call."

"Gotcha. You're on speaker with Chelsey too."

"Where are you?" Chelsey asked in the background.

"Darren and I are parked outside Polly Hart's house. Are you aware of a severe thunderstorm watch? The sky looks nasty."

"Hold on." Chelsey typed at her terminal. "No watch yet. By the way, the background check came back clean on Shawn Massey."

"I could have told you that," Darren said, leaning forward with his elbow resting on the steering wheel and his chin propped on his fist. "Shawn has his challenges, but he's not a bad kid. And he wouldn't turn on his family."

"I ran background checks on Kemp and Megan. Hopefully, something comes up that will help us find Shawn."

Darren chewed his lip and turned away, irritated Chelsey still considered Kemp a suspect. Thunder rumbled.

"We'd better go before it storms," Raven said.

"Fill me in after you finish."

Polly Hart lived in a tiny, two-story white house with no garage. A chain-link fence surrounded the front yard, and a carport leaned over the driveway.

"Appears no one is home," Darren said, stepping into the road.

Raven agreed until the curtain rustled over the window.

"Someone is watching us."

They climbed three rickety steps and rang the doorbell. Footsteps trailed through the downstairs before a teenage girl with honey brown hair opened the door. The girl wore shorts, running sneakers, and a purple T-shirt. She glanced uncertainly at Darren and Raven between the door and jamb.

"Yes?"

"Polly Hart?" Raven asked.

"How do you know my name?"

"Are your parents home, Polly?"

"No, they're at my uncle's house. Are you the police?"

Raven handed Polly her card.

"No. I'm Raven Hopkins, a private investigator with Wolf Lake Consulting. And this is my partner, Darren Holt."

Polly turned the card over in her hand and handed it back to Raven.

"What's this about?"

"We understand you're friends with Shawn Massey."

The girl's eyes widened.

"Did you find Shawn? Where is he?"

"That's what we're trying to determine. Shawn Massey's father hired us to find him. May we talk to you about what happened last night?"

Polly poked her head through the doorway and glanced around the neighborhood.

"I guess you can come inside."

Polly led them into the living room and sat in a beaten recliner with a rip down the side. Raven and Darren took the couch. With the curtains drawn, the gloom poured out of the corners. When thunder rolled outside the window, the teenager turned on the lamp. Raven opened her notepad and clicked her pen.

"When did you last speak with Shawn Massey?"

"A little before eleven o'clock. I dropped him off down the road from his mother's house. He wouldn't let me drive to the house."

"Why not?"

"Shawn was upset. Walking helps him work things out in his head."

"So he was angry with his mother."

Polly bit a nail and nodded.

"I offered to stay, so he had a ride home. He wouldn't let me. When Shawn gets upset, he needs time alone. But after I left, I saw lightning and turned back to find Shawn."

Raven scribbled a note.

"What time was that?"

"Probably ten or fifteen minutes later."

"Did you see Shawn when you returned?"

Polly stared at her knees and shook her head.

"I drove back to his mother's house, even though he'd be angry with me. When I arrived, the lights were off, and the house was open to the storm door."

"Did you knock?"

Polly's eyes appeared haunted. She looked away.

"I got a terrible feeling something was wrong. Wherever Shawn was, he wouldn't have been inside a dark house. So I drove around the neighborhood, looking for him. That's when the rain started. After a while, it rained so hard I couldn't see through the windshield."

"What did you do then?"

"I followed the route he takes to walk home. But when I drove past the park, the river had flooded the bridge. I didn't know what to do, so I drove home and sent a text to his phone. He never answered."

"Have you heard from Shawn since?"

"No. The sheriff visited us after midnight, and the police stopped by a few hours ago. They all asked me the same questions. When did I last speak with Shawn? Did I see him after I drove back to pick him up? It's like he vanished off the face of the earth. The cops think he killed his mother. I'm worried."

"How did Shawn act last night?"

"Angry, but not out of his mind, if that's what you're implying. He wanted to confront his mother. That's all."

Darren leaned forward and clasped his hands together.

"Ms. Hart, can you think of anywhere Shawn would go if he was in trouble?"

Hail pattered the siding as Polly stared toward the window.

"I wished he'd come to me. But I haven't heard from Shawn since I dropped him off."

"What about friends? Someone he trusts."

Polly lifted a shoulder.

"Shawn doesn't have many friends in our class. Most of the people he hangs out with are older. They're all away at college now."

Raven tore a blank sheet of paper from her notepad and handed it to Polly.

"Can you make a list of Shawn's friends?"

"Even if they graduated?"

"Yes."

Polly wiped a tear off her cheek.

"I'll do my best."

"Thank you."

"But Ms. Hopkins? Please find him. I'm scared."

18

Lightning flickered through the backyard. Worried about Scout, Naomi peered through the sliding glass door and looked toward the guest house behind Thomas Shepherd's A-frame. Her daughter was inside the guest house where LeVar lived, researching an investigation for Wolf Lake Consulting. Jack, the dog Thomas rescued from the state park, accompanied Scout. Naomi trusted the gigantic dog to keep Scout safe under normal circumstances. But if a severe storm hit, there wasn't much the dog could do.

Naomi chewed a nail, struggling over whether to call Scout's phone and tell her to come home. The wind ripped twigs off the trees as waves pounded the shore. It was too risky for Scout to return. Naomi had waited too long to decide, and now the storm loomed over the horizon.

Behind her, Serena Hopkins opened the oven and removed a blueberry pie. Sweet dessert scents wafted through the home. Last autumn, Serena accepted Naomi's invitation and joined the Shepherd Systems sales team. Serena's daughter, Raven, expressed concern when Naomi offered Serena the position. Serena was a recovering heroin addict with a long history of substance abuse. She'd pulled her life together after rehab. Since taking the sales position, Serena had surpassed everyone on her team. She became the top salesperson at Shepherd Systems by midwinter, promoted twice in half a year.

"Worried about the weather?" Serena asked, shedding her oven mitts and setting them on the counter. She moved to Naomi's side and joined her at the door. Wolf Lake reflected the jagged lightning. "That little house is stronger than it looks. As long as Scout stays away from the windows, she's safe."

Naomi turned from the glass.

"I'm sure you're right. But I'd feel better if she was home with us. Maybe I should run down to the guest house and—"

Boom!

Lightning struck the lake and lit the downstairs as if a bomb exploded. Serena arched an eyebrow.

"You're not going outside."

Naomi bit her lip and padded to the counter. Blueberry juice bubbled through slits in the crust as the pie cooled beside the stove. Serena and Naomi began baking together last summer. These days, it was more than a hobby and passion. They supplied Ruth Sims and the Broken Yolk with assorted pies, cookies, and breads. Neighbors offered top dollar for Easter desserts. But Naomi refused to sell to her friends and neighbors, instead giving away desserts as gifts until she ran through their supply.

"What's she working on, anyhow?" Serena asked, referring to Scout.

"That missing boy on the news."

"The teenager in Wells Ferry?"

"That's the one. He disappeared last evening, and Thomas discovered the mother dead in her kitchen. Someone stabbed the poor woman."

"Good God, that's horrible. The boy didn't kill her, did he?"

"The sheriff's department won't know until they find him."
Naomi leaned against the counter with her head lowered. "I just
hope this investigation knocks Scout out of her funk."

Serena rinsed her hands in the sink and dried them on a
towel.

"Your daughter? In a funk? I'm not sure we're talking about
the same Scout Mourning."

Naomi raised her eyes to the ceiling and brushed the hair off
her forehead.

"I've never seen her this way. Not even after the accident.
When this damn custody battle heated up, she checked out. Her
grades dropped, she lost interest in her hobbies, and stopped
talking. She barely gave LeVar the time of day this morning, and
you know how much she loves your son."

Serena joined Naomi beside the counter.

"You're right. That doesn't sound like Scout. Has she talked
to somebody?"

A jolt moved through Naomi.

"You mean a therapist?"

Serena draped a reassuring arm around Naomi's shoulders.

"It helped me."

"I suppose it's worth a shot. If Glen backed off, her troubles
would go away. For the life of me, I don't understand why he's
fighting me for Scout."

"Some men are impossible to figure out. They're headstrong
and impulsive. If they opened up and spoke their feelings,
they'd settle their problems. But they keep everything bottled
up."

"For a long time, I pitied Glen. He did nothing wrong."
Naomi flashed back to the accident. She pictured herself in the
passenger seat, fiddling with the radio while Glen waited at a
red light. Then the sudden panic that something huge was
hurtling at them, out of control. She glanced at the mirror a

second before the tractor trailer slammed their vehicle from behind. "There's no reason for Glen to blame himself over what happened. But ignoring his daughter for so long, then taking me to court for custody. It's senseless."

Serena took Naomi's hand in hers and patted it.

"No matter what happens, my family is here for you. And don't worry about LeVar and hurt feelings. He understands what Scout is going through, and he'll be there for both of you."

"Your son is a godsend."

Now Serena's eyes misted over.

"That he is. How he survived my insanity, I'll never know." Serena crossed her heart. "Someone looked over LeVar."

Past the window, the rain let up. The sky brightened as the storm roared over the eastern hills.

"See? There's always hope in the darkest of storms," Serena said, giving Naomi's hand a squeeze.

The tension released from Naomi's shoulders. She walked back to the deck door. The guest house stood unscathed, an impenetrable force against the elements.

"When the pie cools, let's cut Scout a slice and surprise her."

"That's the spirit. I bet dessert for dinner will cheer her up."

Naomi rinsed her hands in the sink. When she shut the water off, Jack began barking from inside the guest house. Great, ear-splitting woofs that lifted the hairs on the back of Naomi's neck. Serena turned to face Naomi with her mouth hanging open. Jack never reacted this violently. Not unless someone threatened his loved ones.

A stranger was in the yard.

19

Officer Avery Neal slid the stapler to the corner of his desk and clicked his case notes together. With his desk arranged to his liking, he checked his messages and glanced toward the door. A half hour ago, he'd called Kemp Massey to the station. The goddamn sheriff would cause a scene if he spotted Massey, so Neal contacted Detective Kowalski and asked to borrow the detective's desk. Kowalski worked in the back corner of the office, out of view from the conference room where Sheriff Shepherd conferred with his deputies. Neal spied the sheriff from the tops of his eyes as the officer pretended to read his notes.

Kemp Massey appeared in the doorway sooner than expected. Neal gave Barber a glare, and Barber hurried to the conference room to run interference. Neal grinned. While his partner kept the sheriff and his deputies busy, Neal crossed the bullpen and motioned Massey to follow him to Kowalski's desk. Massey carried a reusable grocery bag.

"You wanted to speak with me, Officer?"

"Yes. Thank you for coming, Mr. Massey."

Neal noticed Kowalski's nameplate on his desk and turned it

over before Massey saw. He motioned at the open seat and sat in the detective's chair. One day soon, Neal would make detective and finally earn real money with the Wells Ferry PD. Arresting Kemp Massey for his wife's murder would be the feather in the cap that propelled Neal past his peers when the detective position opened.

Neal nodded at the grocery bag.

"I trust you brought what I asked?"

Massey handed him the bag.

"I want it returned when you're finished."

"I'll do my best."

"Why haven't you found my son?"

"I assure you, we're working hard to bring Shawn home. Between the Wells Ferry PD, the sheriff's department, and volunteer searchers, we're covering as much ground as we can."

Massey's jaw tightened.

"You should do more, not sit behind a desk while Shawn runs from a psychopath."

Neal bit his tongue. He wanted to slap the insolence off Massey's face. By sunset, he'd gather evidence implicating Kemp Massey in his wife's murder. This case would finally reach its conclusion. The officer painted on his most genuine smile.

"And I am. I got off the phone with the state police before you arrived. It took some arm twisting, but I arranged for two K9 dogs to help with the search. That's where your son's clothing comes in." Neal lifted the bag without touching its contents. He didn't want to contaminate the scent. "If Shawn is out there, the dogs will find him."

"Why wasn't this done sooner? My boy went missing in the middle of a thunderstorm. The north end of Wells Ferry is under water."

"Shawn is resilient, Mr. Massey. I'm certain he's alive and unharmed." Neal rocked back in Kowalski's chair, picked up a pen, and tapped it against his palm. "Perhaps you can help us narrow the search area."

Battling to maintain his composure, Massey rose from his chair.

"If I knew where Shawn was, don't you think I'd tell you?"

"Sit. It's been a long twenty-four hours. May I get you something to drink? Coffee? Water?"

"I'm not thirsty."

"You're pale, Mr. Massey. Keep your strength up, so you can help me find your son."

Massey huffed.

"Fine. I'll take water."

Officer Neal raised his index finger and strode to the break room. From the drawer, he removed a hand towel and wrapped it around a plastic bottle of water. Then he returned to his desk. Massey stared at his phone, unaware as Neal set the water before him and slipped the towel inside his pocket. Massey cleared the frog from his throat and unscrewed the cap. He nodded at Neal.

"Thank you."

"I'm curious, Mr. Massey. Given your son's school record—fights with classmates, falling grades—I'm worried he makes rash decisions. That's a dangerous combination when he's exposed to the weather, lost, and frightened. We already determined he broke into a private business to get out of the rain."

"If you charge my son with breaking and entering—"

Neal raised a hand.

"Nothing of the sort. There's no damage to the marina, and the owner won't press charges. Why did Shawn head to the marina? Does he have friends who live in the area?"

"Shawn has lots of friends. I'm unsure of their addresses."

"A father should know these things."

Massey ran a tired hand through his hair.

"Yes, I should. I admit I haven't been the best father to Shawn since the separation. It's difficult raising a teenager alone."

"I'm certain it is. But Shawn must have friends he trusts, Mr. Massey. Someone who'd take him in and keep him safe."

The father nodded.

"One would. Mike. I apologize, but I can't recall his last name. A private investigator asked me the same question."

"You don't need a private investigator. We're on the case. Is Shawn's friend a senior at Wells Ferry High?"

"Mike graduated last year. He's a freshman in college. Was it St. John Fisher? Buffalo?" Kemp Massey snapped his fingers. "Nazareth. I remember because Mike gave Shawn his orientation T-shirt." Officer Neal noted the information and closed his memo pad. "Now that I remember, Mike lives a mile or two north of the marina. But he's away at school, so Shawn wouldn't go there."

"That's very helpful." Neal narrowed his eyes. "The marina is a long way from home. In fact, it's in the opposite direction. Putting myself in Shawn's shoes, if someone murdered my mother, I'd run home before I considered an alternative. Unless home was more dangerous than being on the run."

Kemp Massey tensed and sat forward.

"What are you implying?"

Neal grinned inside. He had Massey right where he wanted him. The officer reached beneath his chair and slid the text transcripts from his folder. He slapped the paper on the desk and turned it to face his top suspect.

"Last month you sent your wife a text message. *You only care about power and your career. You're dead to me.*"

The father's eyes darted around the room before returning to the paper.

"We had a fight. You're blowing this out of proportion."

"Am I? *You're dead to me* is an interesting expression, considering someone murdered your wife last night. But you wouldn't have anything to do with that, right?"

Kemp Massey bit his fist and averted his eyes. Neal tapped his finger further down the page and commanded Massey's attention.

"And here you wrote, *He's heartbroken. I'll make you pay for ruining his life.*" Neal leaned back and clasped his hands over his stomach. "Can't blame a father for avenging his son. Did you make your wife pay, Mr. Massey?"

"I'm not answering any more questions. It's obvious where you're taking this."

"When was the last time you visited your wife's house?"

"A year ago. Maybe more."

Good, keep talking, Officer Neal thought. He already knew Kemp Massey tried to kick down his wife's door during a recent fight. The man couldn't keep his lies straight.

"Did you argue about Shawn?"

"That's all we ever fought about, so yes."

"Did the fight turn physical?"

"I wouldn't lay a hand on Megan."

Neal pulled the grocery bag containing Shawn's clothing across the desk and set it at his feet.

"I'll find your son, Mr. Massey. You see, I suspect he had a reason not to run home after he fled the scene. Either he murdered his mother, or he figured out you killed Megan."

"That's ridiculous."

Neal tapped the bag.

"We'll see about that. That's all for now." When Kemp Massey stood, Neal folded his arms. "Oh, and don't leave Wells Ferry. I'll wish to speak to you again. Soon."

"I wouldn't leave town without my son, Officer Neal."

Kemp Massey stormed from the bullpen, almost running

into Barber as Neal's partner crossed the room. Neal shook his head over the father's stupidity.

Ensuring no one paid him attention, Neal removed the towel and wrapped it around the water bottle. Then he carefully screwed the cap on and concealed the bottle inside the grocery bag. The idiot father had left his DNA all over the bottle. All he needed to do was match the DNA and prove Kemp Massey was inside Megan Massey's house.

20

SATURDAY, APRIL 17TH 4:10 P.M.

Naomi couldn't concentrate with Jack barking and tossing himself against the guest house door. Whoever was outside, the dog considered him a threat. Serena moved from window to window, running through the bedrooms before returning to the kitchen.

"There's someone out there, but I can't see who it is."

Naomi wrung her hands. If anyone threatened Scout, Naomi would throw herself in harm's way without hesitation. But indecision froze her in place. She wouldn't rush into the yard without confirming the location of the intruder. Any thief who broke inside the guest house with Jack snapping at the door was a fool. She trusted the dog to keep her daughter safe. Still, she wished for a gun. Anything to deter the intruder.

"We need to get to Scout," Naomi said. "Call 9-1-1 while I check the locks."

Serena's voice traveled through the downstairs as Naomi rushed to the front door. Confirming she'd thrown the bolt and hooked the chain, Naomi turned back to the kitchen. Just then, a shadow passed over the living room window.

"He's in the front yard," Naomi said as Serena ended the call. Serena pressed the air down with her hands.

"Stay calm. It could be a delivery person."

"Why would a delivery person sneak through the yard?" Serena peeked through the sliding glass door.

"There's no one between us and the guest house. I say we make a run for it."

Naomi pressed her lips together and nodded.

"Let's go."

After she peered through the glass, Naomi slid the back door open. Serena followed her onto the deck. Water from this afternoon's rain dripped from the trees, the yard a quagmire of puddles. As they descended the ramp, a man appeared around the corner. Serena drew a breath.

"That's my husband," Naomi said, pulling Serena back. "What the hell is Glen doing here?"

Glen Mourning aimed his phone at the guest house. He made steady, careful steps across Thomas Shepherd's backyard as he recorded LeVar's home, oblivious to Naomi and Serena closing in from the neighboring yard.

"Glen!" He froze at Naomi's shout and almost dropped the phone. Glen turned. Naomi barely recognized him. It appeared her husband had aged twenty years since she last saw him several months ago. His thinning blonde hair stuck out in opposite directions, his eyes black holes sinking into his skull, skin waxen. Almost yellow. "What are you doing?"

"Is this how you keep my daughter safe? By allowing her to hide behind closed doors with a gangster and a murderer?"

"You wait just a minute," Serena said, striding toward Glen. Naomi grabbed Serena and pulled her back. "My son never murdered anyone."

"Oh, I know all about you too. You're the mother, the drug addict, aren't you?"

"Stop it, Glen!" Naomi shouted.

"I won't have these people around Scout. How long before she drops out of school or uses drugs? This is all the evidence I need to prove you've failed as a mother." Glen held the phone in the air like a trophy. "No court will side with you, Naomi. Remove these felons from her life, or so help me, I'll take Scout away from all this and ensure no one harms her again."

"Go back to the house," Naomi said, turning to Serena.

"Not while he's tearing apart my boy."

"Please. Do it for me. I'll fix this."

Serena shot Glen an icy stare that made him flinch. Without another word, she turned and marched back to Naomi's house.

"I hope you're happy, Glen. That's a beautiful woman you upset."

Glen scoffed.

"Sorry for the hurt feelings, but my only concern is for Scout."

"By the way, your footage is useless. LeVar isn't even home today. He's helping the sheriff's department solve a crime."

"Well, he's the expert on criminal activity."

"That's not fair."

"Life isn't fair." Glen's lower lip quivered. "I won't let you put Scout at risk. Not anymore. I'm leaving, Naomi. You'll hear from my lawyer."

Glen trudged up the yard and vanished around the corner of the house. A motor purred along the lake road, and he drove off, leaving Naomi alone in the yard. She cupped her elbows with her hands and let the tears flow. Years of tension burst forth as she fought to regain control over her emotions. At that moment, the lake seemed so vast, so invincible. The water's calming effect disappeared. Wolf Lake intimidated her, warned her of a bleak future she couldn't control.

Inside the guest house, Jack's barking ceased.

As Naomi wiped a tear off her cheek, the curtain parted on the front door. Scout had watched them argue.

21

To Darren, watching Thomas run the press conference was gut-wrenching. He'd met the sheriff last spring and understood Thomas's struggles with Asperger's. Facing a crowd set the sheriff's nerves on edge. And this was no ordinary crowd. A horde of reporters with microphones shouted questions over each other as Thomas shifted his attention from one reporter to the next. It was like watching a novice surfer tackle hurricane-induced waves.

Still, Thomas surprised Darren by maintaining his cool. Perhaps Darren shouldn't have been surprised, for Thomas Shepherd remained the most extraordinary person he'd ever met.

Thomas held up Shawn's yearbook photograph. Darren's throat tightened. The boy appeared so hopeful and full of vigor despite his home life. The kid had overcome long odds, not unlike Thomas. How would Darren live with himself if he didn't find his cousin alive?

"I repeat, we're searching for Shawn Massey." Thomas read Shawn's address. He also gave Shawn's age and a physical description, though the picture said it all. "Anyone who sees

Shawn should call the hotline the Nightshade County Sheriff's Department set up with the Wells Ferry Police."

"Is it true Shawn Massey killed his mother?"

The reporter appeared fresh out of journalism school, his tawny hair parted at the side and slicked, not a hair out of place.

"There's no evidence Shawn Massey murdered Megan Massey."

"But he visited the house at the time of the murder."

"We believe Shawn Massey witnessed the attack. The Nightshade County Sheriff's Department and Wells Ferry Police urge anyone with information regarding Megan Massey's murder to call the hotline. The hotline is anonymous."

"What about the husband?" another reporter shouted from the front.

"Kemp Massey isn't a suspect."

"Explain why he tried to break into his wife's house and sent her threatening messages?"

Darren chewed the inside of his cheek. Someone inside the Wells Ferry PD was leaking information to the press. What kind of police department did they run? This nonsense didn't fly in Syracuse.

Thomas fought to regain control.

"Kemp Massey is a worried father who only wants his son returned."

More questions piled atop one another, a mountain that threatened to topple from the slightest disruption. Darren's eyes flicked to Officer Barber, standing at the back of the room with his arms folded. The officer looked like death warmed over, yet he seemed to enjoy the circus. Darren ignored the temptation to scream at Barber. This wasn't a joke.

Darren's phone buzzed as he turned away from the press conference. A message arrived from Kemp. After scanning the text, Darren searched for Barber again. The officer had disappeared. No sign of his partner, Officer Neal, either. Until the text arrived, Darren hadn't known Neal brought Kemp into the office an hour ago. His stomach churned with consternation. He wished Kemp had consulted Darren first. Darren already harbored guilt for advising his cousin to invite the officers into his home. The minute they set foot inside, they built a case against him. He wasn't sure what Officer Neal was up to. But inviting him to the station felt like a setup. Darren fired a text back to Kemp.

Don't speak to the police again without consulting me first.

Darren awaited his cousin's reply. It never came.

THE GRAY LIGHT peeking around the curtain seemed foreign. Shawn awoke with a start and scrambled off the bed until he remembered where he was. Heart pounding, he stumbled to the window and edged the curtains open. Studying the yard, he found nobody outside.

He breathed again. As he turned around, he caught his reflection in Mike's television screen. His hair stuck out on one side, and the skin hung off his face as though it wanted to slough off and reveal the skull beneath. Shawn fell against the wall and covered his mouth. The vision of his mother's murder flooded over him. He wished he could turn back time and stop the madman. But he'd had his chance and froze like the coward he was. Worthless. What kind of son doesn't defend his mother from an attacker?

I'm sorry, Mom. I did my best.

Though he didn't believe his own words. Not unless running for his life and leaving his mother to die was *his best.* A tiny voice in the back of his head pleaded with him to be fair with himself. The voice claimed Shawn never had a chance to stop the killer.

It happened too fast. The louder, petulant voice tamped the logical argument down. He'd failed his mother.

I know your name.

Despite the gurgling pit in Shawn's stomach, his body ached for lack of food. He recalled the stocked pantry and returned to the kitchen, down the long hall, past the sitting area where he spent too many evenings blasting zombies with his friend. A quick assessment of the pantry caused him to waver between mac and cheese, pasta, rice, and oatmeal. All the choices were quick and easy to cook. He eliminated the mac and cheese—his stomach wouldn't handle a heavy meal, and he didn't trust the butter in the refrigerator. The last thing he needed was food poisoning.

He opened the box of instant oatmeal and poured the cereal into a bowl. After adding water, he stirred the meal and set the bowl in the microwave for ninety seconds. Plain oatmeal tasted bland, but he didn't mind. Less chance he'd regurgitate the food.

The sitting area with the gaming console and wall-mounted television made it too easy for someone walking past to spot him. Not that anyone should be out in the woods. The nearest neighbor was a quarter-mile past the trees. Shawn decided he'd play it safe and keep the lights off. He ate at the kitchen counter, standing in the corner to avoid prying eyes. The oatmeal settled his stomach, so he opted for a second packet. In his imagination, he pictured Mrs. Nash doting over him.

"You're a growing boy, Shawn. There's plenty left over. Stop being bashful."

A smile creased his eyes. He'd do anything to have Mr. and Mrs. Nash open the door and set their bags on the floor. Shawn would have a lot of explaining to do, yet he felt certain they'd understand and help him reach home.

As if home was safe. It was impossible to hide from a murderer who knew you.

He shuffled through the possibilities in his head. Who would hurt his mother? A disgruntled client? Plausible, but Shawn never met the people his mother defended. He'd lost the killer in the woods. It wouldn't be long before the madman tracked him. As much as he longed to stay in this familiar home, he needed to keep moving.

While Shawn thought back to last night, trying to recall details about the masked intruder that would help him identify his mother's murderer, he eyed his clothes piled outside Mike's bedroom. This wouldn't do. The mud dried and crusted over, dirtying the floor. No chance he'd wear the clothes in their present condition. He scooped the filthy pile into his arms and located the basement door past the bedrooms. Carpeted steps descended into a finished basement. A ping-pong table divided the room with a *Pacman* video game machine in the corner. Shawn couldn't stop himself from reading the high scores when he passed. Mike and Mr. Nash held the best scores. Shawn was number four on the list.

The washer and dryer stood against the wall at the rear of the basement. He dropped his clothes into the washer, added detergent, and sat on the floor with his back against the machine. The constant thrum made his eyes droop, this bit of normality grounding him, making last night seem like a nightmare he'd wake up from.

The washer buzzed and pulled Shawn out of sleep. He'd been out for ten minutes or more. On groggy limbs, he moved the clothes into the drier. It would take thirty minutes or more to dry his jeans.

As he padded upstairs, he paused where the hallway opened to the living space. Day waned at the window. The light was a fragile thing that wouldn't hold up against the coming storms. There had to be a way out of this predicament. If only the house had a phone, he could call Polly or his father. Even Mr. and Mrs. Nash.

Beyond the sliding glass door, a crow perched on the deck, assessing Shawn with black, beady eyes. A second landed on the rail and stared through the glass.

Shawn retreated into the shadows. Night was coming, and the killer would be close behind.

22

T hunder rattled the walls inside Wolf Lake Consulting. Chelsey eyed the black clouds beyond the window and closed the blinds. All day, storms had threatened Nightshade County, each round more violent than the last. The severe thunderstorm watch scrolled on the television as she watched a replay of Thomas's press conference.

"Damn them," she said, setting the remote on the desk. "Those media vultures aren't playing fair."

"My advice," LeVar said, glancing up from his workstation. "Turn off the television. There's no reason to put yourself through hell. Besides, Shep can handle the media."

"You're right." Chelsey clicked the remote and returned to her monitor. "It's disgusting how the media drives public opinion with unverified facts and hearsay."

Moments after Chelsey shut off the press conference highlights, Thomas rang her cell.

"Hey, we were just watching you."

"I wish you hadn't," Thomas said, groaning. "That was a no-win situation. At least we got the word out, and people are searching for Shawn. Speaking of which, I have information for you."

"Oh?"

"It took some convincing, but I got the Wells Ferry PD to share the Hanley Stokes case notes. And according to an eyewitness, Stokes visited Megan Massey's house earlier this week."

Chelsey fell back in her chair.

"That's huge. Why haven't we heard about this until now?"

"When you're dead set on pinning a murder on Megan's husband and son, you wear blinders."

"I'm just as guilty as Wells Ferry PD. As I expressed earlier, something about Kemp Massey doesn't seem right. So Stokes showed up at her house. Did they argue?"

"Megan Massey wasn't home when Stokes visited. So we don't know why he went there."

"Maybe he drove to the house, intending to murder her."

"Then returned last night to finish the job," Thomas said in agreement. "Which means we need to find Shawn Massey, our only witness. I'd hate to rely on our teenage prodigy again, but did Scout find anything on Shawn's friends?"

Chelsey released a sigh.

"Scout is having a bad day. LeVar has been messaging with her. Something happened with the father. From what I understand, Glen Mourning showed up at the house and caused a scene."

"Sounds like he's losing control over his emotions. I wish I'd been there to help. All right, so I won't expect a full report from Scout."

"Don't give up on our teenage friend. She has a penchant for coming through in the clutch."

"Truer words have never been spoken. Keep me abreast if she finds anything. The search team is heading out for another sweep of the forest." After a pause, Thomas continued, lowering his voice. "If Wolf Lake Consulting discovered interesting tidbits on Hanley Stokes, I'd be obliged."

"I'm certain we can work something out, Sheriff Shepherd," Chelsey said with a wry grin. "Tell me what you have on our mysterious ex-con."

"He hangs out at a dive called Mahoney's on the east side of Wells Ferry."

"We'll poke around and get back to you."

"Appreciate it, Chelsey. Stokes might be our guy. Talk to you soon."

Chelsey smiled to herself. Her relationship with Thomas continued to blossom. Gone were the days of awkward conversations and worries over their past. He was the same person she remembered from high school, yet different. More sure of himself. Easy to talk to. Lately, he'd expressed interest in Chelsey moving into the A-frame. She wasn't certain she was ready to take that step. But with every passing day, picturing a life with Thomas became easier. Complications existed. What about her tabby, Tigger? The cat would make a fine meal for Jack, and she wouldn't give Tigger up for anyone. Was she ready to sell her house?

A dividing line ran down the whiteboard hanging on the wall. On the left, three photographs surrounded Megan Massey's picture with lines connecting each suspect to the victim. Hanley Stokes, Kemp Massey, and his son. A sheet of paper with a question mark drawn in magic marker represented a fourth potential killer, someone they hadn't considered. On the right half of the whiteboard, Chelsey hung a map of Shawn's last known locations. She peered at the map, piecing the puzzle together. The boy's path led north. After the marina, the searchers lost his tracks. Was Shawn lost, or did he have a destination in mind?

LeVar motioned Chelsey to his desk.

"Found something intriguing."

"What have you got?"

"So I sifted through Megan Massey's phone history. Someone started texting her a few weeks ago. I couldn't trace the messenger."

"Probably a burner phone."

"That's my guess."

"Anything threatening?"

"*I told you to stay out of my business,*" LeVar said, reading the transcript.

"His business? Hanley Stokes runs a business."

"Selling drugs on the east side of town."

"Right. What else do the messages say?"

"*I know all your dirty secrets, you little whore. You've known me long enough to understand I'm the last person you want to cross.*"

"Why would Megan Massey cross the man she defended?"

"Could be she learned too much about Stokes and turned on him."

Chelsey drummed her fingers on the desk, unconvinced. Who was the mystery man sending Megan threatening texts? As Chelsey concentrated, Raven contacted Chelsey through Face-Time. Darren and Raven appeared in the picture. Pine trees framed the background, and a glowering sky hung over their heads. Both struggled to keep their eyes open. Chelsey shook her head.

"Leave the search to the police and sheriff's department," Chelsey said. "The two of you need sleep."

"Not until I find Shawn," Darren said, scrubbing a hand across his facial stubble. "Do we have any leads on his location?"

Chelsey glanced at LeVar, who rolled his chair over and ducked his head into the frame.

"Nothing from Scout yet," said LeVar. "I can contact her, but she's going through a family crisis."

Raven scrunched her face and asked, "It's Glen Mourning again, isn't it? How I'd love to get that man alone in a room for five minutes. Scout deserves better."

"I feel we're running blind," Darren said, glancing into the distance. "We covered the territory north of the park, yet we haven't found tracks since early morning. It's like he disappeared after he left the marina."

"We can't rely on Scout this time," Chelsey said. "I still say catching Megan's killer is the key to locating Shawn. Thomas gave me a lead on Hanley Stokes. It seems Stokes showed up at Megan's house this week when she wasn't home. And LeVar discovered hostile messages sent to Megan's phone. We think they're coming from a burner."

"Pretty brazen to show up at your attorney's house and threaten her after you get out of jail," Raven said.

"No one ever claimed criminals were geniuses."

"Be careful. Stokes has a long record."

"He frequents a bar in Wells Ferry. I'll drive over and check the place out, then swing past his last known address." Raven lifted an eyebrow. Chelsey understood Raven's concern. After Mark Benson shot Chelsey, her struggles with anxiety worsened. She flinched at loud noises, grew nervous when she investigated suspects alone. "Tell you what. After LeVar finishes with Megan's call history, I'll take him with me to Mahoney's." She turned to LeVar. "That work for you?"

"I'm down."

Chelsey's body tensed with new urgency. Though she hadn't zeroed in on a suspect, she sensed the conclusion to this case lay on the horizon. Between the search parties, the Wolf Lake Consulting investigators, and the sheriff's department, the potential of locating Shawn Massey grew by the minute.

Voices called from the background.

"We have to go," Darren said. "Tell us if you learn anything new about Stokes."

"Will do."

Raven and Darren disappeared from the picture. Chelsey fretted over her friends. They should be asleep in their beds, not dragging themselves through the forest. But Chelsey understood. Were it her family, she'd never stop looking, never give up believing in a happy ending.

As LeVar wrapped up his work, Chelsey rummaged inside her desk.

"Heads up."

She tossed LeVar an energy bar and pocketed one for herself.

"What's this for?"

"To hold you over until we find something nutritious. We might be in the field for a while."

"Gotcha. Thanks, Chelsey."

Chelsey released a breath.

"I feel terrible taking you into the field without a weapon."

"I'm ineligible for a private investigator's license until I turn twenty-five."

"But that doesn't mean you can't defend yourself."

"Don't worry about me. If anyone starts drama, it's hammer time."

Chelsey snorted.

"That's exactly what I'm worried about."

23

Standing beside LeVar's sink, Naomi cleaned the dessert plates while Scout worked at the computer. Jack lay beside Scout with his tongue hanging out, a big grin on his face. The dog always smiled when his friends were around, and he loved Scout as much as he loved anyone.

"Are you sure you won't eat dinner? I'll bring it down so you can work without interruption."

Scout rubbed her eyes.

"Maybe in a while. I'm way behind on the research LeVar sent me."

"Tell you what. Ms. Hopkins and I will throw something together and carry it down after we finish. By then, you'll probably have your appetite back."

Serena hadn't accompanied Naomi to the guest house. LeVar's mother cried for a long time after Glen left, frustrated over the accusations. Naomi wanted to smooth things over, but it was best to give Serena space.

She set the plates in a plastic grocery bag and gave her daughter another glance. Clouds raced across the sky and reflected off the lake as Naomi turned down the hallway.

"Mom?"

Naomi stopped and returned to the front room. On the computer monitor, Scout displayed a teenager's social media page.

"Yeah, hon?"

"Why is Dad doing this?"

Naomi leaned against the wall and lifted her eyes to the ceiling, as though searching for an answer.

"I wish I knew, Scout. I've never seen your father act like this. Give me a chance to talk to him."

"I don't want to leave you. I don't want to leave any of this," Scout said, spreading her arms.

"Your father won't take you away. Not if I have anything to say about it."

"It doesn't seem fair. He's saying one thing, his lawyer another. Then we have our own lawyer. But nobody asks what I want. I'm the one who has to live with Dad if the courts decide in his favor."

Naomi touched Scout's shoulder and kissed the top of her head.

"Oh, Scout. It won't come to that. And anyway, the courts will consider your opinion in any decision they make."

Scout dropped her eyes.

"But I don't want to say terrible things about Dad in court, either. As angry as I am, he's still my father."

Naomi's throat clenched.

"There isn't a cruel bone in your body. You'd never hurt your father's feelings." Naomi brushed the hair from Scout's eyes. "Listen, Scout. Nobody can take you from me. I'll talk to your father. Hopefully, this battle never reaches the courts."

Leaning against the arm of her wheelchair, Scout hugged Naomi around the waist. The teenager fell quiet as Naomi stroked her hair.

"I'm sorry for being such a pain."

Naomi knelt before her daughter and held her hands.

"Why would you say that?"

"To you and LeVar, I mean. None of this is your fault. I shouldn't take out my frustrations on the people I care about."

"You didn't hurt my feelings, babe. I understand. Believe me, I do." Naomi paused for a moment. "But it wouldn't be a bad idea to talk to LeVar. He's worried about you."

Scout sniffled and scraped a tear off her eyelid.

"I was such a jerk to him."

"LeVar is on your side, just like I am. Everybody has a bad day once in a while. He won't hold it against you."

"Why did Dad say those awful things about LeVar and Ms. Hopkins?"

"Your guess is as good as mine. But the next time I see your father, he'll get my two cents and then some." Scout gave an uncertain nod and turned back to the computer. "Why don't you tell me about your research?"

Scout explained her methods. She sifted through Shawn Massey's profile, made note of his connections, and investigated his friends. The problem was, Shawn Massey had over five-hundred connections on Facebook, and all those connections needed to be traced so she could verify where each person lived. It would be a long time before Scout found an answer, and it was almost sunset. As much as Naomi wished Scout would rest, this might be the best thing for her. By aiding another teenager, she'd heal herself.

"I support you, Scout. If anyone can save that missing boy, it's you. Work as late as you're comfortable with. We'll bring your food down when it's ready."

Scout thanked her mother and returned to the investigation. Jack followed Naomi to the door. Always the gentleman. She bent low and kissed Jack on the head, scratching behind his

ears and telling him what a good dog he was before she
departed.

At the kitchen table, Serena pored over notes for a new
recipe when Naomi entered through the sliding glass door.
Naomi worried about her shaken friend. Glen's scathing
remarks still echoed in Naomi's head.

"How did it go with Scout?" Serena asked without
looking up.

"She's upset. Who wouldn't be? LeVar has Scout working on
a case, and that's probably good for her. Might be a long night. I
want her to eat so she doesn't get sick."

"What do you have in mind?"

Naomi scratched her head.

"Something easy that I can throw together quick."

Serena set her notes aside and opened the cupboard.

"How about tuna noodle casserole? That always hits the
spot."

"I love it."

"Come on, I'll help you whip dinner together."

As they pulled the ingredients off the shelves, Serena kept
glancing at Naomi from the corner of her eye.

"Serena, I don't blame you for being furious with Glen. He
was out of line."

Serena released a breath.

"The truth is I *am* a recovering heroin addict, and LeVar ran
with the Harmon Kings for years. Glen wasn't wrong. We can't
change our pasts, only command our futures."

"You're none of those things anymore."

"The temptation will always be with me, and LeVar has to
live with his past. Naomi, I wasn't a mother to my children. After
their father walked away, God challenged me to step up and play
the role of two parents. I failed Him. I was a coward, hiding

behind addiction when I should have been there for Raven and LeVar. They raised themselves." Serena set the tuna can on the counter and blew out a breath. "But today scared me. When your husband started yelling, I felt as if I was looking into a mirror."

Naomi set the breadcrumbs down and turned to her friend. "I'm not sure I understand."

"The empty terror in his eyes. That's regret, Naomi. Regret and panic. He's coming to grips with his failures as a father. I went through the same thing, though Glen and I took different paths to avoid our shortcomings. While I turned to drugs, Glen hides behind the legal system and makes us the villains. It's easier to blame others than look into a mirror."

"If he sees himself as a failed parent, why fight for custody?"

"Perhaps it's his way of making up for lost time. If he gives Scout a better life, in his mind, he erases his wrongdoings. Just know that when he climbs into bed every night, he experiences moments of clarity. And they're utterly terrifying. He realizes he's wrong. But in his panic, he doesn't know how to build a bridge back to your daughter."

Naomi sank into a chair and brushed her hair back. Despite her anger, she still loved Glen, still wished he'd never left the family. Now he'd crossed a line. They could never fix their marriage, but there was still a chance for Glen to be the father Scout needed.

"So what should I do?"

"There's nothing you can do," Serena said, sliding into a chair beside Naomi. "You can't force Glen to face his demons. That needs to come from within." Serena touched her heart. "But he needs to do it soon. Time is running out for Scout and Glen. If he doesn't repair their relationship in the coming weeks, he'll lose her forever."

Naomi's heart sank into her belly. She wanted the best for Scout, and the best for her daughter was having a mother and father in her life. Two parents to see her through the tough times and experience her joys. Scout's first kiss, prom and graduation, college. Scout was growing so fast.

Naomi couldn't allow Glen to tear Scout's life apart.

24

Mahoney's reminded Chelsey of every dive bar she'd strolled into. The air held a dusty, sepia quality, as though the room held smoke from the days when lighting up a cigarette inside a bar was legal. A yellowish cast sullied the walls, and a jukebox in the back thumped Aerosmith. The close walls provoked arguments that inevitably ended in parking lot fistfights. A good-looking woman like Chelsey invited games of grab-ass if she dared to venture inside. A three-year-old calendar hung askew behind the bar. Teetering on a stool, a man with a beard full of gray nursed a mug of beer.

The bartender didn't appear as if he belonged here. He was the youngest person in Mahoney's. The bartender wore amber hair parted on the side, the sleeves of his white button-down rolled up to the elbows. He gave Chelsey a baffled, concerned stare, wondering why any respectful woman would risk visiting Mahoney's with sunset approaching. Then his eyes landed on LeVar, and he returned to polishing the counter.

"Help ya?"

The bartender didn't look up when Chelsey sat at the bar with LeVar beside her.

"I'm looking for someone."

"Aren't we all?" The bartender set the rag aside and leaned on the counter with his knuckles. "You a cop or something?"

"A private investigator."

Chelsey fished a card out of her wallet and handed it to the bartender. He glanced at the card and handed it back.

"He a private investigator too?" The man tilted his head at LeVar. "Looks a little young to be a gumshoe. Doubt he's reached the legal drinking age."

Chelsey snickered.

"Gumshoe?"

"Sorry. I'm guilty of reading too many Robert Chandler novels. So what's a private investigator doing inside Mahoney's?"

Three men set their pool sticks down and glared at LeVar from the back of the room. Chelsey recalled LeVar's comment about *hammer time* and hoped the teenager didn't notice the men. She reached into her jacket and removed her phone. Loading a photograph of Hanley Stokes, she set the phone in front of the bartender.

"We're searching for this man. Hanley Stokes. Know him?"

"Pfft." The bartender nodded at a picture of Stokes hanging on the wall. "Our do-not-serve list is one person long. Stokes is the only name on the list."

"Have you seen him around?"

The man scratched behind his ear and gave a warning glance to the three hoods eyeing LeVar.

"Not for three years. We heard he got out of prison. Stokes in trouble again?"

"He might be. Why did you ban him from Mahoney's?"

He shrugged and surveyed the bar.

"Not that Mahoney's attracts a high-class clientele, but Stokes is a known drug dealer. I don't need that problem inside my bar. Before the police arrested him, he pulled a knife on a local guy named Jonas Briggs." The bartender drummed his knuckles against the polished wood. "They were both drunk. Not even sure who started the fight or what it was about. But I draw the line at weapons. Threaten a patron's life, and you don't get to drink in my bar."

"Did Stokes frequently start altercations?" LeVar asked, snacking on a bowl of pretzels.

The man scrunched his face in thought.

"No, he never caused trouble until that night. But one strike and you're out if you pull a knife on someone."

"Would you do me a favor?" Chelsey asked, handing her card back to the bartender. "If Stokes walks into Mahoney's, will you call me? My number is on the bottom of the card."

"Sure, I can do that," the bartender said, slipping the card into his shirt pocket. "But I don't expect Stokes will show his face here. Even for an ex-con, this is a tough crowd."

Chelsey glanced over her shoulder. Despite the drug rumors, Stokes had a clean record until three years ago. The robbery occurred around the time Mahoney's banned him for threatening Jonas Briggs with a knife. What set him off and spun his life out of control?

The bartender assessed LeVar.

"Seems you can handle yourself in a scrap. But the three clowns playing pool aren't choirboys, and I don't want my place trashed."

Chelsey rose off the stool.

"It's fine. We were just leaving."

LeVar gave the bullies a smug grin before he turned away.

"Thank you for your help," Chelsey told the bartender as she pulled LeVar toward the entrance.

"You didn't want to watch me in action?" LeVar smirked in the parking lot.

"I didn't want you spending the night in jail. Can't trust how the cops here will treat you. Even Thomas doesn't trust Wells Ferry PD."

"Next stop?"

"We'll try Stokes's house. But I doubt we'll find him at home."

Hanley Stokes lived in a one-story home on South Seneca Street. The siding had faded to a pale green, and the screened-in front porch was missing a panel. Bugs flew in and out of the missing screen. Chelsey pulled the Civic to the curb and checked the driveway.

"Doesn't appear Stokes is home," LeVar said, leaning his head out the window.

She wanted to tell him to raise the window and pull his head inside before someone shot it off. But when she glanced up the street, she realized they hadn't wandered into gang territory. Stokes's house stuck out among its neighbors. It barely appeared lived in, though Chelsey confirmed the drug dealer had owned the house for a decade.

Chelsey brushed a hand over her gun as she stepped from the Civic. Together, they approached the front door along a chipped walkway. LeVar banged on the screen door. Chelsey didn't see a doorbell. A minute later, LeVar pounded louder. Nobody responded.

"Guess he's not here," Chelsey said, stepping off the porch.

LeVar crossed the unruly lawn and pressed his face against the window. She pictured Stokes aiming a gun at LeVar's head from inside. When LeVar didn't spot the ex-con, he rounded the house and peeked through more windows. He returned to Chelsey and pushed his dreadlocks off his shoulder.

"Nobody's inside. Where to now?"

Chelsey didn't have an answer. Where would a drug dealer hang out after his release? As she considered their next move, a woman with pink hair power-walked down the sidewalk. The woman wore sweatpants, a sweatshirt, and earbuds. She gave LeVar a wary look and hurried past before Chelsey flagged her down by waving her arms over her head. The woman yanked the earbuds out and glanced between Chelsey and LeVar.

"Excuse me. Do you know the man who lives in this house?"

The exerciser shook her head.

"Not personally, but I've seen him around. He did prison time, from what I understand. But I'm not a busybody."

"Have you seen him today?"

"No. Not for a few days, now that you mention it. He drives that damn junker car with the missing muffler. You can hear it from the west side of Wells Ferry. But it's been two or three days since the car came down our road. No way that piece of junk should have passed inspection."

LeVar slipped his hands into his pockets and tried to appear casual. He realized his dreadlocks and physical size made the woman nervous.

"Anybody visit his house in the last week?" he asked, tilting his head at the front door.

"No visitors. But twice in the last couple days I noticed a cop car sitting out front."

Chelsey raised her eyebrows.

"Wells Ferry PD?"

"That's right. What happened? Did the loser break his probation?"

Chelsey handed the woman her card and asked her to call if Stokes showed his face. After the power walker continued down the sidewalk, Chelsey swung around to LeVar.

"Something doesn't feel right. Wells Ferry PD is watching out for Stokes. But they barely mentioned him to the sheriff's department."

"Stokes might have split town," LeVar said, rubbing his chin. "Probably after word got back to the police about Stokes harassing Megan Massey. Stokes didn't want the heat and left."

But was he still in Wells Ferry last night when someone stabbed Megan Massey?

25

SATURDAY, APRIL 17TH 8:05 P.M.

Darren pulled the truck onto the gravel shoulder when the rain became too heavy to see through the windshield. Black clouds rushed overhead, torn tags snaking down and spinning around a vertical axis as wind whipped the car. Raven shot him a nervous look from the passenger seat when the truck vibrated during a gust. To their right, the Wells River crashed through its banks with utter madness. The river's appetite for destruction had no bounds. It ripped chunks off the banks and swallowed the mud, only to spit it out when the river blasted against a dam.

It took ten minutes before the wind relented. Twigs stuck to the windshield wipers. Darren draped his jacket over his head and cleaned the glass, the rain lashing at his face as he wrestled the sticks out of the blades. A decayed, earthy scent mixed with a whiff of ozone. Lightning flashed through the sky.

"That was fun," he said, climbing into the cab with a forced laugh.

Raven didn't respond. Just stared out the passenger window with clenched hands as the river surged out of its banks.

They'd followed the Wells River on a combination of access

roads and scenic overlooks, though there was nothing scenic about nature's wrath. The river would meet the lake two miles to the east. No sign of Shawn. If he'd come this way, the storms erased his tracks hours ago.

Darren and Raven were the only searchers in the field. The sheriff's department, police, and volunteers holed up until the storms rolled through. Between the lightning and flooded roads, the search had taken on a dangerous edge. The various entities wouldn't risk one of their own plunging into the water, though Darren suspected Thomas was out there somewhere, ignoring the mandates.

A police band radio crackled inside the truck. Darren didn't recognize the voices. A new crew had replaced the day shift at Wells Ferry PD. That was a good thing. Darren grew tired of dealing with Officers Barber and Neal, and their insistence that Kemp murdered Megan.

"Ready to move forward?"

Raven glanced across the cab and nodded, though Darren saw through her forced courage. The storms had shaken her, and his Silverado felt puny beneath the boiling sky.

Darren turned the key and pulled the truck off the shoulder. Rivulets streamed across the pavement, dragging silt and mud over the macadam. The tires bucked over the obstruction, only to meet another hill of sludge a few hundred feet down the road. Night had descended on Wells Ferry. Trees along the access road thickened the darkness, made it seem like midnight in January as the wipers ran at high speed.

As he navigated the truck around a myriad of obstructions— fallen tree limbs, gurgling water, more mud—Raven leaned her head out the window with her hand shielding her head from the downpour. She scanned the banks for his missing cousin. Raven wouldn't give up until Darren called off the search.

Which he'd need to do before long. Fate didn't favor Shawn

surviving the last twenty-plus hours in the forest. Darren needed to believe his cousin had found some place to hide from the elements. And from the psychopath chasing him through the wilderness. The alternative was unthinkable.

When the Silverado came upon a tree blocking the road, Darren had no choice but to reverse course. He blew out a frustrated breath as he executed a three-point turn, careful not to back the truck into a ditch. As he shifted into reverse, Raven leaned over her seat and stared through the back windshield.

"Another few feet," she said, chewing on a nail. "Okay, that's far enough."

Despite the tight squeeze, Darren turned the truck around and headed back the way they'd come. He'd need to switch to a different road before they drove east again. The problem was, the alternate routes would take him away from the river.

After they reached town, Raven relaxed. Streetlights hung over the road, cutting through the dark and spilling pools of light over the pavement. Darren switched his high beams on and gave the accelerator extra gas, this road safer than the last.

His phone hummed in his pocket as he gripped the steering wheel. A quick glance at the screen revealed Scout Mourning's name. Darren had almost forgotten about their teenage investigator. This was the first time they'd heard from her since LeVar put her on the case.

He handed the phone over to Raven.

"It's Scout. Put her through the speakers."

Raven fiddled with the truck's Bluetooth connection and answered.

"Hey, Scout. Darren is driving, but he's listening."

"I found a potential hiding spot for Shawn."

Rain drumming against the windshield made it difficult to hear. Darren reached for the volume knob and cranked it higher.

"Where?" he asked, turning down a side street to double back toward the river.

"Does the name Camilla Blanton mean anything to you?"

"Is she a friend of Shawn's?"

"She's Polly Hart's cousin. After I sifted through Polly's profile, I checked her connections and discovered Camilla. Her family has a finished room over the garage, and there are pictures of Shawn partying there with Camilla and Polly. I would have discovered the photos sooner, except Shawn's name isn't tagged in the post. None of their names are."

"Probably because they don't want their parents to catch them," Raven said. "Still, why put incriminating pictures online?"

Darren switched off the high beams when he encountered fog.

"How recent are the pictures?"

"From last summer and fall. It got me thinking. Where might Shawn go if he was in trouble? Camilla posted two days ago that she was going away for the weekend with her parents. Appears to be a college visit."

"Not the smartest information to give up on social media," Raven said.

"If Shawn knew, he'd have a safe place to hide and get out of the weather."

"Shoot me the address."

Scout read Camilla's address. Raven copied it onto a notepad and thanked Scout for the information.

"I'm still working through Shawn's contacts. If I find anyone else, I'll call you."

Raven turned to Darren.

"What do you think?"

"Seems like a long shot, but it's worth checking into."

"Should we head to Camilla's?"

Darren wiped the rainwater off his brow. He was still soaked from clearing debris off the windshield.

"Not yet. If Shawn hid inside Camilla's garage, he's safe. Better to follow the river in case he's lost and trying to escape the storm."

"Scout is usually dead on with her theories."

"She is. Tell you what. Radio the information to Wells Ferry PD. See if they can send a cruiser past Camilla Blanton's place."

"Will do."

While Raven placed the call, Darren divided his attention between the road and his GPS display. Every road to the river dead-ended at a mudslide or another tree across the road. His options diminished. He finally experienced success when he took the truck down Evergreen Road. The river churned ahead, the access road they'd abandoned to the west running perpendicular to Evergreen.

He stopped the truck in the middle of the access road. They were the only fools driving in the deluge, so he was unconcerned about another vehicle coming along. Standing beside the ditch, oblivious to the rain pattering his face, he aimed the binoculars up and down the river. Raven shone a flashlight through the dark. Twice his heart skipped a beat when he spotted something along the banks that looked like torn clothing. Each time the debris turned out to be garbage strewn along the river.

He wiped the rain out of his eyes and called Shawn's name. His voice echoed through the forest and vanished into the night. How could the teenager disappear without a trace?

Raven rubbed his shoulder.

"We'll find him, Darren."

He wanted to believe her. But fear twisted his insides. First Megan's murder. Now Shawn on the run and missing.

And the rain refused to stop.

26

Thomas sat inside his cruiser a quarter mile from the marina, surrounded by the drenched forest. Full dark blanketed the land, interrupted by occasional flashes of lightning over the eastern hills. At last, the storms had moved out of Wells Ferry, and a chilling wind replaced the rain and whipped the trees into a frenzy as he studied the map. He noted Shawn's tracks and the locations of his parents' houses. He sensed he was close to locating Shawn, though he wasn't confident he'd find the boy alive.

Banter carried over the police radio. He filtered it out, only paying attention to where the search crews were. He grumbled to himself. Almost two hours ago, Raven had contacted Wells Ferry PD about Polly Hart's cousin, Camilla Blanton. So far, the police department hadn't bothered to drive past the garage. The odds of Shawn hiding over the family's garage seemed long to Thomas. But it was worth checking into.

Before Thomas set off for the Blanton residence, he radioed his intentions to Aguilar and Lambert, who aided the state police search team a mile east of his position. Search crews swept the terrain between the highway and the lake. The K9 units had found Shawn's scent near the marina before the rains started, but the dogs struggled to pick it up again.

He crossed the town, the cruiser's tires kicking up spray over the flooded streets. The Blanton family lived in a bungalow with a white exterior that glowed in the ambient light. A burgundy roof topped the home, and windows comprised most of the front wall. The lights were off inside. Peepers sang behind the house as Thomas stepped out of the cruiser and flicked his flashlight over the lawn. The closest neighbor lived in a lot two hundred feet away, and poplar trees shielded his view. His shoes swished through wet grass, pant cuffs dampened as he rounded the home and followed the driveway toward the garage.

As he passed windows, he shone the light into the house, searching for movement. A wheelbarrow had toppled over beside the garage, tipped by the storms. A garden shovel with a wicked tip lay in the grass beside the wheelbarrow. Killing the light, he peered at the window above the garage. Darkness pressed against the glass. For a long time, Thomas listened. If Shawn was inside the garage, he didn't want to frighten the teenager.

Sodden earth scents hung heavy in the air. The only sound was the wind shrieking around the house. An image of serial killer Jeremy Hyde flashed before Thomas. The leering murderer held a bloody knife in one hand. Erika Windrow's severed head dangled from the other, the psychopath's fingers clutching the woman's hair. Thomas blinked, and the vision disappeared.

He rubbed his eyes. Since last year's murders, he'd flashed back to the Hyde encounter too many times to count. But never during an investigation. His breath heaved in his chest. Steadying himself, he leaned against the wall and waited until his heartbeat regulated.

A door stood on the side of the garage. He jiggled the knob

and found it unlocked. Turning the flashlight on again, he aimed the beam inside. A wooden staircase led to the room over the garage. Vegetables started from seeds grew beside the windowpanes. As he tugged on the doorknob, a branch snapped in the yard. He froze and stepped into the shadows. Thomas stood with his back against the garage, waiting for the sound to come again. When it didn't, he crept around the rear of the garage, a rickety fence overrun by grapevines to his right. An animal skittered beneath the tangled vines.

The fence curled to his left and divided the rear of the yard from a neighboring property. A rusted swing set stood at the back. The chains swung with screeching noises. He aimed the light into the trees and found himself alone in the yard. The snapping branch could have been caused by the wind. It probably was, he thought.

Then his eyes stopped on a shoe print beneath an elm tree. Just a single indentation where water pooled in the grass. He raised the light and swept it back to the garage, searching for a matching print. Shawn? Or someone else?

He stepped into the shadows and spoke into the radio on his shoulder.

"Trespasser behind the Blanton residence."

He requested backup but knew none was coming. Aguilar and Lambert were fifteen minutes from his location, and the Wells Ferry PD wouldn't lift a finger to help him.

As he stood in the darkness, he studied the room above the garage. If Shawn was here, Thomas might have spooked him. But it didn't feel right. The garage was a logical place for Shawn to hide, but the neighbors lived too close. Someone would have noticed the teenager, especially with his face plastered to the news.

A thump brought Thomas's head around. Someone was outside the Blanton house.

He scanned the yard for danger. Stepping from beneath the tree, he jogged toward the garage and knelt beside the door, a creeping sensation sending goosebumps down his arms. What had he missed? He spotted the fallen wheelbarrow, the closed door leading into the garage, wet impressions in the grass from where he'd walked across the lawn.

The shovel with the sharp point.

It was missing.

The whistle of a deadly object hurtling toward his head warned him of the attack. Pure instinct saved him as he ducked the blow. The shovel missed his skull by inches and smashed against the side of the garage, removing a chunk of wood. With his attacker close, Thomas couldn't draw his weapon. As the shadowed figure readied the shovel for another swing, Thomas drove his elbow into the man's ribcage. The intruder stumbled back a step and grunted. He was fast and strong, a few inches taller than Thomas.

There was no time to react before the man cracked the shovel against Thomas's shoulder. Thomas cried out as stars filled his vision. He lurched sideways when the man swung again. The shovel missed Thomas's head and struck the garage with a deafening crash.

The blast still echoing in Thomas's head, he spun away and pulled the gun from his holster. Brought the gun up and sought his attacker. The man wore black clothing from head to toe, a black ski mask concealing his face, exactly as Shawn had described his mother's killer.

Panicked, the man hurled the shovel at Thomas and ran. The weapon whipped through the air like a boomerang. Thomas covered his head and ducked a split-second before the handle bashed against his skull and drove him to his knees. His head spun.

As he shook off the cobwebs, he searched the yard for his

attacker. Footsteps thumped through a neighboring yard as two dogs barked.

Thomas clutched his gun and stumbled after the killer.

27

"I need you to hold still, Sheriff."

Thomas winced as Deputy Aguilar swabbed the wound above his ear. She covered the laceration with a bandage and blew out a frustrated breath. A paramedic stood next to Aguilar while the ambulance idled curbside. The swirling lights attracted the looky-loos, many in robes and pajamas as they watched from lawns and porches. The paramedic had long flowing hair and a nose piercing that sparkled beneath the streetlights. She didn't look more than a year out of college. As Aguilar finished treating the laceration, the paramedic folded her arms and sent Thomas a disapproving glare.

"He should be in the hospital. That wound needs stitches."

"I told him," Aguilar said with a scowl. "Sheriff Shepherd has a stubborn streak."

The paramedic threw up her hands. After the ambulance drove off, Aguilar rounded on Thomas, who leaned against his cruiser with an ice pack pressed against his head.

"You could have been killed."

"Stop with the lecture. How did I know the killer would be at the Blanton house?"

"Well, you know not to enter a dangerous situation without backup. You're lucky, Sheriff. Did you get a good look at the guy, at least?"

Thomas pinched the bridge of his nose.

"Black ski mask, black clothes."

"Like Megan Massey's killer. They must shop at the same outlet."

"Very funny."

"But you let him get away."

"Like I said, he struck me in the head and ran off before I recovered."

"At least he didn't shoot you. Your attacker did all this damage with a shovel? I'll remember not to invite you over next time I garden. Wouldn't want to trigger you."

"Hey, you didn't see the shovel. That damn thing was a deadly weapon."

Aguilar smirked and looked to the clouds.

"What are we gonna do with you, Sheriff Shepherd?"

Thomas removed the ice pack and felt along the side of his head. He touched a rising bump and flinched.

"Take the night off," Aguilar said. "You're in no shape to hunt through the woods."

"Not until we find Darren's cousin." She rolled her eyes. He glanced away as the neighbors lost interest and staggered inside their warm houses. "We have a problem."

"Besides the headstrong sheriff who almost died an hour ago?"

"I mean Megan Massey's killer. He knew about the room above the garage. This guy expected Shawn to be here."

Aguilar rested her back against the cruiser as a car motored past.

"That makes me consider Kemp Massey again."

"Might be a friend or family member. Hell, it might be anyone with a social media account who saw those pictures."

"That narrows it down to seventy percent of the county." Aguilar tapped her foot. "What are you going to do now?"

"Contact the Blanton family and fill them in on what happened tonight. If we're lucky, they'll give us a lead on who attacked me." Thomas pulled the keys from his pocket and jiggled them in his hand. "The killer is one step ahead of us. He'll go after Shawn again, and we still can't find the kid."

SHAWN AWOKE to the shadow of a black claw raking across the ceiling.

His breath caught before he realized a tree branch outside the window had created the misshapen silhouette. It seemed he awoke every ten minutes to a tree branch crackling inside the woods, or the haunted moan of the wind as it pressed against the cottage, hunting him. All manner of bumps and groans filled the Nash house tonight.

He lay on the carpeted floor beneath a comforter he'd dragged over him. It felt wrong sleeping in Mike's bed. A violation. Though he was certain his friend wouldn't care. Shawn closed his eyes and fluffed the pillow beneath his head, the carpet fibers making his skin itch. Exhaustion crippled him, stealing his will to survive. Every time he drifted off, another sound darted him awake.

Giving up, he tossed the comforter off his body and sat up. Though he'd showered, he hadn't washed away the stench of the forest. He missed his friends, most of whom had left for college last fall. Nine months ago, he'd spent countless hours inside this cottage, swam off the dock with his friends, cracked the top-ten on *Pacman*. His first kiss with Polly Hart had occurred in the lake, their hair dripping wet, bodies pressed together and shivering.

His stomach growled. He hadn't eaten since he microwaved the oatmeal, and he longed for something filling. Could he cook pasta or rice in the dark? Turning on a light would alert a neighbor. He didn't want the Wells Ferry PD screeching into the driveway with flashing lights and sirens blaring. Jail didn't appeal to Shawn, even if Mr. and Mrs. Nash refused to press charges when they returned.

When the sun rose, he'd leave the cottage and figure out a way to call home. His father must be worried sick. Shawn wanted to tell him he was alive and healthy, that he'd return home as soon as it was safe. First, he needed food, energy to keep him on his feet while he hiked through the forest. He contemplated stealing a phone. Perhaps wait outside someone's house and snatch the phone when an opportunity presented itself. He could be quiet when he wanted to be.

Or maybe he'd risk asking for help. He'd need to choose his target carefully, as the entire county hunted him, blaming him for stabbing his mother. If he found someone his age, a person who didn't trust Wells Ferry PD . . .

Guilt lay heavy over his body like sacks of wet cement. His mother's murder kept returning to him. Everything in the cottage reminded Shawn of Megan's house—the knickknacks on the shelves, the stocked pantry, the clean and neat bathroom. Even the smells brought him back. It seemed the Nash family used the same cleaning products as his mother had.

Shawn stood on shaky legs and stretched. The moment he touched the doorknob, a floorboard groaned inside the house. His heart jack-hammered.

He waited at the door, ear pressed against the wood. Silence crept through the hallway. A glance over his shoulder revealed the bedroom window. He'd locked the pane before falling asleep. If he was quiet, he could unlock the window and slide the pane open without drawing attention.

Shadows flashed over the window. Silhouettes of tree limbs, he wanted to believe. Every shadow looked like a stalking killer with a knife.

A thump against the outside of the house sent shock waves through his body. He was trapped. Was the killer in the house or waiting outside the window?

He flipped a coin in his head, gambling with his life, and turned the knob. Stepping into the shadowed hallway, he glanced toward the living space, then toward the door leading down to the basement. The basement was a dead end. No chance he'd escape the killer there. The bathroom loomed across the hall, too dark to make out anyone hiding inside. Logic told Shawn the darkness concealed him as much as it did the killer. Yet he found it impossible not to assign preternatural abilities to his mother's murderer. The psychopath had stalked him through the park in the dead of night, then tracked him to the Nash cottage, though nobody knew he was here. He'd never escape the madman.

With no other choice, he took one step toward the living space, one tiny stride into the dark unknown. The cottage groaned with each gust of wind. He tried to convince himself the sound he'd heard was the house settling.

Yet something hid in the darkness. He sensed its evil presence.

Another step down the hall. His hand brushed a solid object. He pulled back before he recognized the jamb surrounding the entryway to the master bedroom. A few more steps revealed the couch, the silver reflection of the wall-mounted television, the gray light of the cloudless sky washing over the windows. The front door stood ten steps to his left, the sliding glass door to the patio straight ahead. He was close enough to the deck door to confirm nobody had jostled it open. Every window remained locked. Which meant the killer had slipped into the cottage through the front door. How? He'd confirmed the door was locked.

Terror rooted him in place. He swept his gaze across the room, battling the dark as he searched for the killer.

A bellow broke the frozen silence. Then the shadow of a man leapt from behind the couch and hurtled across the room. Shawn grabbed the first thing he saw—the lamp on the corner table. A flash of light glinted off the knife as the killer rounded a lounge chair and lunged.

With a cry, Shawn swung the lamp. The post struck the killer's head and bent his neck sideways. It wasn't enough to stop the murderer or knock him off his feet. But the strike gifted Shawn the precious seconds he needed to rip the door open and lunge through the entryway into the night.

Without looking back, Shawn sprinted across the yard, tree limbs whipping at his face, the killer on his heels and closing in.

He ran blindly. Impossible to find his way in the dark. Everything looked the same inside the forest as the killer's footfalls slammed the earth behind him.

Shawn faked right and dodged left, leaping a hillock and landing on a steep ridge. Somewhere in the night, the murderer cursed. Shawn heard the madman slip and scramble back to his feet.

The teenager pumped his legs harder, heedless of the trees popping out of the dark. His foot struck a rock. Then the night flipped end over end before his back struck the rocky incline. The air rushed from his lungs. Sharp stones tore through his clothes and ripped his flesh. Confused, panicked, he sought purchase as gravity dragged him down and down. A roar grew as he slid down the hillside, as if a devil crawled out of the earth and opened its maw to swallow him whole. It wasn't until he spotted the river rushing up at him that he placed the unholy roar. Then he knew his fate.

Shawn's body launched off the cliff overhanging the Wells River. He hung suspended for a moment, the night deathly silent as though in anticipation. The teenager plunged into the water.

His body slapped the raging current and struck a dam of leaves and tree limbs. In an instant, the river snatched his torso and hauled him over the dam and into its frigid depths. His head sank beneath the water. He couldn't breathe. Black bubbles spun around his face as the cold clutches of the river tossed him like a rag doll. He sank deeper. Struck the river bed.

Darkness enveloped Shawn with dead, icy hands.

28

The lights were off inside the guest house behind Thomas Shepherd's A-frame, the silver glow of the computer monitor the only illumination. Scout typed with growing desperation. She'd crossed off two-hundred of Shawn Massey's connections on a sheet of paper, keeping a handful for further investigation. Of the names she retained, none lived north of the marina. The investigation kept colliding with dead ends.

Her mother snored on one end of the couch behind her, Ms. Hopkins curled on the opposite side. Even Jack gave up the vigil and lay beside her wheelchair, the dog kicking his legs and groaning as he chased a rabbit in his dreams. Scout pushed the mouse away and yawned. Checking the time, she realized how long she'd worked. But there was no time for sleep. A teenager's life was at stake. She reached for the Diet Coke and chugged half the can, clinging to unhealthy energy. Anything to keep her awake and alert.

Each of Shawn's connections blended with the last. As she clicked on another profile, her mind wandered back to her parents' argument. Why would her father make horrible accusations about LeVar and Serena? The Hopkins family members were the kindest, most courageous people she'd ever met. They overcame impossible odds. If only her father could see them as they truly were. Like hell she'd accept living with her father. Though she loved him, her father hadn't supported Scout when she needed him after the accident, hadn't readied her for school each morning and helped her on and off the bus. Her mother deserved better.

Scout crossed another name off the list. This friend lived in Barton Falls, too far away for Shawn to reach on foot. Ready to give up, she called up the next connection on the list. Electricity thrummed through her veins. She crosschecked Mike Nash's profile and confirmed the teenager's parents owned a cottage on Lake Shore Drive north of the marina. She turned around to share the news, stopping herself as Mom and Serena slumbered.

Scout focused on the boy's profile. He attended Nazareth College, close to Rochester. Pictures of college friends, dorm life, and parties filled his time line. She opened his pictures folder and sorted the photographs in chronological order. Focusing on images from last summer before Mike left for Nazareth, Scout dropped her mouth open. Shawn Massey appeared in dozens of pictures, water skiing on the lake, playing video games and eating pizza at the Nash cottage, the smiling boy posing for a photo with Mike's parents. Three photographs depicted an amusing scene—the two teenage boys struggling to erect a tent in the backyard. Scout grinned. The cottage was practically Shawn's second home.

Yet the scenario playing out in her head didn't compute. If Shawn sought protection from the Nash family, why hadn't Mike's parents brought Shawn home to his father? Scout rested her chin on her palm, the hunt for Shawn Massey spiking her adrenaline. She set the soda aside, not requiring caffeine to sustain her intensity.

She returned to Mike's profile. More pictures of college life. The lacrosse team celebrating a victory. Further down, Mike between his parents with a palm tree in the background.

Wait. It was too late to think straight, but Scout knew palm trees didn't grow in New York.

Scanning the descriptions, she rapped her knuckles against the table.

"That's it!"

Naomi bolted awake. Beside Naomi, Serena rubbed the sleep out of her eyes and glanced around the room in confusion.

"What happened?" Naomi asked, sitting up. "Is there a fire?"

"Mike Nash. He flew to Florida for spring break and visited his parents in Key Largo. They're snowbirds. The parents don't come home for another two weeks."

Naomi gave Serena a confused stare. Serena answered with a shrug.

"Don't you get it? Mike and Shawn are best friends, and Shawn spent the summer hanging out at their cottage. He's always there. Shawn is like a family member." Scout minimized the social media profile and loaded a satellite view of the forest outside Wells Ferry. She zoomed in on the marina and pointed at Lake Shore Drive. "The cottage is within walking distance of the marina. That's where Shawn was heading, because he's aware Mr. and Mrs. Nash are in the Keys and Mike is away at college. Shawn must be staying at their house."

Understanding lit Naomi's face.

"Call the sheriff," Serena said, sitting forward. "It's worth looking into."

"I should call LeVar first. He'll know what to do."

Scout located LeVar on her contact list. He answered on the second ring.

"Scout, why are you working so late?"

Hearing LeVar's voice wrenched her heart. She wanted to tell him how sorry she was and make up for the way she'd acted. Even after the way she'd mistreated him, he only concerned himself with her wellbeing.

"I think I found him, LeVar."

"You found Shawn Massey?"

"His best friend lives north of the marina. A boy named Mike Nash."

Scout gave LeVar the address and told him about the pictures she'd found.

"So nobody is home at the cottage," he said. She imagined him jotting a note and running it to Chelsey. "Sounds like a good place to hide. I'll pass the information along to Thomas."

Before he ended the call, she cleared her throat.

"LeVar, I'm sorry for being a jerk."

"Scout, really. It's all right."

"No, it's not. You tried to help me, and I was mean. I've been a bear the last few weeks."

"Everyone understands what you're going through, and we'll always be there for you. *I'll* always be there for you."

Her chest quivered when she exhaled.

"You're a forgiving person, LeVar, and a tremendous friend."

"Tremendous is an understatement. But go on, I'm listening."

She laughed for the first time in weeks.

"Find Shawn, and I'll heap compliments on you for the next month."

"Promise?"

"Scout's honor."

"Ha ha."

"I'll keep going through Shawn's friends, but I'm sure we hit the bullseye this time."

"You're indispensable. I don't know what we'd do without you."

"Probably never catch the bad guys."

He snickered.

"Bet. You're not trashing my house, are you?"

"It's a nonstop party. Our parents are cranking gangsta rap and bouncing off the walls." Naomi gave Scout a confused look. "At least we have Jack to stop them from wrecking the house."

"Pick up the beer cans and pizza boxes before I get home. I can't sleep in a pigsty. You've done as much as you can do tonight. Get some rest, my friend. I'll talk to you in the morning."

29

SUNDAY, APRIL 18TH 2:00 A.M.

Frigid water rolled over Shawn's body as he lay unconscious against the rocks. A wave barreled down the Wells River and slammed over his face, shocking him awake. He sucked oxygen and clawed at the air until he realized he wasn't underwater. A slice of moonlight pierced the clouds and illuminated his surroundings.

The fall came back to him. As his mother's murderer chased him through the forest, he tripped while running down the ridge and tumbled over the cliff. The water's depths saved him from impaling himself on sharp rocks or cracking his head open. Still, it was a miracle he was alive. Albeit barely.

He was so cold he couldn't feel his body. His flesh rippled with goosebumps, teeth chattering as the water soaked him through. The borrowed sweatshirt hung halfway off his body, a laceration cutting from his shoulder to his chest. Swiveling his head, he found himself jammed between a boulder and the riverbank. A cluster of branches and dead leaves pressed against his flesh. Had the swollen river not tossed him into this protective nook, he'd have drowned while unconscious. Dumb luck postponed his funeral. For now.

As he assessed the damage, he remembered the masked killer. He searched the bank and the forest encroaching on the river. How far had the river dragged him? Besides his head, his arms were the only parts of his body which hadn't fallen numb. He pressed his palms against the boulder and pushed himself up. Screamed when searing pain ripped through his right leg. The useless limb bobbed before him in the current. Even in the murky river, he saw the unnatural, crooked bend below his knee. Anxiety ripped through his body. He'd broken his leg and couldn't move. Was the bone sticking through his skin?

He turned his head and searched for a way out of the river. The bank flattened behind him. Beyond the river, the forest climbed up the hillside. The ridge appeared steep, but not as treacherous as the cliffs. He needed to pull himself out of the water before he froze to death, but moving entailed substantial risk. A little to his left, and the rapids would claim him again and tug him down river.

Shawn pressed his palms down and pushed his body up, crying out and collapsing when the pain became too much to bear. In a moment of clarity, he realized the killer would hear him. He wanted to believe the man in the ski mask had left the scene, assuming Shawn died after the fall or drowned. Yet he'd never be free of the killer. Not until one of them lay dead.

With trembling arms, he tore a piece of hanging fabric from the sweatshirt, rolled into a ball, and stuffed it between his teeth. He bit down and struggled to push himself over the banks. The fabric stifled his cries, though they were deafening in his head. His arms quivered like the legs of a newborn calf. The current snatched at his bobbing legs and pulled him away from the rocks. Wincing, he hung on. He spotted another boulder jutting out of the water. Shawn placed his good leg against the rock and pushed. Even his uninjured leg refused to cooperate, it was so numb.

Thick clouds glowered down at him with indifference. He refused to die here. After all he'd gone through since his mother's murder, he wouldn't drown in the river. Shawn pushed until his elbows buckled. Sensation returned to his left leg, just enough for him to press his foot against the boulder and inch himself upward. A wave thundered over his face. He coughed, choking as he tilted his head skyward. Breathing through the waterlogged cloth, he glanced downstream and spied a massive wave tearing between the banks. He wouldn't survive the next onslaught. No chance he'd keep hold of the rocks.

Desperation lending him newfound strength, he pressed himself out of the water and rolled onto the bank. His broken leg sent pain shrieking through his body. The sweatpants had torn from the knee down. The grotesque shape of his leg made him turn his head and vomit. Spitting, he wiped his mouth and dragged himself across the bank, wary of the river surging higher.

Fallen trees covered the banks, and sharp pine scents filled the night. Pressing up to his elbows, he found what he sought— a stout limb just beyond his reach. He inched closer to the branch, every movement sharpening the pain in his shattered leg. At least it wasn't a compound fracture. But he needed shelter. Death by hypothermia was a growing possibility.

His fingers curled around the fallen limb. After he reeled it in, he used the branch for support and battled his way to his feet. It felt as if someone jabbed knives through his leg. The broken leg dragged as he stood on one foot, the branch wobbling as he fought to stay upright. If he fell, he doubted he'd find the strength to stand again. One agonizing step at a time, he plodded toward the ridge. Though the hill would be brutal to climb, he could support himself on the trees and drag himself toward the trail.

Balanced on one leg, he clutched a young spruce tree, his

hands sticky with sap. He pulled himself from one tree to the next and hopped. The numbness subsided, exacerbating the crippling chills rippling through his body. His lips held a sickly blue coloration, the shivers growing in intensity as his head turned cloudy. He needed fire, warmth, a shelter from the elements. If he didn't peel the frigid, soaked clothes from his body in the next thirty minutes, he'd lose consciousness.

Shawn lost track of time as he struggled up the hillside. When the earth flattened, he hardly noticed. He collapsed onto one knee. An insane giggle escaped his lips while he searched the clearing. No shelter anywhere. No sign of human life.

A decade had passed since he was a boy scout, yet he recalled survival tactics. How would he build a fire? The forest dripped from the storms, enormous puddles pooling in the clearing and reflecting the roiling clouds. His eyes landed on a fallen bird's nest, sheltered from earlier rains beneath the over-hanging bough of an evergreen. He limped to the nest. It was dry, thank God. It would make the perfect tinder nest, if he found a few dry branches to start the fire. Every stick he assessed was too wet. Finally, he picked out two branches. A massive log from an oak tree stuck out of the mud and muck. A deep gouge angled across the log, the bark stripped away. Perfect for a makeshift fire board.

Ignoring the pain, Shawn gathered the supplies and carried them to the fire board. Choosing the sharpest, driest stick among the bunch, he sat down and spun the stick against the fire board, his palms blistering as he worked with frantic energy. Heat fled his body, and he understood his time was short unless he started a fire.

Ten minutes later, he collapsed onto his back and wept to the night sky. It was no use. He hadn't started a fire without matches since he was a child, and the forest was too damn wet.

Shawn closed his eyes, content to let sleep take him. Dying in one's sleep wasn't the worst fate.

His head spun. As he drifted unconscious, his mother's voice came to him.

"Wake up, Shawn. It's not your time."

He shook his head and cried.

"Open your eyes, my beautiful boy. There's work to be done."

His senses sharpened. Eyes springing open, Shawn pushed his body into a sitting position and grabbed the pointed stick. His blisters tore. Blood dripped from his palms as he placed the sharpened edge against the fire board. He spun the stick until his arms throbbed and blood slicked the branch. Spun until he couldn't hold the stick.

As night thickened over the clearing, the fire board sparked. Shawn laughed to the clouds, howling like a madman.

But as he loaded the tinder nest, something moved in the forest behind him.

30

SUNDAY, APRIL 18TH 2:10 A.M.

F ueled by caffeine and an invisible clock ticking against them, LeVar and Chelsey arrived at the edge of the forest outside Wells Ferry, where the search teams convened. LeVar counted a dozen officers, many shooting him side-eye glares as if he didn't belong. A twenty-foot tent shielded the officers from the elements. Police and state troopers leaned over a map, while Sheriff Shepherd radioed instructions to the searchers in the field.

Thomas spotted LeVar and Chelsey in the crowd and waved a hand over his head. He cut through the throng to meet them.

"Glad you could make it, but we have more people combing the woods than we need."

"We'll do whatever we can to help," Chelsey said. "Any updates on Shawn Massey?"

"I'm leading a team to the Nash house on Lake Shore Drive. Chances are, it's another dead end. But let's hope he found a way inside and avoided the worst of the storms."

LeVar stood off to the side and gave Thomas and Chelsey space. A table held coffee, soda, and a half-eaten pizza. He reached for a coffee, but a Wells Ferry PD officer with a buzz cut warned him away with a hard stare. Friendly bunch, these Wells Ferry cops. LeVar didn't trust a single one of them. But there was something about Hanley Stokes that made him worry Thomas and his deputies were chasing the wrong guy.

He folded his arms and sat on the edge of the table, observing the flurry of activity. Four troopers, two holding German Shepherds on short leashes, hunched over a map and pointed at landmarks. The troopers conferred with Deputies Aguilar and Lambert, the two Nightshade County deputies dressed in rain slickers. The Wells Ferry cops huddled and spoke in hushed tones. Their eyes kept snapping between Thomas and LeVar.

While Chelsey joined the deputies, LeVar motioned Thomas over.

"We're heading out, so I only have a minute," Thomas said, sipping green tea from a thermos. "Help yourself to a coffee."

"I'd better not."

LeVar peeked over Thomas's shoulder at the police officers and pulled the sheriff out from under the tent. Thomas set his hands on his hips and studied LeVar's face.

"I know that look. You have a theory about the case."

"More of a suspicion. What do you know about Hanley Stokes?"

The sheriff drank his tea and shrugged.

"He did a few years for drug dealing, and Megan Massey defended him in court."

"Chelsey and I drove to his house and knocked. Not sure if you've seen the place, but it's held together by duct tape and Elmer's glue. The porch is ready to fall off the house, the roof has missing shingles, and the siding won't last another year."

"Okay, so the home owner's association won't send Stokes a Christmas card this year. Where are you going with this?"

"Shep, look around you. There's money in Wells Ferry. Lots

of it. Now, let's say you're Hanley Stokes, and you identify a hidden market for drugs in Wells Ferry. You're the only game in town, and the people you sell to have money to spare."

"Right."

"Come on, dude. Stokes is the big cheese. He's running the drug trade in a rich market and living large. But he lives in a house that's one step above ramshackle?"

Thomas scratched his head.

"That seems a little odd."

"And another thing. If Stokes ain't spending money on his house, why did he rob a liquor store?" LeVar let out an exasperated sigh. "This guy has loser written all over him. He hangs out in dive bars and starts fights with the local drunks. Then he pulls a ski mask over his head and tells the liquor store clerk to hand over his cash. Shouldn't this guy own a tropical island by now? I'm not his financial manager. But either Stokes made horrible decisions with his money, or he isn't much of a drug lord."

Now all the Wells Ferry PD officers stared in their direction.

"This feels like a setup," LeVar said, lowering his voice.

"But why? Stokes doesn't have competition."

"Someone wants him out of the way, and I'm not buying Hanley Stokes as the Scarface of Wells Ferry. At best, this loser pushes a little dope here and there, mostly to friends. No way he supplies Wells Ferry."

Thomas squinted in thought. He drank the rest of his tea and slapped LeVar on the shoulder.

"You've given me a lot to consider. But I need to go, just in case Shawn really broke into the Nash cottage."

"Don't doubt our lead investigator, Shep *Dawg*. Scout's always right about these things. Shawn Massey stayed at the cottage. I guarantee it."

THOMAS JOINED the law enforcement officers, most of which had hanging, tired faces. A topographic map lay over a table, the troopers and Thomas's top deputies studying the terrain.

Setting a pin over the park, Thomas pointed to the marina.

"It's a straight line walk from the park to the marina. If Shawn maintained the same trajectory, he'd wind up at the Nash house. Right here." He tapped his finger over Lake Shore Drive. "The teenager saw his mother murdered, and he's been on the run since last night, dodging torrential downpours and a flooded river. If he's inside the cottage, the last thing we want to do is frighten him."

"What if he's the murderer, or he partnered with his father?"

The gruff voice brought Thomas's head up. Officer Barber lumbered through the crowd to reach the table.

"Officer Barber. I thought we sent you home yesterday evening to sleep your cold off."

Barber swiped a hand under his nose.

"Chief called me in. Said all hands on deck. Which means I get to spend the morning with you pricks."

He glanced around for a reaction to his joke. Nobody laughed.

Thomas shared a concerned glance with Aguilar. Officer Barber had caused nothing but trouble for the sheriff's department since the investigation began, and he was dead set on blaming Kemp and Shawn for the stabbing.

"Why don't you coordinate the search from here and save your strength?"

"I don't take orders from you, Sheriff. And I intend to be there when you capture Shawn Massey."

31

Obeying the sheriff's command, Officer Barber doused the lights and siren on his cruiser before they reached Lake Shore Drive. The law enforcement teams had split up while Thomas investigated the Nash cottage. The troopers searched the forest near the marina, while Deputies Lambert and Aguilar trailed Barber's cruiser. Thomas wished anyone but Barber was accompanying him this morning.

They stopped along a winding forest road. A mailbox marked the driveway. A night bird sang from the canopy as Thomas stepped out of his cruiser and edged the door shut. He waited for his deputies to join him. Barber took his sweet time exiting the vehicle, the officer working overtime to grate on Thomas's nerves. The officer coughed into the crook of his arm and stumbled through the mud. He locked eyes with Thomas, a challenge in the man's stare.

Ignoring Barber, Thomas removed Shawn Massey's photograph from his pocket and displayed it to the team members.

"This is who we're looking for. Aguilar and Lambert, take the front door. Officer Barber, follow me around the side. We'll check for an alternate entrance. Remember, keep your lights off and your voices low."

Barber shook his head with derision while he trailed Thomas through the yard. When they neared the deck, the officer rushed ahead and glanced over his shoulder.

"Who put you in charge of the investigation? Last I checked, this was a Wells Ferry PD operation."

"Your chief told me to lead the search. You didn't get the memo, Barber?"

The officer snickered.

"What is it with you, Sheriff? You're convinced Shawn Massey is some kind of saint, and you're the only person not on board with the father as a suspect."

"I just examine the evidence, Officer. All you have is blood in Kemp Massey's sink, and you're ready to send him to the electric chair."

"Because he cut himself when he murdered his wife."

"Where's the blood trail leading out of Megan Massey's house? Did the cut start bleeding after he drove home and reached his bathroom?"

Barber grumbled something under his breath. His heavy frame caused the planks to groan as he climbed the stairs. Darkness hung over the cottage, the clouds suffocating the stars and moon. As Thomas stood beside the sliding glass door, Barber knelt and ran his fingers along the track.

"Well, would you look at that?" he whispered. "The door is off its tracks. Appears your teenage fugitive just added a second breaking and entering charge to his record. The kid is having a busy twenty-four hours."

"Sheriff."

Thomas turned toward Aguilar's voice. She stood beside the deck and watched them between the balusters.

"Find anything?"

"The front door is open, but I don't think anyone is inside. Follow me."

Thomas and Barber rounded the house. Aguilar and Lambert stood outside the entryway. The front door was open a crack, a sliver of gray light visible between the door and jamb. Lambert placed a finger against his lips.

Taking the lead, Thomas entered the cottage with Aguilar and Lambert sweeping in behind him. Barber drew his gun.

Muddy shoe prints marred the floor. Thomas gestured at the tracks so the others didn't disturb them. A quick glance verified the tracks led out of the house before vanishing in the grass.

"The kid left already," Barber said, bending for a better view of the tracks.

Thomas pointed at a second set of tracks moving out of the living space and converging with the prints beside the door.

"Two people were here."

"Maybe the kid had his friends over. Empty house, probably a stocked booze cabinet somewhere. Either that, or the kid doubled back."

"Different shoe sizes. Look at the second set. Larger, right?"

"I suppose. Could be the father's tracks."

"Does that make sense to you? Why would the father hide out with his son in someone else's house?"

Barber muttered under his breath and turned away.

The deputies split up, Lambert taking the rooms off the hallway, Aguilar descending into the basement. The house was dead quiet. Thomas's instincts told him one set of tracks belonged to Shawn.

Barber flicked his flashlight on and swept the beam over the living space. A couch divided the sitting area from the deck doors. The lounge chair sprawled on its side, tipped over. Had the same man who murdered Megan Massey tracked Shawn to the cottage? As Thomas pawed through the room, Aguilar and Lambert returned.

"The house is empty," Aguilar said. "But someone was here. The dryer is still warm, and I found more tracks in the basement."

"Same person dragged the comforter off the bed at the end of the hall," Lambert added. "Found a pillow on the floor and mud ground into the carpet."

Thomas nodded and turned on the light over the kitchen counter. A bowl lay in the dish rack. Water pooled on the tray beneath the bowl.

"He cooked dinner," Thomas said, glancing around the kitchen. "Probably the first meal he ate since yesterday."

"This sounds like *Goldilocks and the Three Bears*," Barber said, folding his arms over his chest. "Kid had it made in the shade. Free room and board, enough trees surrounding the property that the neighbors wouldn't notice anyone inside. Why run off unless he was guilty?"

"Because someone followed him to the cottage. I'm guessing the same person who murdered his mother." Thomas rubbed his chin. "Aguilar and Lambert, dust for prints. I want to know who chased Shawn out of the house."

Barber rolled his eyes.

Thomas walked through the cottage. All the telltale signs were here that Shawn sought refuge in his friend's home. He'd washed his clothes in the basement, taken a shower and hung a still damp towel on the door, cooked in the kitchen. After he finished the walk through, Thomas stood in the yard and searched for tracks, but the grass was too thick. They were only a few hours behind Shawn, but had no way to know which way the teenager ran.

Aguilar joined him in the yard.

"That idiot Barber intends to nail Shawn Massey for breaking and entering."

Thomas sighed and said, "I can talk him down from breaking and entering. But Barber will still go after him for trespassing."

Aguilar peered into the night.

"Hopefully the family won't press charges."

The lake sloshed beyond the trees, and the wilderness stretched for miles.

"Let's get the two K9 units over here."

"Shawn's scent should be fresh. This might be our best chance to catch up to him."

Thomas shifted his jaw. Shawn wasn't alone in the forest. The murderer had stayed one step ahead of them, arriving at the cottage before Thomas, just as the same man had beaten him to the Blanton residence.

If LeVar was correct about Hanley Stokes, who wanted to kill Shawn Massey?

32

The German Shepherds led Thomas's search team through the forest. For the first hour, the dogs had struggled to find Shawn's scent. Now they tugged the troopers forward, dragging them between the trees as they chuffed and sniffed. Back at the cottage, Officer Barber and the Wells Ferry PD controlled the scene. Though Thomas felt relieved not to have the officer breathing down his neck, he didn't trust Wells Ferry PD.

Trooper Vera Simonds began her shift with the search team. The trooper wore her caramel hair above her ears, and her glasses kept fogging in the humid woods. She handled her K9 with expertise as Thomas marveled at the way the dogs sniffed out the missing teenager's scent. One dog bolted ahead of the other, Simonds almost losing her footing as roots clawed at their shoes.

"What's he doing?" Thomas asked.

"The scent is stronger through this part of the trail. We're getting close."

They climbed an incline and weaved between the trees, their boots splashing through puddles. Aguilar and Lambert trailed them, walking fifty feet apart and sweeping flashlight beams through the woods.

"Got something," Lambert called out.

Thomas circled back to his deputy as Trooper Simonds controlled her K9.

"What you got, Lambert?"

"Torn clothing. Appears as if it came from a sweatshirt."

Thomas removed the fabric from a thorn bush. Before he slipped it into an evidence bag, Simonds rushed over with the dog.

"I want to see if it's Shawn Massey's," Simonds said.

Thomas handed the cloth to Simonds, who placed the fabric before the K9's nose. One sniff, and the dog issued a woof.

"Massey's?"

"It's his."

Thomas tipped his cap at Lambert and bagged the evidence. The dogs tugged the team forward as Thomas scanned the trees, knowing they were close now.

"Shawn Massey?"

A second trooper called the boy every several seconds. But a new sound filled the air. A thundering whoosh that could only be the Wells River. The ridge flattened out as the team entered a clearing. The first hint of the new day glowed on the eastern horizon. Then the ridge gave way to a steep drop off, the footing so treacherous even the dogs skittered back and forth as Simonds fought to hold her K9 back. Simond's partner pinwheeled his arms when the rocks slipped out from under his feet. He fell back before gravity claimed him, a minor avalanche of stones leading the way down.

Aguilar descended the ridge sideways. Besides the dogs, she was the only member of the search team able to keep her balance. Thomas took the hill slowly, grabbing hold of saplings to control his descent.

And still the dogs tugged the troopers forward. Thomas shared a glance with Lambert. The rushing river became deafening. Though he didn't see the water yet, the fine spray wet his clothing. Death lay at the bottom of this ridge, and Shawn was somewhere ahead of them.

The dogs pulled up when they reached the cliffs. Confused, the K9 units turned each way and sniffed for a scent that was no longer there. They started back the way they'd came as Simond's directed her dog to locate Shawn.

Thomas stood on the rock shelf and glared at the thundering current. Nobody could survive a fall into the river.

"WHAT DO YOU MEAN, they lost him?"

Darren paced back and forth and tugged his hair, the phone pressed against his ear. Raven glanced at him in question, and he held up a hand. Thomas and his crew were a mile up river, the K9 search and rescue dogs hot on Shawn's trail until they reached the cliffs.

"I understand, Thomas. We'll keep looking."

With a curse, Darren stuffed the phone into his pocket and returned to Raven. They both teetered on the edge of collapse, the need to find Shawn keeping them on their feet. Before long, their bodies would give out, regardless of whether they located his missing cousin. Darren placed a hand on his hip and stared at the river. Around the bend, the current emptied into the lake. If Shawn toppled off the cliffs, the Wells River would drag him downstream and throw his body into the lake. Darren didn't want to assume the worst. Yet he couldn't pull his eyes from the roaring current.

Raven came to him and placed a hand on his back. He

wished this nightmare was over, wished the search teams would bring Shawn home to his father.

"They gave up the chase at the cliffs. It's looking more and more like Shawn fell over the side."

Raven rubbed his back and rested her head against his shoulder.

"We won't give up until we find him," Raven said. "I don't care how long it takes."

Behind them, a New York State Trooper SUV jounced over the terrain and angled toward the river. Darren and Raven walked over to meet the trooper. A lanky man with a limp climbed out of the SUV. Darren recognized Trooper Fitzpatrick. He'd collaborated with Fitzpatrick many times while working for the Syracuse PD. Fitzpatrick did a double take when he spotted Darren approaching.

"Holt? Is that you?"

"Good to see you again, Fitzpatrick. Wish it was under different circumstances."

Darren made introductions.

"Why are you out here before the break of dawn? You part of the search team?"

After Darren explained his relationship to the missing boy, Fitzpatrick softened his eyes.

"I'm sorry, Darren. I didn't know. We're busting ass to find Shawn."

"Why are you setting up beside the lake?" asked Raven.

"Uh," Fitzpatrick stammered, running a hand through his hair. "We have a team arriving within the half-hour. They'll use sonar to check the water. It's a faster process than using divers, and the lake is still icy cold this time of year."

Darren knew what that meant. The troopers believed Shawn fell into the river and drowned. They'd locate Shawn's body with sonar and drag him ashore.

"Hey, man," Fitzpatrick said, patting Darren's arm. "Maybe your cousin made it out of the river."

"He's a strong swimmer," Darren said, pressing his lips together. Who was he kidding? An Olympic swimmer wasn't strong enough to survive those rapids. "Do what you have to do, Fitzpatrick. We'll search along the banks, in case he washed up along the shore."

Darren clasped hands with the trooper. Then he led Raven along the river, their sneakers squishing over the drenched ground. Lily pads covered the shallow portion of the lake where the river emptied its contents. Weedy overgrowth extended along the banks and shielded Darren's view. If Shawn lay unconscious below the weeds, they'd miss him.

The state park ranger peeled back the overgrowth. The river surged five feet away, dangerously close. Raven flashed a light along the bank and crawled onto a boulder. Standing upon the rocks, she gazed across the water to the far banks. The water splashed her face, and she stumbled. Heart pumping, Darren grabbed her.

"Come down before you give me a heart attack."

She leapt the weeds and landed along the bank, her skin slicked from the spray. As she used her sweatshirt to towel her face dry, her phone rang. She glanced at the screen and scrunched her brow.

"It's Aguilar," she said, worry creeping into her eyes.

Darren placed his hands in his pockets and shivered. April mornings were frosty in New York, and the humidity from yesterday's storms hung in the air. He tried not to eavesdrop but couldn't help himself, remembering Aguilar was part of Thomas's search team.

Raven pulled up, her back stiff.

"Are you sure?" A pause. Raven glanced back at Darren, then looked away. "We'll be there as soon as we can."

The seconds seemed like hours as Darren waited for Raven to compose herself.

"What is it? Did they find Shawn?"

"They found a body in the woods. The height and weight match Shawn's build."

"But they have his picture. Surely, they can determine if it's him."

Raven bit her lip.

"It's his face, Darren. Someone hurt him bad. There's no way to identify the . . . wait!"

Darren sprinted up the hillside toward the forest. He had to know.

33

The Nightshade County Medical Examiner's building always gave Thomas a sense of emptiness. Maybe it was the way every sound reverberated off the cold, white walls, or the vacant hallways that seemed to stretch to infinity. Or perhaps he felt the phantoms of every family member who'd identified a lost loved one inside the facility.

He placed a hand against Darren's chest and held him back. "You're not going in there."

"I need to see his face," Darren said, his eyes hazy with tears. Raven stood at his side, one elbow hooked around Darren's in case he lunged for the door. "I want to know what that bastard did to Shawn."

"We aren't even sure it's him." Thomas touched his friend's shoulder. "Give me a chance to identify the victim. Stay here while we examine the body."

Darren raised his eyes to the ceiling. His body coursed with anxious energy.

"How long will you be?"

"As long as it takes. You deserve a definitive answer." Thomas locked eyes with Raven. An unspoken understanding passed between them—she'd keep a vigil over Darren until the ME completed the examination. Thomas started for the door and turned back. "It's best we don't notify the father. I don't need Kemp Massey barging into the medical examiner's office, demanding to see his son's body when we haven't even determined if it's Shawn."

Darren hesitated before nodding.

"I understand. The murder remains between us until you identify the body."

Thomas pushed the door open and entered the examination room. A naked body lay on the table, toes pointed skyward. Virgil Harbough, the venerable medical examiner of Nightshade County, shifted a spotlight over the corpse. His assistant, Claire Brookins, was a russet-haired woman with an amiable smile and enough energy to fuel a power plant. The twenty-seven-year-old was the leading candidate to take Virgil's job after he retired.

"Sheriff," Claire said, donning gloves. She wore a face mask, blue scrubs, and clear plastic over her top.

"What have you determined about our victim?"

Virgil nodded at Claire.

"John Doe is approximately five feet and nine inches in height, about one-hundred-seventy pounds. Light brown hair. That's about all we can determine about his . . . appearance."

"That sounds like Shawn Massey," Thomas said.

"Hard to say. We're struggling to estimate the victim's age with the face so disfigured. I verified full eruption of the second molars. That points toward late teens or adult."

Thomas ran a tentative eye to the victim's face—a bloody pulp, the bones crushed inward. His stomach turned at the grotesque sight.

"Cause of death?"

"Blunt trauma to the skull. Multiple blows, at least two dozen. His attacker wasn't playing around."

"Time of death?"

"Approximate time of death is between four and nine last evening."

The sheriff's gaze moved to the doors. Darren was outside, waiting for an answer. This might be the ranger's cousin.

"Given the size and shape of the wounds," Claire said, continuing. "My guess is the attacker beat the victim with a hammer."

"That's an act of rage. A powerful message, at the very least. Who would do such a thing?"

It was a rhetorical question. Thomas didn't expect an answer from Claire or Virgil. He shone a penlight over the victim's torso. The bugs had feasted on the victim's flesh. Swollen bite marks covered John Doe's skin. Had the killer found his victim in the forest and brutally murdered him? Or did the killer bludgeon the victim elsewhere and dump the body amid the trees?

When the light moved over the victim's shoulder, Thomas stopped and stared. A dirt smudge? No, a permanent marking, almost bruise-like in appearance.

"Stop me if I'm wrong. But isn't that a tattoo?"

Virgil and Claire inspected the marking.

"That's a tattoo, all right," Virgil said. The medical examiner was slight of build, with gray hair and a matching mustache. "It looks as if he tried to have it removed."

"Whoever removed the tattoo botched the job," Claire said, glaring at the marking through a magnifying glass.

Thomas removed his phone and snapped a photo. Not satisfied with the clarity of the picture, he angled the spotlight closer to the victim's shoulder and took another photograph.

"That's a prison tattoo," Thomas said, scratching his chin. "Which means this might not be Shawn Massey."

"That's good news. But who is it?"

"Give me a minute, and I'll find your answer."

Thomas left Virgil and Claire with the body and exited the examination room. He turned away from the lobby and padded down the long hallway, not wanting to involve Darren until he learned more. As he walked, he studied the photograph on his phone. The tattoo was partially removed, making it difficult to identify. At the end of the hallway, he located the staff break room and slipped inside, turning on the lights. The small kitchenette featured a dorm-size refrigerator, a microwave, one coffee maker, and a table with four chairs. He rested his back against the counter and phoned Deputy Lambert.

"Lambert here."

"It's me. Where are you?"

"Back at the office. I plan to crash for a few hours before I rejoin the search team."

"Take all the time you need. Can you do me a favor before you turn in?"

"Sure thing."

"I'm sending you a photograph. It's a tattoo from our John Doe."

"Tattoo, eh? Sexy. What kind?"

"Might be a prison tat. Put the picture through the database and see what pops up."

"Roger that."

The inmate database included vital statistics on current and former inmates, including tattoos and unique markings. Lambert placed the phone down. In the background, the deputy pounded away on his keyboard. Thomas tapped his foot, hopeful Shawn Massey wasn't lying dead at the far end of the hall.

A minute passed. It felt like an hour. Lambert picked up the phone and gave a low whistle.

"I found a match on your tattoo."

A wave of relief poured through Thomas. The victim was a former inmate. That ruled out Darren's cousin.

"Who is our John Doe?"

"Thomas, it's Hanley Stokes."

"Stokes. Are you sure?"

"It's him. Even with the tattoo partially removed, the database spit back a perfect match."

Thomas fell back against the wall. His number one suspect in Megan Massey's murder lay dead in the county morgue, and he still hadn't found Shawn. After the call ended, he raced toward the lobby, stopping for a moment to tell Virgil and Claire he'd identified the victim. When he reached the lobby, he found Raven consoling an irate Darren.

"Don't do anything you'll regret," she said.

Darren wiped a hand across his mouth in frustration before he noticed Thomas in the entryway.

"This is bullshit, Thomas."

"What happened?"

"Wells Ferry PD are out of control. They arrested Kemp for murder."

34

F ate ripped Darren in opposite directions. Though Thomas determined the John Doe was Hanley Stokes, not Shawn, Wells Ferry PD had arrested Kemp Massey for murdering his wife. One piece of good news followed by a gut punch. It seemed impossible, as though he'd walked into a *Twilight Zone* episode.

Raven urged him to slow down, as he weaved the Silverado through traffic and sped toward the highway, Wells Ferry twenty minutes away. It almost felt as if the Stokes murder was a diversion, a trick to preoccupy him while the police moved on Kemp. He brushed the hair from his eyes, his shoulders thick with fatigue. He didn't trust the officers, but this wasn't the time for conspiracy theories.

"We'll get Kemp the best representation," Raven said.

"Ironic, but the best criminal defense attorney in Wells Ferry was his wife, and she won't be taking the case." He slapped the steering wheel. "Wells Ferry PD blamed Kemp for the murder from the moment they arrived at his house. It's my fault. I never should have told Kemp to let them inside."

"You couldn't have known they'd railroad Kemp. And let's be honest. Your cousin wasn't forthcoming about the blood."

Darren pulled his lips tight. The evidence was circumstantial, and there wasn't enough to warrant an arrest. So what else did the police have on Kemp?

The Wells Ferry exit materialized along the shoulder. Darren coasted down the ramp and swung the truck toward the center of town.

"Think this through, Darren. If the police catch you inside Megan's house, they'll arrest you next. It's an active crime scene."

Darren clicked his tongue. His eyes moved to the mirrors when a police cruiser pulled onto the street behind them. He adjusted the mirror and peered at the cruiser until it turned onto a side street. He released his breath.

"Someone murdered my cousin's wife, and the next day, her client ended up in the morgue. It's not a coincidence."

"No, it isn't."

"Megan knew something about Hanley Stokes, and I'm afraid they both died because of it. I need to see her files."

Raven's legs drummed. She didn't approve of Darren's plans, but she didn't argue, either.

Darren paused at a stop sign and checked each way for police cruisers. Then he pressed the gas. The truck rumbled into the east side of town. When he stopped the truck outside Megan Massey's house, he searched the windows for movement. The crime scene investigators had moved on. Police tape covered the door.

He climbed down from the cab and crossed the lawn with Raven beside him. At the door, he glanced over his shoulder. Nobody watching. He ripped the tape aside and held the screen door open, shielding Raven with his body as she jiggled the lock pick. The locking mechanism unlatched with a loud click. Darren shoved the door open.

They stood in the entryway, the curtains drawn and the downstairs overrun by darkness. Bits of glass covered the hallway floor.

"Where is her study?"

"Upstairs," Darren said. Kemp had mentioned in passing once that Megan converted a bedroom into a home office. He turned on his flashlight. "Here goes nothing."

He led the way up the staircase. The murder had occurred in the kitchen. After he found the Hanley Stokes case folder, he'd search the kitchen and see if the police missed anything. Not a stretch, considering the shoddy work they'd displayed since the investigation began. As he searched for Megan's office, his mind returned to the lake shore and Trooper Fitzgerald. The troopers were using sonar to detect Shawn's body. At any second, Darren might receive notification that the troopers had dragged his teenage cousin out of the lake.

Wearing gloves, he pushed open each bedroom door until he found the office. There wasn't much to the room. Just a mahogany desk, a black leather rolling chair, and a vertical filing cabinet stuffed into the corner. He paused at the computer and jiggled the mouse. The screen prompted him for a password. He was short on time and cracking passwords wasn't part of his skill set.

Raven opened each drawer on the desk. Darren moved to the cabinet and froze when something knocked against the house. Raven met his eyes; Darren killed the light. They stood in absolute darkness, a thin line of gray sliding beneath the closed door. He sensed, rather than heard Raven moving closer to him. Now they breathed in the dark beside each other. The house was silent now. Down the street, a horn honked twice before a vehicle motored past. Darren clicked the flashlight again.

He tugged on the cabinet drawers. Locked, as expected.

"Work your magic," Darren said. "Then let's get the hell out of here."

She slipped the lock pick into the top drawer and gave a twist. Darren slid the drawer open and angled the light over the folders, each labeled with a name and arranged in alphabetical order. The last folder ended with Givens.

He shot a worried look over his shoulder. If the police returned, he'd have a lot of explaining to do.

"Skip the second cabinet," he said. "Try the third from the top."

Raven knelt beside the lock. Darren directed the beam over the cabinet and cupped his hand around the light, preventing stray illumination from wandering around the blackout shades covering the windows. He wished he'd had a room this dark while he slept after overnight shifts. It only took a few seconds for Raven to unlock the cabinet. She slid the drawer open and sifted through the names, whispering each.

"Pascall. Spraggins. Stanley. Welch." She looked back at him. "No Stokes."

"Are the folders out of order?"

Raven peeled through each folder a second time and shook her head. Either Megan Massey kept the Hanley Stokes file in a secret location, or someone had taken her case notes.

Then the door opened. A flashlight beam shone into Darren's eyes.

"Freeze! Hands in the air."

~

CHIEF WINTRINGHAM STOOD over Darren and Raven with his knuckles on the desk.

"You want to explain why you broke into an active crime scene and searched through Megan Massey's filing cabinet?

Because I need a reason why I shouldn't throw both of you in jail for breaking and entering. And interfering in my investigation. You should know better. Especially you, Holt."

Darren stared at his hands. He'd met Wintringham a few times during his run with the Syracuse PD. The chief had noticeably aged from the last time Darren ran into him, ten or more years ago. Standing three inches taller than Darren, Wintringham remained an imposing force. Gray eyebrows narrowed at the bridge of his nose, and his handlebar mustache puffed as he spoke.

"We believe Hanley Stokes's death is related to Megan Massey's murder."

"No shit. That doesn't give you the right to tear down my police tape. You a half-ass private investigator now like your partner?" The chief tilted his head at Raven.

"Just helping my cousin find his son."

"So you're aiding a murderer."

Darren crossed his arms.

"Kemp Massey didn't murder his wife."

"That's not what the evidence says."

"You haven't shared the evidence with me, so how can I argue?"

Wintringham threw up his hands.

"You want to see the evidence? You're lucky you aren't behind bars. The only reason I haven't thrown the book at you is I respected your work when you were a cop. Now, tell me what you found in Megan Massey's office."

The chief glared from Darren to Raven. Raven lowered her face into her hands and rubbed her eyes.

"Nothing," Raven said. "And that's the problem. Someone stole the Stokes file."

"Or she tossed it out."

"A criminal defense attorney of Megan's stature keeps everything."

"You're aware a witness placed Stokes at Megan Massey's house, correct?" Darren asked.

"We're all aware," Wintringham said, stroking his mustache. "My last dollar says Stokes stole his file."

"Why?"

"If I had to guess, his attorney had damaging information on Stokes, something that could send him back to jail if it got out."

"Or Stokes knew something about the man who killed his attorney," Raven said. "And the killer murdered Stokes to keep him quiet."

"Even if that's true, that doesn't give you the right to enter Massey's home. You could have contaminated the scene."

"We didn't. Darren and I wore gloves. There was nothing of note in the cabinet."

Wintringham chuckled.

"Well, then. I guess you did nothing wrong, and I should allow you to walk out of here. What were you planning to do with the folder, if you found it?"

"All we wanted was to connect Stokes to Megan's killer and locate Shawn."

"Shawn Massey aided his father. They both had motive to murder Megan Massey."

Darren stared at Wintringham through the tops of his eyes.

"You don't believe that, do you? Your evidence is circumstantial. Unless you link Kemp Massey to the scene—"

Wintringham held up a hand. He crossed his office, shut the door, and pulled the blinds.

"I'm only telling you this because I've had good dealings with you in the past, and you were a respected cop before you walked away. We lifted the husband's prints from Megan Massey's kitchen."

Dammit. Kemp claimed he'd given up on Megan and never visited her house. Yet he'd attempted to kick the door down in a fit of rage, and now the police placed him inside the kitchen.

"There has to be a logical explanation."

"There is. Kemp Massey stabbed his wife, and Shawn was in the room when it happened."

35

So cold.

Shawn's eyelids fluttered open to sunlight pouring through the canopy. He sensed it was a mild morning, but the warmth refused to penetrate his flesh. He pushed himself up to his elbows and fell back, fingers digging at his eyes as pain rocketed up his shattered leg. How long had he lain in the clearing, exposed? What remained of the sweatshirt curled in the leaves. Ants scurried across the clothing. The sweatpants lay beside his feet, shredded at the cuffs. In his underwear, he scratched his skin and squinted at the mounds rising off his flesh. Bug bites. Hundreds of them. Pus oozed from a sore between his nipples.

His eyes drifted to the fire. He vaguely recalled waking up to toss tree limbs onto the flames, yet it had burned out hours ago, judging by the thin tendril of gray smoke lifting off the coals. The memory of awakening pulled his attention to the surrounding forest. Something had watched him during the night, plodding through the trees at the periphery of his vision. The killer? Or an animal waiting for Shawn to succumb to the elements?

Nowhere was safe. The ski masked killer had found him at the Nash cottage. How had he known Shawn would seek refuge in his friend's vacant house? Before Shawn fell off the cliffs and dropped into the river, the killer had been right behind him, closing the distance. He wanted to believe the madman had given up the chase, assuming Shawn was dead. Intuition told him otherwise. The killer was still out there, still hunting Shawn. Unless the police fished Shawn's body out of the river and declared him dead, the killer would never give up the chase.

He needed to restart the fire. That was the only way he'd survive. Despite drying beside the fire pit for several hours, the sweatshirt and sweatpants remained damp. Intuition told him not to pull the clothes over his body. Better to let the sun dry the clothing while he worked on the fire. But he was too frozen to listen to reason. He wanted clothes on his body, even though the risk of hypothermia increased.

Shawn coughed and wiped his nose. His forehead was hot to the touch, body wracked with bone-deep aches. It felt as if someone had scraped his throat with a razor, his mouth and lips too dry to swallow. He had a fever. If he didn't act fast, his body would shut down.

It occurred to him his last drink had been with dinner when he microwaved oatmeal. Two tall glasses of water would hold him over a little longer. But not forever. A peek at the sky—puffy white clouds against a backdrop of blue—told him rain wasn't coming soon. And that was good, because the Wells River couldn't handle more rain.

He pawed through the dead leaves and weeds covering the clearing. The last of the kindling had burned with the fire before sunrise. Shawn clutched a handful of leaves drying under the morning sun. Then he loaded the leaves onto the smoking coals and waited for the tinder to smolder. Blowing on the leaves, he invoked a flame. Before he lost the fire, he dropped twigs on the leaves. It took five minutes before he had the fire popping and crackling. Too bad the heat couldn't melt the invisible layer of ice plating his skin. He tossed larger limbs onto the fire, the smoke billowing and bending with the wind.

His gnarled leg hung askew below the knee. Every movement sent white-hot agony through his body. Two stout tree limbs lay beside his stack of firewood. The limbs would serve as a brace and stabilize his lower leg, except he needed a rope to fasten the branches. It seemed fate had given him two choices—drag himself to his feet and find a way out of the forest, no matter the pain, or keep the fire going and hope someone would spot the smoke and rescue him. The second option made the most sense. He wouldn't get far walking, not with his fever building. But smoke would act as a beacon and lead the killer straight to him. No, he needed to be careful. Survive the morning, break the fever, then figure out how to escape the forest.

Giving up on fashioning a splint, Shawn dropped the sticks into the fire. The warm glow reached his skin, and his shivers ceased as he stoked the flames. It was a small fire. Just enough warmth to keep him alive, not enough smoke to attract attention unless the killer wandered through the clearing.

Wearing the damp sweatshirt and sweatpants, he struggled to his feet and hobbled on one leg. The fuel wouldn't last long. As he collected firewood, dragging waterlogged branches into the sunlight to dry, his mind wandered to his father. Was he somewhere in the forest, searching for Shawn? Or was he home, a sitting duck? Shawn needed to warn his father. The killer knew where they lived.

The wind moaned through the trees. He thought he heard a voice. A rescue worker searching for Shawn? He doused his hopes when the voice didn't come again. Below the steady susurration of the wind, the Wells River thundered through the valley. He pictured its black, churning waters. How he'd survived the fall into the river, he didn't know. And he'd need to cross the river again to reach home.

Wincing as he hopped across the clearing, he dropped a load of firewood beside the pit. Another voice carried on the wind, and this time he was certain it was a man. It made no sense for the killer to announce his presence. The ski masked murderer moved in silence and struck when Shawn let his guard down. Unless it was a trap—the killer posing as a rescue worker.

Shawn moved from tree to tree and stepped down the ridge. The forest blocked his view of the river, though the volume of its unholy roar spiked with each step. If someone was searching the forest, Shawn didn't see him. His good leg throbbed from exertion. He knelt beside an evergreen and peeled the branches back. The river barreled over rocks and splashed over its banks. No search crew, no savior come to rescue him. Maybe he'd hallucinated.

He waited several minutes until he was certain nobody was below the ridge. Then the distinct crackle of a police radio brought his head around.

"Affirmative," the voice said from the darkness. "Consider Shawn Massey armed and dangerous." A pause. "That's right. Barber arrested the father for murder. The son was involved."

His father? Arrested? A twinge of panic ripped through Shawn when he imagined his father locked in a jail cell. This was typical Wells Ferry PD, twisting the facts to close a case fast. Shawn hid behind a tree as the officer marched through the forest, parallel to the clearing. The teenager glanced up the ridge. If the officer smelled smoke, Shawn wouldn't escape.

As if a benevolent force watched over him, the wind shifted and blew the smoke in the opposite direction. Keep walking, Shawn urged until the officer disappeared into the woods. The authorities weren't searching for Shawn to rescue him. They wanted to arrest him as they had his father.

And that made him wonder. The police refused to consider other suspects besides him and his father. Why were they dead set on turning him into a murderer?

36

SUNDAY, APRIL 18TH 10:30 A.M.

D arren parked his truck a hundred yards from the tent. During the ride from Wells Ferry to the forest, Raven had remained quiet. She suspected the police were right about Kemp, and he didn't blame her. His cousin had lied about never visiting Megan, displayed volatility, and given a lame excuse for his injured finger and the sink full of blood. Now the police had fingerprint evidence tying Kemp to the murder scene.

Still, he didn't buy Kemp as a murderer. The man in the ski mask chasing Shawn wasn't the teenager's father in disguise. There had to be another explanation, something they'd missed. Dammit, he wished he'd found the Stokes file.

The authorities wouldn't welcome Darren inside the tent, and news of Wells Ferry PD catching them inside Megan Massey's house probably dominated the conversation. As he climbed down from the cab and emerged from behind a state trooper's SUV, he spotted a scattering of troopers and police beneath the tent, conferring over coffee. An officer with a jutting chin and his cap pulled down to his eyes noticed Darren and turned away.

"Wouldn't it be better if we searched on our own and avoided the police?" Raven muttered from the side of her mouth.

"I need to know where they're looking and if they have evidence implicating Shawn."

"They won't share information with you."

"Cops are a bunch of hens. Get us together, and we can't shut up."

Raven wasn't convinced. Nor was Darren. The search crews focused their efforts on the lake and river, dragging the water for Shawn's corpse, while a skeleton crew checked the forest. At this rate, they'd never find Shawn alive.

The police officers moved away and whispered when Darren and Raven stepped beneath the tent. Darren relaxed his shoulders when he spotted a familiar face. Trooper Fitzgerald held court with his cohorts. Fitzgerald raised a hesitant hand when he noticed Darren. His partners strolled away.

"How did it go at the lake?"

Fitzgerald swiped a hand across his forehead. After a chilly morning, the heat and humidity had returned.

"The only thing the sonar found was an old tire."

"So Shawn is still alive."

"Let's hope so."

Darren ran his gaze across the tent and lifted his chin at the officers.

"I take it we're not welcome."

"Word spreads fast," Fitzgerald said, lowering his voice. "Once the news broke about Wells Ferry PD catching you inside the house, they started wondering about your motivations. What were you thinking?"

Darren shook his head.

"I'm not convinced my cousin hurt anyone."

"Don't take this the wrong way, but we can't form unbiased opinions when our families are involved. If you were still on the force, your chief wouldn't allow you anywhere near this case. But if you must know, the evidence against Kemp Massey keeps growing."

"I understand the police lifted his prints from the victim's kitchen."

Fitzgerald narrowed his brow.

"Who told you that?"

"I have my sources."

"I understand you were inside Kemp Massey's house when the police found blood in his bathroom sink."

Darren nodded.

"Kemp claims he cut his finger fixing a hinge."

"Enormous coincidence, your cousin slicing his finger open at the same time someone stabbed Megan across town."

"Doesn't it bother you Megan Massey's client ended up dead in the woods after someone murdered her?"

Fitzgerald glanced away and folded his arms.

"Are you suggesting the same killer murdered Hanley Stokes? The MO's are different. A stabbing and a blunt force attack."

"Why would Kemp attack Hanley Stokes?" Raven asked. "I'm not seeing the connection."

The trooper shrugged and kicked at the dirt.

"Your guess is as good as mine. But the rumor is Kemp Massey resented his wife for putting her career above her family. Stokes was a client."

"Should we expect Kemp Massey to murder all of his wife's clients? That's a stretch."

"Well, he can't murder anyone from behind bars."

"You're drinking the Kool Aid," Darren said. "These cops have you believing my cousin is a murderer."

"He's already behind bars, so there's no point arguing. My job is to help you find Shawn."

"And throw him in a cell with his father. Every cop here thinks he conspired to murder his mother, and that makes no sense. Where's the evidence implicating Shawn?"

Fitzgerald raised his palms and glanced over his shoulder. The officers were too far away to eavesdrop.

"We go way back, Darren. And that's the only reason I'm telling you this. Wells Ferry PD found hair matching Shawn's in the kitchen. DNA tests are pending, but the color is a perfect match."

"But it's already been established Shawn ate dinner with his mother every week," Raven argued.

"The hair was on the victim."

"Which suggests Shawn helped his mother after the lunatic stabbed her," said Darren, losing patience with his friend.

"That was my first thought too. But so far, the only people we've placed inside the kitchen are Kemp Massey, his son, and the victim." Fitzgerald adjusted his belt. "Look, I'll help you find your cousin. But my orders are to arrest Shawn."

THE LIGHT POURING through the window prevented Thomas from falling asleep. Every time he closed his eyes, he pictured Hanley Stokes with his face bashed in, the mangled skull, blood staining the whites of his eyes. Thomas sighed and rolled onto his side, pulled the pillow over his head, breathed in the dark until he couldn't take it anymore. He tossed the pillow aside. Jack lay at his feet. The dog lifted an eye and fell back to sleep.

Down the hall, Lambert snored from the guest room. The sheriff had practically twisted his deputy's arm into taking a nap. If Lambert had his way, he'd work two days straight until they rescued the missing teenager. He'd only agreed to sleep a few hours because Thomas promised he'd wake him by noon so they could continue the search.

Thomas pushed the blankets off his legs and walked to the window. No lights shone inside the guest house. LeVar was asleep after a long night, and Scout had stayed up past three in the morning until Naomi forced her to return home. Scout's research had led Thomas to the right place, but he'd been too late. The killer beat him to the scene. Again.

His mind returned to the attack outside the Blanton's garage. The killer knew Shawn's hangouts. Was the killer one of the teenager's friends? Or the father? He'd heard the news about Kemp Massey after he identified Stokes as their John Doe, and the arrest ate at him. He couldn't come up with a reason Shawn's father or a friend would murder Stokes.

Accepting he'd never fall asleep, Thomas dressed and walked downstairs, careful not to wake his deputy. He fried three eggs in the pan, plated the eggs with a side of toast, and poured a glass of orange juice. As he ate at the table, he observed the lake through the deck door. There were already boaters on the water, the locals taking advantage of the amiable weather after days of storms. The water level had risen over the last week, flooding boat houses across the lake.

He yawned into his hand and glared at the clock. If he'd slept three hours since the murder, he couldn't recall. Thomas picked his phone off the table and dialed Chelsey at work.

"Thomas, you promised me you'd go home and sleep."

"I went home, but my mind won't sit still. This case has me tied in knots."

"Tell me about it." Chelsey groaned. "Every hour that passes, the odds of finding Shawn alive shrink."

"You heard about Hanley Stokes, I take it?"

"Raven filled me in."

Thomas eyed his pale reflection in the glass and ruffled his hair.

"He's the key to breaking this case. Trouble is, our department is stretched thin, and Wells Ferry PD won't cooperate. I need a research team."

"Just say the word. Wolf Lake Consulting is at your disposal."

He strolled into the kitchen and set the kettle on the burner.

"Tell you what. I'll give Lambert another hour of sleep, then we'll meet you at your office. How does noon sound?"

"I'll be here. And so will LeVar. He set his alarm and will arrive before lunchtime. What do you have in mind?"

Upstairs, the floorboards squeaked. Lambert was awake.

"We'll bypass Wells Ferry PD and the state police and solve this case ourselves."

Chelsey's voice smiled through the phone.

"I like this rebellious side of you."

37

SUNDAY, APRIL 18TH 12:00 P.M.

Thomas pulled into the Wolf Lake Consulting parking lot a second before LeVar. The teenager blasted hip-hop from the speakers of his black Chrysler Limited as his tires bumped over the blacktop. LeVar lifted his chin at Thomas and slammed the car door, juggling his keys in his hands.

"You ready to work, Shep Dawg?"

Thomas squinted at LeVar.

"How do you have this much energy?"

LeVar laughed without answering and motioned Thomas to follow. As they walked toward the entrance, Deputy Lambert drove his cruiser into the lot and parked between Thomas and LeVar. Lambert appeared as if he hadn't slept in a week. LeVar held the door for the sheriff and his deputy. Thomas scowled down at his muddy boots. He slipped them off, banged them together beside the bushes, then set them on a floor mat.

Chelsey rounded the corner as Thomas stepped into the hallway. Their eyes met for the briefest of moments, and the smile pouring out of her gaze warmed his chest. She turned into the kitchen. The silverware tray rattled open. As Thomas padded down the hallway, his socked feet slipping on the mopped floor, Lambert and LeVar headed to the investigation room.

Thomas stopped inside the kitchen doorway and admired her. Chelsey was a whirlwind of activity. She portioned sandwich meat on sliced rolls, adding toppings as she hummed to herself. The light through the window caught her complexion and haloed her face, making her appear angelic. And she was an angel. After all she'd gone through between her teenage and adult years, she always thought of others and placed their needs above hers.

"Let me help you with those," he said.

She waved him off.

"I've got this."

She glanced down at his socked feet and grinned. He lifted his shoulders.

"Force of habit. My mother would have my hide if I tracked mud into the house."

Chelsey set the sandwich fixings aside and crossed the kitchen. Taking his face in her hands, she pressed her lips against his. Heat rolled through his body. Her shampoo was redolent of wildflowers and honey. After their lips parted, she pulled him close and wrapped her arms around his shoulders. He hung his arms at his sides for a second, overcome by her sudden display of affection. Then he moved his arms around her back, the sounds from the office melting away, as though the two of them drifted out to sea on a raft. A quiver ran through Chelsey's body, and when he tried to pull away and question her, she tightened her grip. A long time passed before she let go.

"What was that for?"

"Nothing," she said, giving his nose a *boop*. "Do I need an excuse to hug my boyfriend?"

Thomas watched her from the corner of his eye as she

returned to the sandwiches. He'd sensed fear during their embrace. Yet this had nothing to do with panic attacks, and everything to do with him.

"Hey, you don't need to worry about me."

She glanced away, but not before he caught her eyes misting over.

"Just be careful. Okay, Thomas?"

"I always am."

She set a hand on her hip and shot him a *you-can't-fool-me* glare.

"How long have I known you? I have a bad feeling about this case."

"If this is about the attack outside the garage, it was supposed to be a simple search."

"And the Jeremy Hyde case. Rushing into Alec Samson's house without backup. Don't do everything by yourself. You're just one man."

"I have two deputies."

"Then take them with you and stop traipsing around the forest on your own." She released a breath and set the tray aside. "This killer is smart, Thomas. He's always one step ahead of us. My advice? Trust nobody."

Inside the office, they gathered around the murder board. Thomas mulled over Chelsey's warning before she appeared in the entryway with the tray of sandwiches.

"Are those from the deli?" Lambert asked, touching his stomach.

"Heck, no. These are homemade. I have roast beef, turkey, and chicken. Take your pick."

Lambert plucked a turkey sandwich off the tray. Thomas wasn't hungry, but he didn't expect another meal before nightfall. He let LeVar and Chelsey choose first, then grabbed the remaining sandwich which turned out to be roast beef on an onion roll with lettuce, tomato, and a horse radish sauce. He placed the sandwich on a paper plate and set it beside Chelsey's computer. She dumped a handful of veggie chips next to the sandwich and gave him a wink.

"They're good for you. Eat up."

"What's wrong with good ole potato chips?"

"Don't argue with her, Shep," LeVar said. "She's on a healthy eating kick."

"Fine," Thomas said, popping a veggie chip into his mouth. Not bad. He palmed a few more.

"I should adjust the murder board," Chelsey said. She peeled Stokes's photo off the suspect list and placed it beside Megan Massey's picture. "There. That's better." She turned her attention to Thomas. "We're coming down to the finish line on the Shawn Massey case. How can Wolf Lake Consulting help the Nightshade County Sheriff's Department?"

Thomas gestured at the board with a chip.

"Now that Hanley Stokes is off the suspect list, it's time we alter our strategy. We're not only searching for people who wanted Massey dead, but also anyone who had a beef with Stokes."

"The bartender at Mahoney's mentioned a fight. How about the guy Stokes pulled the knife on?"

LeVar lifted himself onto the edge of his desk.

"Nah. That was a drunken brawl gone wrong. No reason for Jonas Briggs to hunt Stokes down after the dude got out of prison."

"So who wanted Stokes dead?"

Lambert chewed his sandwich and said, "If Stokes sold drugs in Wells Ferry, maybe someone wanted in on his territory."

"Now you're talking," said LeVar. "Follow the money."

"Another dealer?" Chelsey asked. "I didn't realize Wells Ferry had an underground drug war."

Thomas shook his head.

"If there was a war, we'd have more bodies on our hands and more suspects to look into."

"Perhaps Stokes cheated someone on a deal, or somebody sought revenge after a loved one overdosed."

"This doesn't strike me as a drug deal gone bad," Lambert said. "More like someone wanting Stokes out of the way."

Thomas sipped from a water bottle.

"It's possible. But Megan Massey doesn't fit into that theory. Why would anyone encroaching on Stokes's territory kill Massey?"

The others fell quiet. After a moment of thought, Chelsey spoke.

"I ran background checks on Hanley Stokes and Megan Massey. Except for Massey representing Stokes, their paths never crossed. I crosschecked every name that came up, but didn't find a common thread."

"We're missing something. The problem is, between searching for Shawn and hunting down Megan Massey's contacts, my department has a full plate. And Wells Ferry PD already decided Kemp Massey killed his wife with Shawn's help. I need Wolf Lake Consulting to dig into Stokes's past. Interview his friends, his enemies, anyone who'll shed light on our case. Someone wanted Stokes dead, and the same person targeted Megan and Shawn Massey."

"We'll start with Stokes's associates."

"Shake the bushes. See what falls out. Remember, the killer beat me to the Blanton house. He suspected Shawn would seek refuge inside the garage."

"And the killer was there when Shawn broke into the Nash house on Lake Shore Drive," LeVar said, narrowing his eyes. "I'd focus on Shawn's friends. But why would a teenager kill Hanley Stokes?"

"We keep running into dead ends. Let our department concentrate on Megan Massey's murder. Hit the streets and learn everything you can about Hanley Stokes. There's a common thread between them. Let's find it."

Chelsey produced a list of names she'd compiled during the Stokes background check.

"I'll take LeVar with me. As soon as we learn something, I'll contact you."

The group broke up. Lambert grabbed his keys and headed for the door, while LeVar carried half of his sandwich to the refrigerator. As Thomas turned to leave, Chelsey grabbed him.

"Promise me you'll be careful."

"I should ask you to make the same promise," he said, studying her eyes. What was she so afraid of?

"Humor me."

"All right, I promise."

She kissed his lips.

"I can't live without you, Thomas Shepherd. Come back to me."

38

Scout waited outside the guest house for Jack to do his business. The skies had cleared, but there was something inherently untrustworthy about the day. Like a smiling old woman outside a house of gingerbread holding a hatchet behind her back. She squinted at the sun, wondering where the sense of foreboding came from.

"Are you done, boy?"

Jack gave a woof and strutted into the house with his tail wagging. Before Scout wheeled inside, she gave the sky another skeptical glance. She shut the door and pushed herself into the front room. The majestic view of Wolf Lake unfurled before her. Scout should have been exhausted. After staying up late, she'd awoken at seven, scarfed down her mother's pancakes, dried the dishes, and hurried to her bedroom. LeVar had been asleep inside the guest house, and she hadn't wanted to bother him. Instead, she worked on her laptop, crossing off more names as she perused Shawn Massey's connections. A little before noon, LeVar's Chrysler Limited roared to life in the neighboring driveway. After he drove off, she kissed her mother and told her she'd care for Jack and spend another hour researching the investigation.

"You did your job," Naomi said with a curious smile. "Why don't you play with Jack in the yard, or sit by the lake?"

"It doesn't feel right. I missed something important."

Now she typed at the computer, each of Shawn's connections starting out with false promise before she accepted the friend couldn't be the killer. She'd heard about the Hanley Stokes murder. It was all over the news. The murders seemed unrelated, except Megan Massey had acted as Stokes's attorney.

Scout returned to Mike Nash's profile. Her assumption about Shawn hiding at the cottage had proved accurate. What good had it done anyone? The killer found Shawn before Thomas.

She searched Mike Nash's posts and pictures, then cross-referenced his other social media accounts—Twitter, Instagram, even his YouTube profile. There was nothing to suggest a falling out between Mike and Shawn. No jealous battle over a girl, no reason Mike would turn on Shawn and attack the teenager, let alone murder Shawn's mother.

In a separate window, she studied the photographs from Camilla Blanton's garage. Shawn posing with Polly, his eyes holding the hazy glaze of the inebriated, the girl's lips pressed against his cheek even as her eyes smiled toward the camera. Camilla leaning over Shawn as he curled inside a sleeping bag, Polly ostensibly shooting the photo as Camilla draped a fake Halloween spider web over Shawn's face. Shawn felt comfortable over the garage, just as he did at the Nash cottage, where Mike's parents accepted Shawn as one of the family. The killer had to be a friend. Someone who read Shawn's profile.

She set the mouse down in frustration. Then a jolt shot through her body.

No, it couldn't be.

She'd phoned LeVar after discovering the connections

between Shawn, Camilla, and Mike. Each time, LeVar alerted Thomas, who shared the theories with the search parties. The killer was on the search team.

CHELSEY WAITED inside the Honda Civic with LeVar and closed the FaceTime meeting with Darren and Raven. Chelsey's partner and the state park ranger were dodging Wells Ferry officers along the river and ignoring the chief's mandate to stay out of the investigation. While the search crews concentrated their efforts on the river and lake, Darren and Raven tracked through the forest between the park and marina, convinced they were close to finding Shawn Massey.

Chelsey eyed the white duplex. Two cars and a pickup truck clogged the driveway. Darrell Mack lived in the apartment on the second floor. As they climbed the stairs, a dog barked and clawed at the door of the first-floor apartment. Mack's name had emerged during the background checks. The police listed him as a known accomplice to Stokes and a possible drug pusher.

Mack answered after a minute of knocking. The man wore a week's worth of scruff on his face, and his belly hung over the waistline of his bluejeans. He glanced around Chelsey and LeVar as if he expected someone else.

"Darrell Mack?" Chelsey asked.

"Who wants to know?"

"My name is Chelsey Byrd, and this is LeVar Hopkins. We'd like to ask you a few questions about Hanley Stokes."

"I'm not talking to no cops," Mack said.

He pushed the door shut, but Chelsey blocked it with her foot.

"We're not the police."

"Bullshit."

Chelsey displayed her card.

"I'm a private investigator with Wolf Lake Consulting."

Mack swept the greasy hair back on his head and gave the hallway another wary stare.

"I got nothing to say about Stokes."

"Please, Mr. Mack. It's important we learn what happened to your friend. A teenager's life is at stake."

"A teenager? Stokes didn't know no teenagers. You got your facts mixed up."

"All I ask is you lend us five minutes of your time. Then we'll get out of your hair."

Mack studied LeVar. He clearly wasn't comfortable inviting the imposing teen into his apartment. Mack narrowed his eyes at Chelsey.

"Anyone see you come inside?"

Chelsey glanced at LeVar in question.

"I don't think so."

"The cops know you're here?"

Thomas did, but Chelsey sensed admitting the truth would be a deal breaker.

"Nobody."

Mack held the door open and motioned them inside with a sweep of his arm. The second Chelsey and LeVar entered the apartment, Mack locked the door, threw the bolt, and connected the chain for good measure. Stokes's accomplice glared through the peephole for a long second before he invited them into the kitchen.

The apartment appeared upscale for the east side of Wells Ferry. Solid walls, a fresh paint job, long windows with unobstructed views of the town. The lake shimmered in the distance. Despite Mack's appearance, the man had money. He'd need money to afford this apartment. The clutter told a different story. Dishes piled in the sink, a plaid shirt with a rip down the sleeve dangled off a chair, and an empty dog dish lay in the corner with bits of crumbled kibble dirtying the tiled floor.

"You have a dog, Mr. Mack?" Chelsey asked.

Mack's lip quivered. He wiped a hand across his forehead.

"*Had* a dog, yeah. Ripper."

"Did Ripper pass? I'm sorry for your loss."

Mack shrugged a shoulder and peered at the bowl with a glazed eye.

"He was a five-year-old pit, powerful as a tank. Came home from work two weeks ago and found him dead in the living room."

"That's terrible. What happened?"

"Vet said he got into some bad food. But the cupboards were closed. There was nothing he could have gotten into."

Concern flashed in LeVar's eyes. Chelsey crossed a leg over her knee.

"We understand you were friends with Hanley Stokes."

"We go back, sure."

"Did you speak to Stokes after his release?"

Mack's foot tapped beneath the table.

"We met for drinks once. Two days after he got out, if memory serves."

"At any point during your discussion, did Stokes complain about someone wanting to hurt him?"

"No, and it would be best if you left. I don't wanna talk about my dead friend."

"Please, Mr. Mack. We're trying to help."

"There's nothing you can do to bring him back. I want you to leave."

"What about—"

"Go. Now."

"You're afraid of something," LeVar said, resting his forearms on the table.

A protest formed on Mack's lips. His gaze traveled back to Ripper's bowl.

"Not afraid of nothing."

"Someone murdered Stokes. Bashed his face in with a hammer. Where I come from, you don't do something like that unless you're sending a message."

"I wouldn't know anything about that."

"Yeah? Did the same person send you a message while you were at work?"

LeVar nodded at the bowl. Mack chewed his lip.

"You ask too many questions. Anyone ever tell you that?"

"Questions that might get me killed?"

"If the wrong person finds out . . ."

Mack twirled a finger in the air, as if doing so explained who killed Hanley Stokes.

"We'll offer you protection," Chelsey said, removing a notepad from her bag. "Tell us the truth, and we'll ensure the killer won't hurt you."

A humorless smile spread across Mack's face.

"Who's gonna protect me?"

"My firm has a close working relationship with the Nightshade County Sheriff's Department. If you tell me who threatened Stokes—"

Mack leaned his head back and laughed at the ceiling.

"Don't you get it? I can't go to the cops. If I could, I would have years ago."

Chelsey met LeVar's eyes. He gave her a quick shake of his head, a warning not to push Mack. She ignored it.

"I'm personal friends with Sheriff Shepherd. He doesn't trust the Wells Ferry PD, either."

Mack waved a hand in the air.

"Not interested. Get the hell out of my apartment and take your thug friend with you."

"It's a cop," LeVar said, glaring at Mack. The man lowered his eyes to the table. "Who?"

Nobody spoke. Outside, a car rumbled past, and Mack's gaze darted to the window. When the motor faded away, the tension released from his neck. Chelsey reached out and set a hand on the man's forearm.

"This bastard killed your friend, broke into your home, and poisoned your dog. Give me his name. We'll end this."

Mack settled back in his chair. He appeared drained, defeated, a man who'd given up believing in new beginnings.

"I can't tell you the guy's name, but he's a cop." Mack settled his face into his hands. He breathed between his fingers and gathered his thoughts. "Three years ago, Stokes ran drugs on the east side of Wells Ferry. Mostly dope, no hard stuff, nothing that would hurt anyone. He'd lost his job and was struggling to make ends meet. We both were. So I helped him out, and he gave me a cut on each sale."

"What happened?"

"A few weeks later, we were parked behind Tootie's, a restaurant on the shore. This muscular guy walked up to the car, and Stokes figured the guy wanted to buy. Instead, the jerk leaned inside the window, real casual and cocky, and said he'd shut us down if we didn't cooperate."

Chelsey's belly shifted in worry.

"What do you mean by cooperate?"

"Said he wanted a piece of the action. A finder's fee, he called it. As long as we paid, he'd allow us to stay in business."

"Are you're certain he was a cop?"

"He never flashed a badge or nothing. But we could tell. Guy smelled like a pig."

LeVar rubbed his chin and said, "So he made you pay to play."

"Yeah."

"But it was never enough."

"Every few weeks, he'd hit up Stokes for more cash. Got to where we were losing money on each sale. So Stokes quit selling and got himself a job over at that mechanic's place on Route 13. But the guy kept coming back for his pay, even after Stokes told him he'd gone out of business. Stokes was giving the guy half his paycheck just to keep the heat off his back."

"That's why he held up the liquor store."

Mack stared at the wall, remembering a different time and place.

"Stokes wasn't a gang banger, and he never hurt anyone pushing dope. But he was desperate. Poor guy couldn't pay his mortgage." Mack shook his head. "Why the hell did I let him get into that business?"

Chelsey wrote a note on her pad.

"Did either of you seek legal protection?"

"Not me, but Stokes did. And look where it got him." Mack flashed a rueful grin. "He took the last of his savings and hired a lawyer. Two days later, the police found drugs in his house." Mack made air quotes around *found*. "He kept the same lawyer after his case went to trial. Still ended up in prison. You can't fight a corrupt system."

"You're aware someone murdered his attorney?"

Mack didn't answer, just chewed a thumbnail.

"Mr. Mack, did Stokes's attorney contact you after he got out of prison?"

"She did."

"When?"

"The day before Ripper died."

39

SUNDAY, APRIL 18TH 1:55 P.M.

"I don't understand why we're checking the forest again. We should concentrate on the river. That's where we'll find the kid."

Thomas stared at Officer Neal. They wandered somewhere south of the Nash cottage, pushing through the woods with the Wells River crashing through its banks below the ridgeline. Why had the Wells Ferry PD written Shawn off as dead? Even if the police believed the teenager had drowned, they were obligated to search for Shawn.

"Keep looking. The dogs led us in this direction. It's possible he didn't fall off the cliffs, and the rain washed his scent away."

"Then you need an education on K9 units, Sheriff Shepherd. The trail was still fresh when the troopers brought the dogs down. If Shawn Massey came this way, they would have found him."

The sunny afternoon perished beneath a boiling gray sky. Wind rattled the trees, and a black cloud rolled over the lake, angling toward the forest. The connection between the Stokes and Massey murders twisted around in Thomas's head. He'd pondered the mystery since leaving Wolf Lake Consulting. Someone set up Stokes, and Massey knew about it.

He didn't want to believe a cop murdered Stokes and Massey. But the evidence pointed toward law enforcement. Twice, Scout relayed information about Shawn's friends, and the killer showed up each time. It had to be a trooper or a police officer. They were the only people privy to the information.

Barber.

The Wells Ferry police officer had obstructed the investigation at every turn, challenging Thomas's authority. He'd also arrived at Megan Massey's house moments after Darren and Raven searched the office. Had the chief not intervened, Darren and Raven would be sitting in jail cells now.

Thomas studied Neal as he trailed the officer. Though Neal displayed arrogance, he'd demonstrated leadership during the search through the town park. How could Thomas approach Neal with his concerns? Barber was Neal's partner, and an obvious camaraderie existed between the two officers.

The ground gave way beneath Thomas's shoes. Gravel cascaded down the ridge and into the river. Mudslides had ravaged the hills, bending trees into submission, blanketing the terrain with a treacherous silt that could give way. He edged away from the cliff. Neal looked back at him and continued on, unconcerned.

A half-mile from the marina, Neal stopped and scanned the trees.

"Did you hear that?"

Thomas listened. Nothing but birdsong and the distant groan of thunder.

Neal shook his head and said, "Thought I heard someone in the forest. Must be my imagination. Come on."

As they pushed through a tangle of trees and undergrowth, Thomas caught a whiff of smoke. They'd strayed too far from the neighborhoods for the smell to come from a grill, and nobody in their right mind would camp until the weather cleared and the flooding subsided. If Neal smelled the smoke, he didn't say. Yet Thomas noticed when the officer angled deeper into the forest toward the fire.

The sheriff hoped Shawn Massey was alive and had built a fire to survive. If so, the smoke would lead them to the missing teenager.

"Somebody started a fire in the woods," Thomas said, climbing over a fallen tree.

"Might be from the marina. There's a grill behind the building."

Thomas didn't think the smoke came from the marina. The marina stood behind them, while the wind blew straight at their faces. Neal's muscles tensed.

"How long have you partnered with Officer Barber?"

Neal scowled back at him.

"Three years. Why?"

"A few years ago, the Syracuse newspapers ran a story on suspected corruption inside the Wells Ferry Police Department."

The officer shook his head and laughed, the humor never reaching his eyes.

"Here we go. I'd hoped you differed from your predecessor, Sheriff. But it seems the apple doesn't fall far from the tree. Sheriff Gray was a class-A prick. Just wanted you to know that." Neal pulled up and turned on Thomas. The officer stood almost a head taller. "For the record, the corruption rumors were just that. Rumors. The papers never found proof. Just unsubstantiated claims from a reporter looking for attention."

Thomas raised an eyebrow.

"So it's impossible a bad egg or two sneaked into your department?"

"What's this have to do with Barber?"

"Walk with me," Thomas said. "And keep an open mind."

Fallen trees forced them closer to the cliffs. Thomas ran a wary eye toward the steep drop off. A person could disappear into the ravine and never be found.

"I'm listening."

"There's only one reason the same man would murder Megan Massey and Hanley Stokes."

"If this is another baseless accusation, I'm not interested."

"Massey represented Stokes, and I doubt Stokes was the drug kingpin the Wells Ferry PD made him out to be."

"Explain," Neal said without looking back at Thomas.

"His house, for starters. It's tearing apart at the seams. And the liquor store robbery. Why rob a store when you're swimming in money?"

"Because Stokes is a sociopath."

"Someone hit up Stokes for money. Could have been a rival pushing in on his territory. But then I remembered the corruption scandal. What if a cop got rid of Stokes because Stokes refused to cooperate?"

"Nice story. You're a regular Dan Brown. But why did your fictional cop murder an attorney?"

"Stokes told Massey about the corruption, and she was building a case against the Wells Ferry PD." Thomas stopped and waited until Neal turned. "Darren Holt searched Massey's office for the Hanley Stokes case notes and came up empty."

"Which proves nothing."

"Wells Ferry PD had access to the house during the investigation. If the killer knew where to look—"

Neal waved his hands.

"I'm not listening to your bullshit. Take your lies to the press and see how far it gets you."

"Officer Barber impeded this case from the moment he

arrived. He was the first to show up and catch Darren and Raven inside Massey's office. Isn't it possible Officer Barber—"

Neal whirled on Thomas, giving the sheriff no time to react. The nightstick whistled at Thomas's head and struck his temple.

Thomas's eyes rolled back in his head. As the forest somersaulted, his fingers clutched at the air.

The nightstick slammed against his face. He toppled backward, sliding, falling, until there was nothing below his feet but air and a two-hundred-foot plunge into the ravine. He reached for the cliff and snagged the edge with his fingers. Neal strolled to the precipice and grinned down at Thomas. Without a word, Neal ground his shoe on Thomas's fingers.

"See you in hell, Sheriff."

Thomas fell into the ravine.

40

For the third time in the last five minutes, Chelsey called Thomas and got his voicemail. LeVar drove the Civic, Chelsey in no condition to drive with so many worries flying through her head. Darrell Mack had identified Officer Avery Neal when Chelsey showed him a picture. Like Thomas, she'd believed Officer Barber killed Megan Massey and Hanley Stokes. It made sense. Barber received notifications when Thomas relayed Scout's information about Camilla Blanton and Mike Nash. But so had Officer Neal.

To make matters worse, the search coordinator claimed Thomas had requested Neal as a partner when Chelsey phoned the tent. No doubt Thomas wanted to discuss his concerns about Barber with Neal. Now Thomas was alone in the forest with a murderer, and he wasn't answering his phone.

"Drive faster," Chelsey said.

"As you wish."

LeVar pressed the gas and threw Chelsey's head against the seat. She phoned Darren and Raven and filled them in on Officer Neal. Wells Ferry PD hadn't taken her seriously after

Mack identified Neal as the killer. Deputies Lambert and Aguilar were already searching the forest for the sheriff.

A weightless tingle of fear moved through Chelsey's chest. They were too late. She sensed it. Why hadn't she figured it out sooner? It had to be a cop. Nobody except law enforcement had access to Megan Massey's files.

"He'll be all right," LeVar said, not taking his eyes off the highway. The Wells Ferry exit loomed ahead. "Shep faced worse trouble than this and survived. Trust him."

"I do," she said, her throat parched, the words sounding like lies. "Help me find him, LeVar."

INFINITE BLACK. Somewhere, the rush of water.

Wetness plunked his face—blood? No, not blood. Another droplet splattered his forehead. Rain.

A million razors sliced through his spine, his back screaming.

Thomas fluttered his eyelids. Above him, the world lay on its side, the trees jutting over and angled across his vision, as though the law of gravity had fallen on its head. He blinked and stared at his surroundings. Didn't understand where he was or how he got here.

The attack flashed back to him. Something had happened. Yes, the officer struck him with the nightstick.

And then . . .

And then . . .

He'd fallen over the cliff. So why was he still alive?

Officer Avery Neal was the killer, and he was going after Shawn next.

Something rough bit into his back and neck. He swiveled his head and found himself flush against a tree, a stout trunk growing out of the hillside at a nearly horizontal angle, the upper branches curling toward a benevolent god. When he shifted his body, he didn't feel his legs. No tingle of pins-and-needles, no pain. Just a hollow nothingness.

This couldn't be happening. The bullet from the Los Angeles gang shooting had come within an inch of paralyzing or killing him. He'd survived after serial killer Jeremy Hyde broke inside the A-frame in the dead of night, and he'd defeated murderer Alec Samson in his house of horrors. For over a decade in law enforcement, he'd tempted fate. And she'd come back to bite him.

Maybe the shock had numbed him from the waist down. He pressed his elbows against the trunk and sat up, urging the blood to flow into his lower body. His legs refused to respond.

He lay his head back and closed his eyes. Issued a prayer. Even with full mobility, he couldn't climb out of the ravine without falling into the river. The spray wet his back. The water was close now. Hungry. Ten or fifteen feet beneath him.

Lightning tore through the sky. In response, the heavens opened. Though it seemed as if the gates of hell burst forth. Rain poured down on his face, choking his mouth and nose as he gasped and coughed. The tree trunk grew slick beneath his body. Heart hammering, he braced his arms around the tree as the cloudburst ravaged the land.

Another peel of thunder. The rain let up, rogue sprinkles seeking his eyes every time he blinked. He searched the terrain. Two more trees hung off the cliff walls to either side beneath him. If he reached the trees, he might find the strength to swing sideways and drop onto the riverbank. That is, if the river didn't rise and submerge the bank again.

As he considered the lifetime of paralysis awaiting him, if he lived through this ordeal, he pictured Scout. The teenager was stronger than Thomas. She'd accepted her fate and carried on, while he lay here, giving up on life.

He clung to one desperate hope. Blunt force trauma to the spine could cause temporary paralysis and numbness. How long the paralysis lasted, he didn't recall. Perhaps it varied based on the trauma's magnitude.

Touching his holster and pockets, he closed his eyes and issued a grim chuckle. He'd lost his gun during the fall. Worse yet, he'd dropped his radio. The phone was still in his pocket, the screen shattered, the back ajar. He clicked the power button with a resigned moan. As he figured, the phone refused to power on.

When Thomas cocked his head at the neighboring tree five feet below his body, a tingle moved through the toes of his right foot. He held his breath. Tried to wiggle his ankle. His leg didn't respond.

He gazed down at the river. The water had risen another foot. A little more, and the river would engulf the trees and cut off his escape route. Thomas wrapped his arms around the trunk and hung his useless legs over the water. Now what? The neighboring tree appeared a mile away. As he hung suspended, the river lapping at his boots, he struggled to hold his dead weight aloft. His biceps pulsed and quivered. He'd fall within seconds if he didn't jump.

Swinging with his core, he threw himself toward the lower tree. As he reached out, a surge of adrenaline kicked through his body. He wouldn't make it. At the last moment, a split-second before the river swallowed him, his hand clutched a stout branch. His torso struck the tree trunk, ribs buckling. Thomas cried out, bit his lip, and drew blood. He sucked air into his chest as he giggled maniacally. Somehow, he'd made it.

The bank lay below. Not far. He dropped, accepting his legs wouldn't support him when he landed. Bracing himself, he landed hard on his backside. Stars rocketed through his vision. The air driven from his lungs, he curled into a ball, a gangling root scratching his cheek. The water smashed through the banks just past his shoes. Creeping higher. He needed to move.

Dragging himself up the hillside, he crawled on his elbows. A jagged rock tore through his pants and gashed him below the knee.

And he felt it. Yes, sweet pain.

He glanced back at his legs, as though acknowledging their existence would bring them back to life. Sensation ebbed through his lower body. Fleeting, but it was there.

Thomas reached for a sapling and yanked himself to his knees. It was a two-hundred-foot climb to escape the ravine, and Officer Neal was hunting Shawn in the forest.

And he had no way to contact Chelsey or his deputies.

41

Deputy Aguilar gripped the cruiser's steering wheel and squealed the tires around a hairpin turn. The forest offered poor visibility, the trees flying past her windows at warp speed. She scanned the woods as she drove. When last she'd spoken with Thomas, he'd hiked between the marina and the cliffs, working his way through the wilderness with Officer Neal. But she lost radio contact with the sheriff, and nobody could reach Neal.

Anxiousness twisted her stomach into knots. Something terrible had happened and caused two law enforcement officers to fall off the face of the earth. She thought of the Wells River, the psychopath in the woods, the thunderstorm that rolled through an hour ago. Too many dangers.

An access road whipped past. She hit the brakes and backed up, glaring down the long, gloomy path. Branches lay strewn across the road, as if nature conspired to keep her from entering. Aguilar yanked the wheel and took the cruiser down the access road. The tires jounced over fallen limbs, and a leafless elm tree hung suspended above the cruiser. One sudden gust of wind, and the tree would crush her. The roof clipped the tree, followed by the fingernails-on-chalkboard screech of bark ripping metal. Thomas wouldn't be pleased. If she found the sheriff alive, she'd gladly listen to him complain about caring for their vehicles.

She eyed the GPS. The cruiser followed the winding road between the marina and the cliffs. There were no cabins, no mailboxes, no evidence of human life. With the windows lowered, she could hear the river. A branch poked through the opening and scratched her neck. She pulled the wheel to the right just as a shadowed form lurched into the road and flopped down in a puddle.

Aguilar stomped the brakes. The tires slid across the silt and mud, the full weight of the vehicle bearing down on the prone figure.

The cruiser thumped over an obstruction and came down, shocks bouncing.

"Please, let that be a tree limb I hit."

She was too sickened to look over the dashboard. But she had to. Duty pulled her out of the cruiser. As she pushed the door open, a bloody hand reached over the hood and grabbed hold of the grille.

And Aguilar thought, "My God, I ran over Shawn Massey."

But when she spied the waterlogged mop of hair, she hissed. "Sheriff!"

She dropped to her knees and supported Thomas, who clung to the grille like a lifeline. A broken log lay beneath the wheels. Thankfully, she'd stopped an inch short of the sheriff's body. Scrapes drew blood from his temples and arms. His legs trembled as though he'd lost control of his lower body.

"What happened?"

"Neal." Thomas turned his head and hacked out a broken-glass cough. On his hands and knees, the sheriff hung his head. Red-tinged spittle dangled off his lips. "He's going after Shawn Massey."

Aguilar slung his arm over her shoulder and hoisted him to his feet. He slumped over, and she used the cruiser to brace his body and keep him upright.

"I'm calling an ambulance."

"No. Get me into the passenger seat. We need to stop Neal."

Realization struck Aguilar like ice water. Officer Neal had killed Megan Massey and Hanley Stokes. No wonder Neal pinned the murders on Kemp and Shawn. Was Barber involved too?

Ignoring the sheriff's protests, she radioed for an ambulance and told dispatch she'd bring Thomas to the search party tent. The tents were a ten-minute drive away, and she doubted an ambulance could traverse the access road.

"Move your feet, Sheriff," she said, hauling him around the cruiser.

She didn't like the way his legs dragged, sometimes finding purchase before falling limp and useless. What had happened to Thomas in the forest? Sweat pouring off her brow, her body straining under his weight, she grunted and shoved him into the passenger seat. He lolled over and draped over the center console. And she kept thinking, "Please, let this be exhaustion. Don't take Thomas yet. This isn't his time, not yet."

Aguilar threw the cruiser into reverse and completed a three-point turn. Heedless of the obstructions covering the road, she gunned the motor and rushed forward, wary of the elm tree she'd seen hanging over the road. When she encountered it again, the tree inched lower like the gates at a madman's railroad crossing. The trunk ripped another gouge through the roof. She glanced over at Thomas, hoping for a flippant complaint. None came. The sheriff muttered something indecipherable, his eyelids fluttering as he slouched against the seat.

"Hold on, Thomas. Just a little longer. I'll get you help."

He didn't respond.

It occurred to her Officer Neal must have planted evidence at the murder scene. He'd taken Shawn Massey's comb before CSI discovered the boy's hair on his dead mother's clothing. Then there was the water bottle in Megan Massey's kitchen with Kemp's fingerprints on the plastic. The bastard. Neal might have offered Kemp a bottle of water when he brought him to the station for questioning. Then Neal placed the bottle inside the kitchen and made it appear Kemp had visited the house on the night of the murder.

She lifted the radio as she gave Thomas one last glance. Someone had to stop Officer Neal.

But Thomas was thirty minutes from the nearest emergency room.

42

Officer Barber steered his SUV with one hand as the other hand pressed the hankie against his nose. The fever had worsened since morning. Probably because every time he put his head on the pillow, the idiot chief called and demanded he return to duty. Over the last ten minutes, the crackle of voices had boomed through the radio and amplified his headache. It was the same old crap—yes, we're checking this set of coordinates. No, there's no sign of Shawn Massey. Blah. Sick of the banter, he turned off the radio. As far as Barber was concerned, he wasn't on duty until he reached the search tent and accepted his orders. Until then, he was on his own time. And if the chief didn't like it, the dinosaur could pound salt.

This case needed to end.

Why were the officers so concerned with finding Shawn Massey? The teenager partnered with his father and murdered Megan Massey. Neal had seen the truth from the beginning, and though Barber had expressed doubt, all his misgivings vanished after he saw Kemp Massey's bathroom sink full of blood. Afterward, CSI matched hairs on the victim to Shawn

Massey, and Kemp Massey's fingerprints were inside the kitchen.

An open and shut case. The kid was a dangerous fugitive. If he drowned in the Wells River, so be it. That was God's way of serving justice.

Still, there was one puzzle piece that didn't fit. The Hanley Stokes murder. It didn't feel right. The murder kept worming around in the back of Barber's brain. Why would Kemp Massey murder a drug dealer?

He coughed into the cloth and spat phlegm through the open window. County Route 7 was a mess of puddles and potholes, murder on his suspension, but this was the most direct route to the search tents outside Wells Ferry. Though the temperature was in the seventies, his teeth chattered from the chills crawling beneath his skin. He should be in bed, not chasing ghosts.

His gaze moved to Avery Neal's ranch house, a half-mile up the road. After they caught Shawn Massey, Barber's partner would be a shoo-in for the detective position. Jealousy burned a hole in Barber's chest. He had five years of experience on Neal But Neal solved more cases than anyone on station. The guy just had a nose for ferreting out criminals and finding evidence.

Barber almost passed Neal's house before he spotted the officer's BMW in the driveway. He never understood how Neal afforded a pricey car on a cop's salary. Neal claimed he'd purchased a used model, but Barber read the odometer the last time Neal picked him up, and the car only had twelve-thousand miles on it. Barber slowed the SUV to a crawl and parked along the road. Neal was supposed to be in the forest.

The officer turned off the motor and monitored the house. Dark windows, closed doors. The engine ticked. A gusting wind blew cloying humidity through the SUV.

Maybe Neal got a ride from one of the boys. That would

explain why his car sat in the driveway. But there was something piled in the backseat, a black, bulky silhouette visible through the windows.

Barber edged the door open and stepped into the road. Eyed the BMW, then the house again. No movement inside. What the hell?

He swallowed and instinctively moved his hand toward the holstered gun. He wanted to get a good look inside that car, though he couldn't say why. Just a hunch.

Barber was two steps from the rear bumper when the front door of Neal's ranch opened. He pulled to a stop when he spied his partner with a gym bag thrown over his shoulder and a pair of car keys dangling off his finger, as if Neal had a pressing workout session to get to. Neal strode with purpose down the steps before he noticed Barber in the driveway. A stunned expression froze Neal's face. Then the shock faded behind a smile that appeared faulty to Barber. Contrived. Even dangerous.

"You lost, Barber?"

Barber nodded at the gym bag.

"You're not in uniform. Why aren't you with the search teams?"

"I was. All morning, in fact. Chief gave me the afternoon off." Barber hacked and wheezed.

"Doesn't seem right. Here I am, sick as a dog, and the department calls me in." Barber took another step forward, and as he moved closer to the BMW, Neal circled the vehicle and cut him off. Neal's eyes flicked to the backseat before returning to Barber. This time Barber peered into the windows. Neal had packed the BMW with boxes, bags, even his hunting rifle. "You headed on vacation, Neal?"

Neal glanced back at the house and pushed his fingers through his hair.

"Gotta crash at a hotel for a few nights. The roof is leaking again. You know how it is."

"And you're taking the rifle?"

"I'm not leaving it unattended."

The corner of Neal's mouth twitched. Almost imperceptible, but Barber saw. What was Neal hiding?

Barber coughed into the crook of his arm and cleared his hazy eyes.

"I suppose I'll head to work. Still seems like bullshit the department gave you the afternoon off and called me in after I requested sick leave."

Neal lifted his palms.

"Wish I could help, but that's Wintringham for you. Chief doesn't know his ass from a hole in the ground, and he doesn't care about your health, as long as you get the job done and make him look good." Neal cleared his throat. "But don't repeat that. I still need the old bastard to hire me for the next detective position. Right, buddy?"

As Barber stood his ground, Neal inched closer to the BMW. His hand drifted toward a bulge in his front pocket. If Barber wasn't crazy, he'd suspect his partner hid a weapon in the pocket of his jeans. But not Neal. Barber had partnered with the man for three years and trusted him.

"Mum's the word," Barber said, pantomiming a zipper across his lips. "I'd better go before the chief has my ass."

Neal's shoulders relaxed. Another oddity that pulled Barber's eye. Barber turned when the phone buzzed inside his pocket.

"I'll let you get that," Neal said. "Catch you at the tents after eight, all right?"

"Sure thing."

Barber swiped the phone. A text arrived from Deputy Aguilar from the Nightshade County Sheriff's Department.

Barber didn't like the damn sheriff, and he'd learned not to trust the deputies after years of conflict between the two sides. Yet Aguilar seemed okay. Tough for a broad. He respected her. Barber wouldn't mess with Aguilar on her worst day.

He read the message and didn't comprehend the words. It seemed like a cruel prank.

A hot wire of electricity pulsed through his veins. Neal murdered Megan Massey and Hanley Stokes, and shoved Sheriff Shepherd over the cliffs outside Wells Ferry. Impossible.

But as Barber's eyes flicked to his partner, understanding crossed Neal's face. Barber reached for his gun. Too slow. Neal retrieved the knife and closed on Barber before the officer reacted. The blade jammed into Barber's abdomen. A strangled cry pushed out of his throat. As he slumped against Neal, the murderer whispered in his ear.

"Sorry it had to be this way, old buddy. But for the record, I never liked you."

Barber's eyes widened when Neal gave the knife a cruel twist.

Officer Avery Neal watched Barber slump to one knee. Once the officer hit the driveway, Barber would be too heavy to lift. And Neal couldn't leave the fat uniformed officer in his driveway. People tended to notice dead cops beside the road.

Neal tossed the knife aside and supported Barber beneath his armpits, holding him steady as he worked him toward the back of the BMW. The afternoon wasn't going as planned. Sheriff Shepherd knew too much, came too close to the truth. He'd believed Barber the killer, an idea that struck Neal as hilarious. Barber couldn't orchestrate two murders, plant evidence, and get away with it. Neal's partner was too dull and pigheaded.

In time, Shepherd would have discovered the truth. So Neal did what he needed to do. He attacked the sheriff and tossed him into the gorge. By the time the authorities fished his dead body out of the river, Neal would be long gone.

Except he never found Shawn Massey. Last summer, he'd chased the punk kid and his friends after raiding their party. Shawn was an ingrate, a product of his power-hungry mother. And Megan Massey had built a case against Neal. Neal didn't wish to leave a loose end. But the damn teenager had eluded him until Neal ran out of time. Neal had smelled the wood smoke in the forest and come so close to catching the teen.

With a groan, Neal popped the trunk and shifted Barber toward the opening. As the overweight officer muttered something in between death throes, Neal hauled him over the bumper and dropped him into the trunk. The BMW bounced from the dying man's weight.

The trunk slammed shut, like the jaws of a monstrous devil consuming its prey.

43

The doors swung shut on the ambulance. Lights whirled, and a siren shrieked as the emergency vehicle drove away from the tent with Sheriff Shepherd in the back. Chelsey Byrd's green Honda Civic hung close to the ambulance's bumper with LeVar Hopkins behind the wheel and Chelsey inconsolable in the passenger seat.

Seeing Chelsey's reaction had been the worst. Aguilar almost had her emotions under control before Chelsey broke down, frantic and helpless as the paramedics loaded the man she loved into the ambulance. Chelsey held his hand until they wheeled him inside the ambulance, then called his name as the troopers moved her away from the vehicle.

Deputy Aguilar's lips quivered. She shook off her anxiousness, convincing herself the sheriff would want her to catch Officer Neal, not waste time grieving over him. But she couldn't exorcise the memory of Thomas's pallid skin, the way his legs flopped uselessly behind him as she hauled him into the cruiser. He hadn't spoken a word after he warned her about Neal. How the sheriff crawled out of the ravine, she'd never comprehend.

Lambert met her eyes across the tent, and a silent understanding passed between them. She'd never seen Lambert worry. Not until now. Lambert swiped an arm across his eyes, pretending to wipe away sweat.

All around them, the troopers and police officers scrambled to gather their belongings. Aguilar didn't like everyone abandoning Shawn Massey. But catching Neal was the priority, and they needed as many vehicles as they could gather to shut down his escape routes and prevent the killer from fleeing the county.

Her phone rang. She read Raven's name on the screen.

"Where are you?"

"A mile west of the tent," Raven said. "How's Thomas?"

Aguilar bit her lip. She didn't want to upset Raven, but now wasn't the time to mince words.

"There's something wrong with him. He couldn't control his legs, and he stopped responding after I got him into the vehicle."

Raven relayed the information to Darren.

"He'll be okay, right?"

Aguilar squeezed her eyes shut. A tear trickled out.

"I'm sure he'll be fine."

Please let him live, she thought.

"We just heard about Officer Neal," Raven said. "Is it true? He killed Massey and Stokes?"

"And attacked Thomas, yes. Every law enforcement officer in Nightshade County is looking for Neal. We'll catch him. Just find Shawn Massey. He's still out there."

"We will, Aguilar. Let us know the minute you hear from the hospital."

Aguilar ended the call and checked her messages. Still nothing from Officer Barber. She'd chosen to send a direct message to the officer because he partnered with Neal. Better to learn the truth from a fellow law enforcement officer than from a news reporter. But Barber hadn't responded, and he was due to arrive for work ten minutes ago.

Lambert came to her side as Trooper Fitzgerald strode up to them. Fitzgerald knew Darren Holt, and the trooper had organized the sonar search for Shawn Massey.

A dark thought popped into Aguilar's head. She pictured Barber running into Neal on his way to work and trusting his partner. The possibility also existed Barber was involved and had helped Neal kill Massey and Stokes. It was Barber who caught Raven and Darren inside Megan Massey's home office, so he might be working with Neal.

"Let's run a trace on Barber's phone," Aguilar said.

Fitzgerald squinted his eyes.

"You think Neal went after Barber?"

"Or Barber aided Neal. Either way, Barber should be here by now. Something doesn't feel right."

"I'll contact the cell company."

Aguilar and Lambert followed Fitzgerald to his cruiser, where the state trooper requested an emergency trace on Barber's phone. While he pressed the phone to his ear, he reached across the cab and retrieved his laptop bag. After booting up the computer and logging in, he handed the laptop to Aguilar. She popped the trunk and set the laptop down. After she loaded the tracking software, a triangulated approximation of Barber's position appeared on the screen. And it was moving.

"He's on County Route 7," Lambert said, tapping the screen. "He's heading away from the search tents."

Fitzgerald pocketed his phone.

"Wells Ferry PD received a report of a black BMW driving at high speed along CR-7 about four miles from here."

Aguilar pictured the road map in her head.

"CR-7 links up with the highway near Barton Falls."

Fitzgerald gave them a grim nod.

"And once Neal hits the highway, he'll have multiple routes

to choose from," Lambert said. "He might reach Pennsylvania or Ohio before we zero in on him again."

Aguilar pulled the keys from her pocket.

"Let's go."

They piled into their vehicles. Tires kicked up mud and stone as they wheeled toward the access road. Aguilar pressed the gas and hung close to Fitzgerald's bumper. Reds and blues from Lambert's lights spun in Aguilar's mirror, her partner's cruiser a car length behind. One eye on the GPS, Aguilar followed the red squiggly line toward its conclusion. They'd cut Neal off a mile short of the highway. That is, if Neal wasn't driving faster than them. As if Trooper Fitzgerald read her thoughts, he pushed his vehicle faster.

The broken white lines of the access road shot toward them in a blur. Fitzgerald increased his speed to eighty-five, Aguilar right behind him. The radio buzzed with reports of additional sightings. An officer spotted Neal's BMW near the intersection of County Route 7 and Harriot Lane, a tenth of a mile from Milton's gas station. Neal must have been driving one hundred mph to be that close to the highway. They were losing him.

A second call came over the radio. Neal had turned onto West Geneva Road. It was a roundabout route toward the highway, but less traveled than County Route 7. This was the break Aguilar needed. Fitzgerald led the three-vehicle convoy toward West Geneva Road.

When they reached their destination, Aguilar skidded to a halt alongside the trooper and formed a roadblock with their vehicles. Lambert pulled to the shoulder behind them. Two miles up the road, a glint of black metal poked over the horizon. Fitzgerald raised binoculars to his eyes.

"It's Neal. He's coming fast."

Did the fugitive officer intend to slam through the barricade?

Aguilar, Lambert, and Fitzgerald shielded themselves

behind their vehicles, guns trained on the approaching BMW. Sirens wailed in the distance, and the whirling lights of a pursuing Wells Ferry PD cruiser appeared behind Neal. They'd boxed him in. No side roads to turn onto, just farms and meadowland for as far as their eyes could see.

Neal kept coming. Motoring forward like a black shooting star. Aguilar ground her teeth, prepared to leap out of the way if the psychopath barreled into their vehicles. A hundred yards shy of the roadblock, Neal slammed his brakes and stopped the BMW.

They spied the killer through the tinted glass, his shadow almost imperceptible against the dark interior. Where was Barber?

The Wells Ferry PD officer blocked the road behind the BMW and stepped onto the blacktop with his gun drawn. Fitzgerald communicated with the officer via radio. More sirens shrilled over the horizon. Soon, half the county's law enforcement officers would surround the fugitive.

Neal didn't budge. He sat inside his car, unmoving.

Trooper Fitzgerald spoke through a bullhorn.

"Avery Neal, step out of the vehicle with your hands in the air."

No response.

The uniformed officer closed on the BMW from behind, the young officer's eyes holding the terror of a rookie who'd never encountered an armed hostile before. The rookie had reason to worry. Avery Neal was a veteran of the force, a trained shooter.

"Avery Neal, come out of the vehicle with your hands up."

The door edged open. Aguilar's finger tensed on the trigger. For a second, she believed the arrest might end without gunfire.

But as she peered through the tinted windows, she spotted an elongated object in Neal's hands.

She had a half-second to yell, "Rifle!"

The gun blast punctured Fitzgerald's window and ripped through the door, missing the trooper by inches. Fitzgerald ducked and regrouped. Before he spun into position, Aguilar squeezed off three shots in succession. Lambert fired beside her.

The BMW's door swung open. Neal lurched onto the blacktop and dropped to his knees, the rifle on the ground beside him. Blood poured from his chest and shoulder. Insanity tainted his eyes, his face twisted into a rictus of pain.

As the officers rushed forward, Neal fell flat on the roadway. He died with open, haunted eyes.

44

"He has to be close."

Darren scanned the forest beside Raven. He used a digital map on his phone to narrow down Shawn's location. On the map, he noted the marina's position, the Nash house a mile to the north, and the cliffs.

"This is where Neal attacked Thomas," Raven said, pointing at the steep drop into the ravine. A shiver rolled through Darren's body as he stared into the Wells River at the bottom of the ravine. How had Thomas survived the fall? "Neal led the search, and my guess is he'd figured out where Shawn was hiding."

She tapped a finger on the map and drew an invisible radius. Darren scratched his head. The cliffs lay behind them. That's where the dogs had lost Shawn's scent. If the boy dragged himself out of the river, he wouldn't get far. Shawn must be injured and exhausted.

"Somewhere in here," Darren said, indicating a clearing amid the heavily wooded area to their west.

"That's as good a guess as any."

They pushed through the trees, the going slow. There were

no trails, no worn walkways to quicken their search. Darren missed the manicured state park trails. This was akin to struggling through a jungle. Branches snapped at their faces, and roots tripped them up. He eyed the sky. Three hours until sunset.

Halfway to their destination, Raven stopped and placed a hand on Darren's chest. He fell silent and glanced at her.

"What's wrong?"

"Do you smell that?"

He sniffed the air. At first, the only scent he caught was the thick humidity of the waterlogged terrain. Then his eyes snapped toward the clearing.

"Smoke."

Darren and Raven rushed ahead, each calling Shawn's name as they searched for a break in the trees. The clearing was close. He saw it on the map, though the trees conspired to shield his view. The wood smoke was fleeting. Darren assumed the fire had burned out hours ago, the residual scents hanging in the air.

"There he is," Raven said, picking up her pace.

Darren followed her eyes to the white-fleshed figure splayed beyond the tree line. His heart quickened. He ran with renewed vigor, shoving branches aside and bursting through pricker bushes to reach his cousin. He burst into the clearing with Raven steps behind. Shawn didn't respond to Darren's voice. The boy curled beside a long dead fire he'd encased with a circle of rocks. A pair of shredded sweatpants lay beside the fire pit. The sweatshirt hung off Shawn's body with one sleeve missing, long tears cutting through the fabric as if some beast had clawed through the boy's clothing.

Darren fell to his knees beside Shawn and touched the boy's neck. No pulse. His stomach shot into his throat. No, this wasn't possible. He'd searched for Shawn since Friday night, always a step behind the boy and the killer who pursued him.

He couldn't die. Not after they'd come so close to rescuing him.

Raven knelt beside Shawn and sent Darren a helpless glance.

"Is he—"

Darren shook his head. He refused to accept the inevitable. His fingers moved along Shawn's neck and found nothing but gelid, dead flesh.

Then the tips of his fingers settled on a faint pulse. A weak thrum beneath the surface. Darren rolled Shawn over, ripped his jacket off, and placed it beneath the teenager's head. The boy's skin was a lunar surface of festering bug bites. The state park ranger placed his ear beside Shawn's mouth. Thank God, the boy was breathing. Raven phoned their position to the state trooper barracks, as Darren glanced around the forest, wondering how a medical crew would reach them. No roads for the ambulance. The clearing was too small to land a helicopter, and Shawn didn't have time to wait for a rescue aircraft.

Shawn quivered. It was the first time Darren had witnessed movement from the boy.

"Shawn, it's Darren. You're going to be all right, but I need you to open your eyes. Can you do that for me?"

Shawn didn't respond. As Raven read the coordinates to the dispatcher, Darren removed his shirt and draped it over Shawn's bare legs.

"Hypothermia," Darren said as he met Raven's eyes. "He's going into shock."

Shawn's body temperature had dropped, the teenager unable to produce enough heat to compensate for the energy he'd lost. Had the fire not burned out, Shawn might have staved off hypothermia. But he'd exposed himself to the rain and wind for too long.

Darren felt the heat leeching off his body and into Shawn's.

He needed to cover the boy until Shawn's body warmed. Even then, he wasn't confident he could turn the boy's fate around.

"Come on, Shawn. Stay with me."

Darren rubbed the boy's arms and legs, hoping to get Shawn's blood flowing. The teenager muttered something with slurred speech. His eyes fluttered open and closed again. Darren hadn't lost his cousin. Not yet.

"The ambulance is on the way," Raven said. "There's a dirt road southwest of here."

"How far?"

"Half a mile."

Indecision tore Darren in opposite directions. If he carried Shawn's limp body to the road, he'd spare the boy precious time. But the flesh pressing against his chest remained frigid to the touch. Shawn might die from shock before they reached the ambulance.

"Search for kindling," Darren said. "Get that fire going again."

Raven nodded and rushed away to gather firewood. She brought a load back to the fire pit and dropped it.

"Now what?"

"In my jacket, there's a lighter in the inside pocket and a plastic bag of cotton balls." As she reached beneath Shawn's head, Darren studied the boy's face. He wanted to believe there was more color than when they'd first discovered the teen. "I always have a backup plan when I hike through the state park."

Raven bunched the kindling into a pile and flicked the lighter. The cotton balls caught first, then the kindling. Darren was about to tell her to arrange the smaller branches over the kindling first. He didn't need to. Raven already knew what to do.

Darren placed his faith in Raven to get the fire going. He concentrated on keeping Shawn warm. He never stopped speaking to his cousin, though no replies came.

"That was smart of you," Darren said. "Hiding inside your friend's house. I wouldn't have thought of that." Darren snickered. "Can't wait to see their faces when you explain why you broke the deck door and ate their oatmeal."

He glanced down at Shawn. If Darren used his imagination, he might have perceived a wry grin curling the corners of Shawn's mouth.

"Your father is fine, Shawn. But he's worried sick about you. So is Polly. Come back to us and you'll see them before sunset. How's that sound?"

The fire roared beside their bodies. Blissful heat poured off the flames.

"Don't get too close," Raven said, gauging the wind's direction as smoke curled over Darren's head.

She was right. The fire snapped at the wood with hunger, growing by the second. He needed to pull Shawn to the other side of the fire, away from the smoke.

With Raven's help, he positioned Shawn on the opposite end of the fire pit. The smoke snaked away and angled toward the dirt road, giving the emergency workers a beacon to follow.

Shawn coughed. Darren sat up and supported Shawn's upper body in his lap as blood rushed into the boy's cheeks. This time, Shawn opened his eyes. He gazed up at Darren, unsure where he was.

"Welcome back. Do you know who I am?"

Shawn gave Darren a hazy look before moving his eyes to Raven. He scratched a bug bite on his stomach.

"What are you doing here, Darren?"

Darren smiled. Beyond the forest, an ambulance siren grew in volume.

"Hang in there a little longer, buddy. Help is on the way."

45

After sunset, the ICU doctor located Chelsey in the waiting room. He told her she could spend five minutes with Thomas, but the sheriff needed rest. She followed the corridor past the nurses' station, nervous over what awaited her.

Thomas was sitting up with his legs dangling off the bed, as if he intended to march out of the hospital on his own. Tubes hung from his arms. An intravenous solution pumped into his veins.

"What are you doing up?"

His mouth tightened into a grimace.

"Lying against the mattress is killing my spine," he said, reaching around to touch the small of his back.

The tubes stretched, and Chelsey fretted Thomas might inadvertently tear the IV out. His legs moved on their own. She released the breath she'd held for several hours.

"So you can feel your legs?" she asked, hope featherlight in her chest.

He wiped his eyes and glanced down at his legs, as though they were alien appendages he didn't recognize.

"I'm sore, but full mobility returned. Fate was on my side. The saplings growing off the ridge slowed me down until I struck the tree. The doctors say the impact to my spine caused temporary paralysis. It would have gone away on its own."

"Don't start with the *I-shouldn't-be-in-the-hospital* nonsense. When Aguilar found you, you were hanging by a thread." She pictured Thomas, injured and soaked, dragging himself out of the gorge without use of his legs. It seemed impossible, yet he'd made it to the road. "You're a fighter, Thomas. But one lesson I've learned this year—we should accept help from people who care about us. And right now, you need medical attention."

He raised an arm and touched the IV. Studied it, almost uncomprehending. It broke her heart. The tubes pumping fluids into his body and the probes attached to his skin irritated him worse than loud noises. Thomas understood why he needed the fluids, but the IV and probes tested his patience. She touched his shoulder. He met her eyes.

"Lie back," she said, cupping a hand behind his head and nudging him backward. "Don't think about the IV. It's not even there, okay?"

He obeyed, but not without a long, dragged out sigh.

"How's Shawn Massey?"

"Darren checked on him fifteen minutes ago. Shawn is dehydrated and recovering from hypothermia. He'll need a few days of rest, and he'll wear a cast. But the doctors say he's out of the woods."

"No pun intended?"

He smiled for the first time since she'd come to him. The levity brightened the gloomy room.

"Glad to see you found your sense of humor. Shawn is one tough kid. He was suffering from hypothermia when Darren and Raven found him. Another hour, and I'd hate to fathom what might have happened to Shawn."

"Is he conscious?"

"Yes, and he already spoke to the police."

"What about his father?"

"Kemp arrived at the hospital an hour ago. The police released him after they determined Officer Neal killed Megan Massey and Hanley Stokes."

Thomas rubbed a frustrated hand across his mouth.

"I should have suspected Neal. But I was dead set on Barber being the killer."

"Don't blame yourself, Thomas. Neal had everyone fooled, including his own partner. While you were in the gorge, Barber stopped to visit Neal on his way to the forest. Neal stabbed Barber and hid his body in the back of his BMW."

"Is Barber dead?"

Chelsey gave Thomas a grim look, and he raised his eyes to the ceiling. A knock on the door brought their heads around. Chief Wintringham waited in the doorway in full uniform.

"How is he?"

Chelsey didn't trust Wintringham or his officers. Wells Ferry PD had botched the investigation from the beginning, and Neal murdered three people before the authorities caught on to him.

"He's alive, no thanks to Officer Neal."

"If I may speak with the sheriff."

"You may." Chelsey took the chair in the corner. "But I'm staying. Whatever you say to Thomas, you can say it in front of me."

Wintringham nodded and took the chair beside Thomas's bed.

"I want you to know how sorry I am, Sheriff. Officer Neal pulled the wool over my eyes."

"You allowed him to arrest Kemp Massey."

"Neal provided damning evidence. He tricked the husband into leaving fingerprints on a water bottle. Then Neal placed the evidence inside Megan Massey's kitchen. My department will conduct a full investigation of Neal's activities over the last three years. From what we've gathered, Neal threatened to arrest Hanley Stokes if Stokes didn't share profits with Neal. After Stokes broke the agreement, Neal planted drugs inside Stokes's house."

"Yet you never suspected Neal."

Wintringham stared at his shoes.

"I didn't. In retrospect, it seems obvious. Neal led the raid and knew exactly where the drugs were. Said he'd received a tip, and I believed him. Some narcotics we recovered—heroin, coke, meth—aren't trafficked inside Wells Ferry. Our town has its share of problems, but we rarely hear about hard narcotics." Wintringham rubbed his eyes. "We sent an innocent man to prison and allowed an extortionist and future murderer to protect and serve."

"What about the evidence Stokes gave to Megan Massey, implicating Neal?"

The chief blew out a breath.

"Neal stole the file. That much is obvious. We haven't uncovered the file yet, but Neal had access to Massey's office." Uncomfortable silence lingered inside the room, the beeps of the monitors keeping time with the night. Wintringham set a hand on the bed rail. "If I may speak frankly, Sheriff. I only have a few years until they kick my sorry behind out of the department. Before I go, I'd like to repair our relationship."

Chelsey glanced up. The request surprised her. Though she distrusted the local police, she read the sincerity on Wintringham's face.

"Respect is the foundation of a healthy relationship," Thomas said, and Wintringham lowered his eyes again. "And I respect you." The chief looked up, surprised. "Darren Holt speaks highly of you and says you're an honest man. We don't always spot the evil in others. I don't blame you for Neal's actions. He fooled everyone in your department, and I never suspected him, either."

"Still, I should have noticed. While I appreciate Darren Holt's words, actions speak louder. Expect a better working relationship between Wells Ferry PD and the Nightshade County Sheriff's Department, starting now."

Thomas reached out and offered his hand. Wintringham shook it.

"I'll leave you to heal," Wintringham said, pushing himself up from the chair with a groan. "See you soon, Sheriff."

46

Darren waited outside Shawn's ICU room, arms folded, his tired back braced against the wall. Raven rested her head on his shoulders. It felt as if they'd marched through the forest for months. He was watching a nurse wheel an elderly woman down the hall when Raven shook his arm. Kemp Massey exited Shawn's room. A uniformed officer waited beside the door with additional questions for Kemp, but the officer gave the father a moment to confer with Darren and Raven.

"How's Shawn doing?" Raven asked.

Kemp glanced over his shoulder, unable to pull his attention from his son.

"His color looks a lot better, and his speech isn't slurred anymore. The doctor wants to monitor him, but she expects a full recovery."

"That's a relief," Darren said, patting his cousin's shoulder.

"We have you to thank. Both of you. If you hadn't kept Shawn warm . . ."

Kemp's words trailed off.

"Shawn is a fighter. He'd have found a way to survive."

"No thanks to me," Kemp said. Darren and Raven shared a glance. "So much of what happened could have been avoided if I'd been truthful from the start. After Megan and I separated, I blamed her for destroying our home. But we'd had problems for years. We hid it from Shawn, but kids are smart. They recognize the signs. There are only so many times you can argue behind closed doors before your child figures out what's going on."

"Marriages end," Raven said. "It's an unfortunate fact of life. But staying in an unhealthy relationship makes things worse for everyone, including the child."

"True. But blaming Megan for the separation prevented Shawn from moving on. He harbored misplaced anger toward his mother for years. And that's my fault. I failed my son."

Darren pressed his lips together.

"Kemp, tell me the truth. Did you try to break into Megan's house the night you argued?"

The police officer glanced up. Kemp pushed his hands inside his pockets and shuffled his feet.

"I never stopped loving her, Darren. Even after I poisoned my son into believing his mother was the devil, I wanted to work things out, to pull our family together. That night, I drove to Megan's house, intending to ask her for a second chance. She didn't take me seriously, and I lost my cool. We argued on the steps before she told me to go home. After she closed the door in my face, I lost control. In my mind, she was giving up on Shawn, not just me. I regret my actions."

"Does Shawn know?"

"I'm certain he suspects the truth." A tear crawled out of Kemp's eye. "I still love Megan, and I can't believe I'll never see her again."

"We're here for you," Darren said, clasping a hand around Kemp's arm. "But you need to be a father to your son. Time ran out for you and Megan. Don't let it run out for you and Shawn."

Kemp wiped his cheek and nodded.

"I'd better answer the officer's questions and get back to my boy."

"Give Shawn a hug for us," Darren said, draping an arm over Raven's shoulders. "See you in the morning."

47

Naomi hated herself for tricking LeVar and Scout. But what choice did she have?

She stood five steps back from the window, the pane open to the screen, the lights off so neither LeVar nor Scout would see her watching. Glen stood beside Naomi with his hands on his hips.

"Why did you call me here, Naomi? I don't approve of my daughter conversing with a hood. Didn't I make myself clear?"

"Just watch. And listen."

The late April sun painted the yard in vibrant spring colors, the grass a rich green after so much rain. The breeze off the lake ruffled the pages in Scout's notebook, and LeVar's folder slid off the table and landed on the lawn. She snickered as he retrieved the folder. This time, he combated the wind by setting a text-book on the folder. Naomi touched Glen's arm, and the rigidity loosened in his body. His jaw pulsed as his eyes locked on the former gangster sitting across the picnic table from Scout.

Yesterday, Naomi had asked LeVar to help her carry the picnic table from the lake shore to their yard outside Naomi's bedroom window. LeVar didn't understand why Naomi wanted the table moved. Nothing beat grilling in the backyard and eating beside the water.

"It's a beautiful spot for you and Scout to study together," she'd said, drawing an unconvinced stare from LeVar. "If it doesn't work out, we'll move it back next week."

Naomi understood she'd never convince Glen to give LeVar a chance. Her stubborn husband needed to see the truth for himself. Now she lingered beyond view, her husband's glare never leaving LeVar.

Scout glanced up from her textbook.

"What are you reading about?"

"Criminal profiling," LeVar said, scribbling a note as he scanned his book.

"You mean catching serial killers?"

"All criminals. Thieves, Peeping Toms, drug dealers, anyone."

"Give me an example. Profile someone we know."

LeVar cocked an eyebrow.

"*Aight*. How about the girl who keeps asking questions because she needs excuses not to finish her homework?"

"Ha. You're a million laughs, LeVar. So after you take this course, you can help Thomas and Chelsey catch creepers."

"I already help Thomas and Chelsey catch creepers."

"But you'd be good at it, finally."

LeVar gave Scout a deadpan stare. It took a moment before they broke into giggles. LeVar tapped a finger on the blank page in Scout's notebook.

"Get to work."

Hidden in the shadows beyond the window, Glen chewed his lip. He put on a convincing front, but Naomi saw the ice melting off her husband.

"He's going into criminal justice? Does he want to be a police officer or something?"

Naomi nodded.

"LeVar came from nothing and fought his way out of Harmon. He's brilliant and kind, and he wants to help others."

In the backyard, Scout's tongue protruded from the corner of her mouth as she turned pages and scanned the reading assignment. LeVar wrote at a frantic pace as he focused on the criminal profiling textbook.

"Heard your mom is buying your sister's house," Scout said.

"Mmm."

"And she's buying a car. That would be really cool to have her around more often. But I'll miss Raven." Scout chewed her pen. "Hey, do you think Raven and Darren will visit after she moves into the cabin?"

"You're not doing your homework."

"I mean, I don't want the investigation team to fall apart. We still have cases to solve."

LeVar sighed. He placed his elbows on the table and rested his chin on his fists.

"Raven and Darren need their privacy. But that doesn't mean they don't enjoy seeing you. The team isn't breaking up. You'll always have me around."

"And you'll always have me to teach you about music."

Shaking his head, LeVar flipped the page. As he returned to his studies, Jack announced himself with a loud woof and bounded off the deck behind the A-frame. Thomas watched from the doorway and raised a hand at Scout and LeVar. Naomi felt relieved the sheriff was back on his feet. The doctor had ordered Thomas to take two weeks off from work. Naomi doubted Thomas would last through the weekend before he returned to the office.

As Glen and Naomi observed in silence, LeVar read Scout's homework over her shoulder and answered a pressing question. Then Scout proofread LeVar's term paper and offered suggestions to help the paragraphs flow together. LeVar and Scout were a perfect team. They might have been brother and sister, for the way they meshed.

Glen turned away and checked his phone, but not before Naomi caught his eyes glistening over.

"I need to go," Glen said. "Something came up at work."

"I wish you'd stay for lunch. Scout would love to spend time with you."

As she leaned against the wall and assessed him, he brushed the thinning hair out of his eyes.

"I'll come see Scout when I have more time." Glen fretted with his hands as she narrowed her eyes. "I promise."

Naomi walked him to the door. He paused in the entryway, an enigma she'd never fully understand. She wanted to tell him the accident wasn't his fault, that he shouldn't blame himself for Scout's paralysis. But she'd told him these things many times. Until he acknowledged these truths, she would never reach him.

"I suppose I'll hear from your lawyer by the end of the week."

Glen stared into the distance and jiggled the car keys in his hand.

"No, I don't believe you will."

Her heart hammered.

"Glen, are you dropping the suit?"

"Whatever problems exist between us, we'll work them out. We have to think of Scout."

He clomped down the ramp without looking back. Then he was gone.

～

NAOMI SERVED TUNA SANDWICHES, pickles, and chips to LeVar and Scout. After LeVar ensured Scout completed her homework, Naomi asked him to grab one side of the picnic table.

"You already decided it's better by the water? Could have told you that."

She laughed.

"You're always right, LeVar."

After they set the table and benches beside the lake, she hugged him. LeVar gave her a curious stare.

"What was that for?"

"For being the big brother Scout needs. You're a good man, LeVar. I'm proud to call you a friend."

Naomi walked back to the house, grinning. Still the tough guy who never cried, LeVar turned toward the water and coughed into his hand. And in that moment, she loved him like a son and hoped he'd always be their neighbor.

She found Scout in the kitchen, tilting her upper body over the wheelchair arm to retrieve a soda from the refrigerator.

"Let me help you with that," Naomi said, grabbing the cola off the top shelf.

Popping the top, Naomi handed the can to her daughter.

"Dad stopped by."

Scout coughed and wiped her mouth.

"Dad was here? When?"

"While you were doing homework with LeVar."

"But he didn't yell or say mean things about LeVar. Why didn't he speak to me?"

Naomi wrung her hands and slid into a chair beside the table. Scout swiveled the wheelchair to face her.

"It took LeVar's mother to help me see the light, but I think I figured out your father. He still hates himself because of the accident, and he's worried he's losing you."

"Dad isn't losing me. Why does he feel that way?"

"He sees the men in your life—Thomas, LeVar, Darren—and recognizes how much you've grown."

"He's jealous?"

"Not exactly. I'd say he's worried he's lost his place in your life."

Scout's face twisted with concern.

"But I love him. Just because I'm friends with LeVar doesn't mean I don't want a father."

Naomi tapped her nails on the table.

"Maybe you should tell him that."

"I will. What about the custody battle? When is he taking you to court?"

"There won't be a custody battle, hon."

"He told you he dropped the case?"

"Not in so many words. But I know your father. He understands no court is powerful enough to build a bridge between the two of you. That's his duty."

Scout's eyes traveled to the deck door. LeVar stood beside the shore, skipping stones into the lake.

"I want you to understand something, Scout. I'll always love your dad, and I want nothing more than for your father to be a part of your life. But there's no going back to the way things were."

"You're asking him for a divorce."

Naomi considered her daughter's words for a moment.

"Eventually, yes. He broke my trust, and it's time I moved on. But he's your father, and he'll always be a part of our family."

48

Beside the water, Thomas leaned on a walking stick and watched the boats slide across the surface of Wolf Lake. LeVar tossed a Frisbee to Jack while Scout shouted encouragement to the dog. Sweet smoke curled up from the grill where Darren and Raven flipped burgers and hot dogs and belly-laughed with Sheriff Gray. Turning to face the A-frame, Thomas winced. His legs ached from overexertion, though he'd done nothing strenuous today. Just casual walks to the trail and back. His doctors told him to expect a rough week before he regained his strength. He needed to be cautious with his back. After the gunshot wound and the fall into the ravine, his spine had taken too much trauma. His body required time to heal.

Through the windows, he could see Chelsey inside, pulling the baked beans from the oven, while Naomi and Serena readied their latest baking masterpiece. Thomas Shepherd smiled. The family was back together again, and for the first time this spring, the sky was an honest blue with no hint of rain.

A shout pulled his attention to the state park trail. On the worn path, a teenage boy waved a hand over his head. It was good to see Shawn Massey enjoying the perfect April day. His father pushed Shawn in a wheelchair, a cautious hand on the teenager's back as they navigated a bumpy patch on the trail. They'd taken Darren's advice and stuck to the smooth portion of the lake trail.

A horn honked in the driveway. Salutations followed before Deputy Lambert arrived with Aguilar. Lambert cornered Gray on the deck and held court, the deputy and the former sheriff clinking beer bottles together in a toast.

"Where's your walker, old man?"

Thomas snickered as Aguilar descended the yard and joined him at the shoreline. She wore a blue cotton skirt and a tank that showed off her biceps, a baseball cap pulled over her head.

"No hospital can hold me, Aguilar."

She looked at him quizzically.

"You sure you're okay? Maybe you shouldn't push yourself."

"The doctor told me no high impact sports, no heavy lifting."

"So I won't twist your arm and force you to join me at the gym."

"Recovery has its benefits."

She laughed, but there was a darker substance lingering behind the smile. Guilt and regret.

"It's not unusual to experience anxiety and guilt afterward," he said, touching her shoulder.

Aguilar turned her head away.

"I don't know what you mean."

"Remember the advice you gave me after the Jeremy Hyde and Thea Barlow cases? You told me I'd done nothing wrong, and I should stick with my therapy."

"I remember."

"And?"

Her shoulders slumped.

"Can I tell you something, Thomas?"

"You can always talk to me, Aguilar."

Aguilar kicked a stone with her sandal and pulled her lips tight.

"I've never shot anyone before, let alone killed a person. And to think it was a cop."

Thomas nodded.

"It's painful. But you did what you had to do. Avery Neal was a wolf in sheep's clothing, and he gave you no choice. If you and Lambert hadn't opened fire, he would have killed both of you. And Trooper Fitzgerald."

"I keep telling myself that. It's like there are two voices in my head, and the irrational one is the loudest. What should I do?"

"First, I'll address you as your supervisor. County policy dictates you'll attend therapy until your doctor deems you're fit for fieldwork again." He held up a hand when she opened her mouth. "It's the law. You'll remain on desk duty until you're ready. I promise, it won't be long."

She folded her arms and pouted her lips. On the lake, a family rode a motorboat over the waves and pulled a young girl on water skis.

"And now I'll speak to you as a friend." He waited until she turned to him. "You did the right thing, Aguilar, and you're the best cop I've ever worked with. It will take time before you come to grips with what happened. Give yourself as much time as you need. And hey, who's to say your bullet took down Neal? Lambert fired his weapon too."

The corner of Aguilar's mouth lifted.

"Lambert couldn't shoot an outhouse from twenty paces."

"But I'd pay money to see him try."

Aguilar smiled contentedly out at the water. The longer she watched the waves slosh against the rocks, the more her muscles relaxed.

"You know, just standing beside the lake helps. Like my worries are drifting away with the waves. Is that weird?"

"Not at all. People have flocked to the water for centuries. It has to do with the negative ions produced by flowing water."

He stopped himself. A few years ago, he would have recited any of the dozens of studies he'd memorized on bodies of water and their effects on human psychology. He could be too literal, and had been since he was a child. It was better to enjoy the simple things and live life.

Thomas cleared his throat.

"Anyhow, if the voices inside your head ever get too loud and you want a place to relax . . ." He swept his arm across the shore. "Mi casa, su casa."

She grinned up at him.

"You speak Spanish now, Shep Dawg?"

"Not exactly. But I see you're getting your nicknames from LeVar."

They took their time strolling back to the others. Aguilar surprised Gray with a hug. Watching the former sheriff dangle a beer in one hand and wonder if he should embrace Aguilar made Thomas chuckle to himself.

While Scout talked LeVar's ear off about criminal profiling, Darren sliced a hot dog and tossed pieces to Jack. The massive pup snatched the chunks out of the air and swallowed them whole.

Thomas set the walking stick on the lawn and relaxed in an Adirondack chair. It felt wonderful to rest his legs. After setting the baked beans on the picnic table, Chelsey fell into the chair beside him. She gave him a wink and dropped her head back. As the sun poured golden warmth over the yard, he wanted to ask her to move in. Every moment beside Chelsey was worth cherishing.

"If these cookouts get any larger," she said, closing her eyes, "we'll have to rent out the football stadium."

"There'll always be enough room for friends and family." He touched his heart. "Love is limitless."

Thank you so much for reading.
Ready to read book six in the Wolf Lake thriller series?
Download and start reading now!

GET A FREE BOOK!

I'm a pretty nice guy once you look past the grisly images in my head. Most of all, I love connecting with awesome readers like you.

Join my VIP Reader Group and get a FREE serial killer thriller for your Kindle.

Get My Free Book

www.danpadavona.com/thriller-readers-vip-group/

SHOW YOUR SUPPORT FOR INDIE AUTHORS

Did you enjoy this book? If so, please let other thriller fans know by leaving a short review. Positive reviews help spread the word about independent authors and their novels. Thank you.

ABOUT THE AUTHOR

Dan Padavona is the author of the The Darkwater Cove series, The Scarlett Bell thriller series, *Her Shallow Grave*, The Dark Vanishings series, *Camp Slasher, Quilt, Crawlspace, The Face of Midnight, Storberry, Shadow Witch*, and the horror anthology, *The Island*. He lives in upstate New York with his beautiful wife, Terri, and their children, Joe, and Julia. Dan is a meteorologist with NOAA's National Weather Service. Besides writing, he enjoys visiting amusement parks, beach vacations, Renaissance fairs, gardening, playing with the family dogs, and eating too much ice cream.

Visit Dan at: www.danpadavona.com

Made in the USA
Las Vegas, NV
29 June 2022

50874847R00163